NYXIA WHITE COLLECTION

ORLANDO A. SANCHEZ

though
THEY BITE
BOOK ONE

ABOUT THE STORY

Sleep tight...don't let the bedbugs bite...when the monsters come hunting, call Nyxia White.

Nyxia White isn't entirely human. She sees the things no one else can. She never counted on being called to The Seven, it was an offer she could've refused...if she wanted to die.

Now she's one of the beings tasked with protecting humanity.

When creatures start escaping the darkness and claiming human lives, Nyxia is the one who will stand against them. Together with her demon partner, Acheron, and dark magic, she will fight for those who can't fight for themselves.

When monsters come hunting...she will be their nightmare.

ISBN: 9798472670470

Everyone is a dark moon and has a dark side which he never shows to anybody.
-Mark Twain

ONE

The smell hit me first.

"Blood," I said, sniffing the air. "That way."

I loved New York City at night, especially after a hard rain. The park smelled of cut grass and fresh earth. For a few brief hours, the world felt clean, washed of the impurities I knew existed beneath its facade.

I pointed down the worn path. We moved through the trees, careful to remain silent as we closed in on the creature. I came upon more traces of blood, smelling rather than seeing them.

"Only blood," my partner said, crouching down to touch the small puddle, bringing his finger to his tongue and tasting it. "A recent kill from the taste of it."

"Do you have to do that?"

"Do what?" he asked, innocently. "It's not like I'm lapping it up. I have some decorum, you know. Besides, it's type O... boring. I prefer A."

"If the blood is here," I said, looking around, "it must have fed close by."

"There," my partner said, pointing to the right. "A body or what's left of it, over there."

I adjusted my night vision, bringing the body into clear view.

A half-eaten corpse lay in the trees—a young man in his mid-twenties, missing his lower half. His torso was empty of all major organs. Judging from his expression and the scent around his body, he died hard and scared.

"Definitely a *Minoras*," I said. "Look at those claw marks; definitely a Dragondog."

"Was this the target? Doesn't smell nearly powerful enough."

"He wasn't the target...just unlucky," I said, examining the body. "Wrong place, wrong time."

"Not half the man he used to be," my partner said, looking at the victim. "He did not die well."

"Demon humor is seriously twisted," I said, glancing over at my partner. "Not half the man he used to be?"

"I can't help what I am any more than you can, Nyx," he said. "Otherkin humor is fairly distasteful, even for a demon."

"True. It's not you, Acheron," I said, taking a deep breath and letting it out slow. "This thing has me agitated. How did it even get out? Black Cleavers?"

"Cleavers would never be this sloppy," Acheron said, looking at the body. "This looks freelance. Revenge-cast maybe?"

"That is monumentally stupid. Especially with a *Minoras*."

"I didn't say the summoner was smart, just not a Cleaver."

Black Cleavers were self-appointed sorcerers that hunted demons. Most of them were dangerous. All of them were egocentric idiots. Only a small handful were actual threats. The real issue was that they numbered in the thousands, scattered all over the world.

"More likely a summons," Acheron said. "Someone was

using magic above their pay grade"—he looked down at the body—"maybe this unlucky bastard."

"No," I said. "There'd be a circle somewhere. He wasn't powerful enough for a free-cast. He just ended up being a snack."

"More like half a snack," Acheron observed. "It's moving fast if it didn't even bother to finish its meal. What's the rush?"

"It's still bound," I said, looking at the trail of blood. "This has to be a reverse-cast."

"Which means it's headed to the locus of the cast."

"The summons," I said. "It's heading to the summoner."

"Who is in for a very rude and lethal surprise."

"This is totally going to suck."

"And not in a good way either," Acheron added, looking into the night. "It's angry. Demons don't appreciate being summoned, bound, or imprisoned. I should know."

I nodded.

"It's going to try and break the bond," I said, moving silently through the trees. "I'd prefer not having to fight this thing."

"I'm not in any rush to face it, either," Acheron said, keeping his voice low. "The creature will be stronger after this."

"It's still feeding," I said, looking down at the small traces of blood leading away from the body. "That way."

"Must have taken the organs to go. At least it's being neat."

I stared at my partner.

"Neat, really?" I asked. "That's what you get from this?"

"What? There was hardly any blood," he said, pointing behind him. "It really drained the victim dry. I give it a solid E for effort."

I shook my head and sighed.

"This is what I get, having a demon for a partner."

"Hey, you summoned me, not the other way around," he said as we moved deeper into the trees. "Not my fault you used the wrong binding spell. What were you thinking?"

"I wasn't," I said, recalling the night I called Acheron into my circle...and broke it, nearly killing myself in the process. "I wasn't expecting...you."

I had only survived because Acheron was a Demon Lord who was more interested in his freedom than my life. That, and I was an Otherkin, not exactly an easy or soft target.

"Yet here I am," Acheron answered with a small bow. "A glorious mistake."

"A mistake I regret every day, trust me."

"I'm stuck with you too, you know."

"I'm going to guess—escaping hell means you got the better end of this deal."

"True," Acheron said with a quiet chuckle, then grew silent. "We have to kill it. You know we can't let it leave the park...at least not alive."

"I know," I said. "The Seven will lose their shit if it gets out."

"Especially Victoria...and she tolerates you."

"We have to maintain the bond, at least until we deal with it," I said. "If it..."

"If it breaks the bond," Acheron said, "it will be buffet time. Right now, it just wants the summoner. All bets are off if the bond is broken."

"Don't remind me," I said, moving faster. "Just be happy it's only a *Minoras*."

Acheron shuddered.

"You say that like it's a good thing," Acheron snapped. "*Minoras* are angry balls of fury on a good day. Once summoned, they become blenders of death."

"Up ahead," I said, lowering my voice and pointing. "There."

Several meters ahead of us, in a large summoning circle, stood a petrified young man who was quickly realizing he was in deep shit. The *Minoras*—a lower demon—looked like a hybrid between a large dog and a small dragon. Its body was covered in red-orange scales, each of its six legs ended in claws, and its canine-shaped head contained enormous fangs.

It paced slowly outside the summoner's circle. This was a reverse-cast. Stupid and dangerous for all but the most experienced sorcerers. In a reverse-cast, the summoner would call forth the creature and then bind them to service, while standing in the protection of the circle.

The safest way would've been to go traditional: stand in a protective circle, summon the creature into a binding circle, and compel it while it was still inside. The riskiest method was reserved for only the most powerful sorcerers: a free-cast. No circles on either end. Free-casts usually ended in a bloody mess...for the sorcerer.

The *Minoras* continued pacing around the circle, focused on the sorcerer inside, oblivious to everything and everyone outside of it. Every few seconds, it would growl and lash out at the edge. A small burst of orange energy would accompany every lash, leaving an afterglow delineating the protective boundary of the circle.

"It's focused on him...for now," Acheron said in a hushed tone. "You want to try and talk it down?"

"Do I look like a demon-whisperer?"

"Do you want me to answer that?"

"Shut it," I said, approaching the circle. "If this goes wrong..."

"I'll make sure to identify your body," Acheron deadpanned. "I'll bring flowers to your grave every year, too...when I remember."

I proceeded to give Acheron a one-finger response as I approached the circle...and the demon.

TWO

"Looks like you have a problem," I said to the sorcerer in the center of the circle, while staying back far enough to avoid the *Minoras*' orbit. "What were you planning to do with it?"

"I'm...I'm going to control it," the sorcerer stammered. "I can do this. They're going to pay."

"The real question is: what are *you* going to pay?"

"I can cover the cost of this...I have blood."

He pulled out a small bottle filled with a dark liquid. I glanced at the bottle and then at the pacing *Minoras*.

"That seems a little short for this demon," I said, keeping my voice low. "Do you have more?"

"Not on me, no."

"You do," I said, shaking my head slowly. "Not on you, but in you."

"Listen, I know what I'm doing. I don't need help, thanks."

He had guts. I gave him that much. Suicidally stupid, but large in the *cojones* department.

Summoning was not for the faint of heart.

You were asking something—not someone, something—

dangerous from another world to step into this one...forcefully. Try to remember being grabbed by the ear and dragged somewhere as a child. Now multiply that by one million, and you have an idea how the summoned feel...just to start.

It didn't matter what you were summoning. If you were not strong enough, you could end up dead on principle alone. Being summoned by a lesser being was insulting. If the summoned creature was considered benevolent—and I used that term lightly—it meant they would at least listen to your proposal before blasting you to bits, or ripping your arms and legs off, all while laughing at your mortal ass.

Malevolent creatures would straight up try and kill the summoner...much like the *Minoras* and the clueless sorcerer I was looking at. They wouldn't entertain a conversation, and the sooner they could dispatch you, the sooner they could get back to whatever they had been destroying when they had been summoned. To them, summoners were just a tasty distraction.

This reverse-cast was partially smart. Using the park at night meant it was mostly deserted—little chance for collateral damage, except for the unlucky victim. It also had several points of exit. Smart, if you needed to escape an angry demon. Not so smart if you used the wrong containment method, like a reverse-cast. If the *Minoras* killed the caster in the circle...it was free.

A free *Minoras* was a nightmare to consider. It would go on a rampage, killing everything in sight—and they had excellent sight.

The last, and most dangerous component of a summons, was the cost. Every summons had a cost, a price that had to be paid. Blood was usually the currency of choice; it needed to be enough to motivate the creature in the circle to obey. If the offer was unsatisfactory, and the summoner was incredibly lucky, they would just leave. I had never met anyone that lucky.

The sorcerer in the circle tonight was not one of the lucky ones.

"Your funeral," I said, taking a few more steps back, and waving him on. "Don't let me stop you. Please, proceed."

I noticed the sigils. Definitely not Black Cleaver work. Whoever this summoner was, he was in way over his head. He began an incantation. By the third verse, I knew he was going to die.

"You better stop him," Acheron said from behind me. "I don't know where he learned those verses, but any second now, he's going to be dinner for that demon."

"Are you going to deal with the demon?" I asked, letting the frustration creep into my voice. "Because I'm not going to be able to talk it down from munching on Clueless here, *and* stop him from finishing the verses at the same time."

"Hmm," Acheron said, pulling a book out of his coat and leaning against a tree, "I'm not on the clock. Besides, my contract only deals with keeping *you* safe, not idiot sorcerers who are too stupid to live. This is a classic example of Darwinism in effect."

"Acheron..."

"Fine, I'll distract the Sorcerer Supreme, you deal with the angry demon dog," Acheron said, closing the book. "You owe me dinner."

"We'll do Fong's later."

"Excellent," Acheron said, approaching the circle as I sidled close to the *Minoras*. "They have a new platter... the Carolina Reaper Special. It was so hot, I heard it nearly killed someone."

"Hello?" I said, waving a hand. "Sorcerer...focus?"

"Right," he said, licking his lips. "Dinner later. Save suicidal sorcerer now."

"Good plan," I said, stepping closer to the demon. "Go distract him and make sure he doesn't finish that incantation."

"I still think we should let natural selection sort him out."

"Go," I said, pointing at the sorcerer, "now."

Even though the *Minoras* were lower demons, they were intelligent and capable of language if you knew how to speak to them. Being an Otherkin meant demontongue came naturally to me. It was how I communicated with Acheron in public, even though he enjoyed showing off his skills as a polyglot.

Demontongue was similar to some of the original languages on earth—full of clicks, grunts and sounds not natural to what was considered 'civilized' culture.

I stepped as close as I dared to the *Minoras,* without getting too close.

"This one is not worth your attention, great demon," I said. Demons had egos the size of mountains; it never hurt to stroke them. "He's not even a meal. Look how thin and frail he is."

"Even one as frail as he, bleeds," the *Minoras* answered without looking at me. "I will feast on his blood and chew his bones."

Its voice was a combination of a low dog growl and an angry dragon roar. Menacing enough to force your body into a pucker factor of ten, and make you want to run away screaming. A fear reflex raced through my body, and my legs wanted to follow.

I stood my ground...barely.

"I'm afraid I can't let you do that," I said when I found my voice again. "He made a mistake summoning you."

"One he will pay for with his life."

"Can't let you kill him, either," I said, a little more boldly. "I'll have OSA deal with him."

The *Minoras* turned its head, as if noticing me for the first time...a good and a bad thing. It sniffed the air and focused on where I stood. Its orange eyes fixed me with its gaze.

"You speak my tongue, but you are not of my kind," it said. "Do you wish to end your life this night?"

"That's going to be a hard no," I said. "Why were you summoned?"

"This foolish human wishes to exact vengeance," the *Minoras* spat after a low growl. "He dares to summon me? I will feed on his entrails."

"Let's hold off on the feeding on his entrails," I said, holding up a hand and looking for an opening. "Perhaps, we can reach an agreement."

Minoras were covered in scales, except for a small spot beneath their jaws at the bottom of their necks—a vulnerability I had nearly lost an arm to discover, years ago. If I was going to stop this demon, I only had to get past a mouth full of razor-sharp fangs, half a dozen lethal claws and supernatural reflexes to get at that spot.

A walk in the park. If that park was located in the middle of a minefield.

"You have no concern here," the *Minoras* answered, swiveling its head back to the petrified sorcerer Acheron was trying to coax out of the circle. "This is not your summons. Do not make it your night to die."

The timing had to be perfect. If Acheron managed to get the sorcerer out of the circle before I subdued the *Minoras*... well, dead sorcerer and then a hungry, free demon. Which would mean we were next on the menu.

"*Any luck?*" Acheron mentally asked from the other side of the circle. "*This sorcerer is being surprisingly uncooperative.*"

The demon-bond we shared allowed us to communicate silently, if we were close enough; distance interfered with the process. If we were too far away from each other, we would be met with silence.

Acheron couldn't enter the circle; being a demon prevented him from crossing the outer boundary. It didn't mean he couldn't affect the sorcerer, just that most of his options tended to be on the extremely violent and petrifying side, likely resulting in a dead sorcerer. If the sorcerer died, the *Minoras* was free, leaving us to deal with a hungry, unbound demon. A recipe of nastiness that put us back on the menu.

I needed the sorcerer alive…at least for now.

"May have something to do with the angry demon waiting to shred him the moment he steps out of that circle," I answered. *"This is a revenge-cast. Tell him to shut it down and we can help him. If not, we leave him to the demon. Convince him."*

I refocused on the *Minoras* when I heard a scream from behind me.

"What are you?" screamed the sorcerer, scrambling away from Acheron, but staying inside the circle. "Stay away from me!"

"You know how you're scared of that demon over there?" Acheron said with a smile. "I'm the thing that scares the demons."

Acheron had partially revealed his true-self. Most human brains couldn't process the image of a true-self without short-circuiting and driving the person insane instantly. A partial reveal would frighten, but not push a mind to insanity—just scare the person shitless. Great.

There was no way the sorcerer would leave that circle now. That left Plan B.

I hated Plan B.

The *Minoras* turned to face me now, fully engaged. It sensed the immediate threat and acted accordingly. In its mind, the sorcerer could wait.

I was the appetizer before the meal.

"What are you?" it asked, turning its body. The six claws raked the ground. "You are not Brood."

"I'm the thing creatures like you fear."

"I fear nothing."

"Wrong answer."

I leaped.

The night embraced me in its caress, and for a few silent seconds, hanging suspended mid-air, I felt peace. I landed on the *Minoras,* claws first, and shredded through a layer of scales. It howled in pain and anger.

Then it lunged.

I jumped back and rolled away from a deadly swipe. It snapped its head around, attempting to bury razor sharp fangs in my side. I raked its eyes and clawed its side. With a howl, this one more anger than pain the demon lashed out, slamming a fist into my midsection.

I landed several feet away and rolled, the pain of the blow a dull throbbing in the back of my mind. It pounced forward, landing next to me. I punched it in the ribs and nearly broke my hand. It whipped its tail around preternaturally fast. I ducked under the mace-like appendage and caught a back kick in the chest with a *whomp* sound escaping my lips.

I landed hard and bounced a few times before catching my breath again.

"Ouch," I grumbled, getting back to my feet. "I felt that."

"We don't have all night," Acheron said in my head. *"Its presence will attract others soon. Finish it."*

"Easier said than done," I answered. *"You want to try?"*

"And deprive you of a sense of accomplishment? Hell forbid."

The scales were becoming a nuisance. I let my hands transform into claws again, and slowly licked my lips, heightening my sense of smell.

I ran forward.

The last thing it expected, but welcomed, opening its maw in anticipation. I slid under it at the last possible moment and buried my claws in its neck, striking its vulnerable spot.

It howled one last time as thick, black ichor poured from the wound. I slid away, barely avoiding its claws, and got slowly to my feet as it stumbled away. It collapsed several meters away before disappearing in a small blaze of demon-flame. I kicked dirt over the napalm-like substance, making sure it was completely out before walking over to Acheron.

"I don't think he's convinced," Acheron said, pointing at the sorcerer. "Says he's never leaving the circle."

"Drop the circle," I said, my voice low. "Do it...now."

"Are you insane?" the sorcerer said. "Do you know what *that* is next to you?"

I looked over at Acheron who smiled and waved.

"You cast a circle with the express purpose of exacting vengeance," I said. "You put hundreds, if not thousands of lives in danger. Drop the circle...or you get the same treatment as the demon...the *other* demon."

"No," the sorcerer answered, bolder now that the *Minoras* was gone. "You can't touch me as long..."

I ran into the circle and grabbed him by the neck, careful to make sure my claws were retracted. I didn't want to accidentally perforate his neck.

"As long as what?" I asked, squeezing until he wheezed, turning several shades of pink. "Did you think I was a demon?"

He nodded.

"Mistakes like that can get you killed," I said, shaking my head. "Are you planning on summoning more demons?"

He shook his head vigorously.

"Damn straight you won't," I said, punching him square across the jaw with my free hand. He passed out immediately.

I dropped him to the ground outside of the circle, where he crumpled, unconscious. I stepped over to where Acheron waited. "Call OSA and have this idiot picked up."

OSA—the Order of Supernatural Affairs, or Bears, as they were called, were the ruling magical police force in the world. They were formed a thousand years ago, with various branches dealing with different aspects of sorcery and the supernatural all over the world. The only group older than the OSA was The Seven, who'd been around since the Unveiling.

"Did you kill him?" Acheron asked, looking down at the sorcerer. "You know the Bears don't like it when we use excessive force."

"He's alive for now," I said. "Can't say how long he'll remain that way if he casts again. I'll recommend an ablation of his casting for his own safety."

Acheron nodded and pulled out his phone.

"Order of Supernatural Affairs, please," he said into the phone. "Yes, I'll wait."

I stepped over to the circle and broke the outer boundary with my foot. Something about all of this was off. There was no way this third-rate sorcerer should have been able to summon a *Minoras*. An imp, maybe—if he was lucky—but not a *Minoras*...unless he had help.

I examined the circle again and my blood turned to ice.

We had a problem.

THREE

"Acheron, over here," I said, still crouched over the faintly glowing circle. "What do you make of this?"

Acheron stepped over to where I was and looked into the circle. He formed an orb of demonflame and held it high to get a better look at the summoning circle in the darkness. The demonflame was for my benefit. My night vision was exceptional and only exceeded by carpenter bees. Acheron's night vision made me, and the bees, appear blind by comparison.

No one escaped a demon in the dark.

I rubbed my nose as the acrid stench of demonflame hung in the air. There was no way I would ever get used to the odor of rotten eggs and burning meat mixed together. It was an assault on my heightened sense of smell.

"What, exactly do you see?" he asked, peering into the circle. "These are typical sigils."

"You don't see it?" I asked, tracing the odd sigil in the dirt next to the circle. "There's a symbol in here, nested into the others. This one."

Acheron looked down at the symbol I had traced and his face darkened.

"Are you certain?" he asked. "This is the exact symbol you see?"

I nodded my head.

"It's hard to see, because it's hidden behind some of the others, but it's there," I said. "You really can't see it?"

"No," Acheron said, his voice low and dangerous. "That concerns me."

"What kind of sigil is this?"

"That's *not* a Black Cleaver sigil," Acheron said, suspending the flame in the air above us to get a better look at my tracing. "That appears to be a powerful, ancient design, highly volatile. Far too dangerous for a novice sorcerer to know, along with that incantation he was mangling."

"Did you make out what he was saying? The parts I caught practically guaranteed he was going to be shredded."

"He would have been...if we had allowed him to finish."

"Why do they do this?" I asked, mostly to myself. "Summon demons, I mean."

"The awareness among humans has always existed," Acheron said, slipping into professor mode, and pushing his glasses up on the bridge of his nose. "The fascination with the unseen and supernatural is practically a feature with them."

"There's nothing wrong with searching for something greater than yourself," I said. "In many cases it makes us humble, wiser. It helps us grow and become enlightened."

Acheron gave me a soft golf clap.

"It can also be twisted, perverted, and turned into a form of control and evil," he added. "Most of the religions humans pursue and create are a form of control. More wars have been fought in the name of deities than I care to remember."

"But you're a demon," I said. "Doesn't that mean some of them were right?"

"You do realize that demons are considered demons because we are fallen?" Acheron asked softly. "You know what we're fallen from?"

"A great height?" I answered with a grin. "And you, in particular, landed on your head? Explains plenty, actually."

"Otherkin humor is just as bad as demon humor," Acheron answered with a small smile. "Angels...we are considered fallen angels."

"Is that true?" I asked. "Were you an angel?"

"Demons and angels are just names for beings that are unknown to humans." Acheron answered, waving my words away. "Things the human mind cannot comprehend."

"I've never met an 'Angel'. Are they like demons, but with manners?"

He shook his head with a sigh.

"All it means, is that they don't understand *what* I am," he answered. "Even science, if sufficiently advanced, can appear to be magic. Most religions are ancient, rooted in traditions questioned by no one, just blindly followed. What some call demons, others call angels. It's all made up and artificial. Humans trying to understand what their brains can't possibly comprehend."

"Was that just a long winded way of you saying 'I don't know'?" I asked. "It's okay to admit you don't know something."

"I worry about you sometimes," he said shooting me a glare. "Humans have always delved in areas that don't concern them. They like to poke the dark...they just don't like it when the dark pokes back."

"Almost every demon I've met—present company excluded—has tried to kill me," I said, crouching down in the circle. "I never had the opportunity to reach out and understand them. They were too busy trying to shred me."

"That's about right," Acheron said with a nod. "Seems humans and Brood have more in common than they know."

"That's a scary thought."

"I know."

I traced the ancient symbol with my finger, burning it into my memory.

"What are you doing?" Acheron asked, concerned. "Don't touch that. You don't know where it's been."

"I'm storing it"—I tapped my temple—"in case I need to use it later," I said. "You said it was powerful. Sounds important, possibly useful."

"I also said it could be highly volatile and dangerous," Acheron added. "Did that part not register? Especially if I can't see it. That means…"

"It was hidden," I finished. "Someone didn't want demons to see this sigil."

"Demons, or just me?" Acheron said. "This feels off."

"That's why we're looking into it."

"Again, what part of dangerous are you not understanding?" Acheron said. "If someone masked the sigil, its presence in this summoning circle was deliberate."

"Exactly," I said. "Dangerous, highly volatile and powerful, sounds like it can come in handy at some point."

"I strongly advise against using *that* sigil," Acheron cautioned. "It may have been used in this summoning, but that doesn't make it safe. It almost got him"—he pointed at the sorcerer—"painfully killed."

"I know," I said with a slight smile. "That's the whole point. Whoever helped him out knew it was volatile and dangerous. That's information I can use later."

"I don't like it," he said. "Especially the part about you being the only one seeing it."

"That's why we get paid the big money," I said. "We take on the impossible cases."

"Paid? I don't get paid except in aggravation."

"Then you are due a bonus," I said, looking down at the sorcerer. "And this case is going to pay you in spades."

"I think," he said, stepping back, while staring at me, "you are more dangerous than that sigil. Ancient, unknown sigils are to be avoided, not stored for future use—or in your case, abuse."

"Someone helped him," I said, keeping my voice low. "They knowingly gave him this sigil. They knew it would summon something too powerful for a novice sorcerer to control, much less survive. This was almost a murder by proxy."

"Or they could have been erasing their tracks. Unleash a *Minoras*, kill the summoner in the process, and wreak havoc on the populace."

"Destroy the circle," I said, stepping away from the summoning circle with a nod, "before the OSA gets here. No need to complicate this further."

"Who would gain from this?" Acheron asked as he destroyed the circle with a burst of demonflame. "Do we know who he is?"

"This smells like Cleavers," I said. "Except I don't see any of their usual work. The havoc and destruction is their M.O., but not the demon summoning. Could be they're getting smarter, operating at a distance, using middle men, or victims in this case."

"If the purpose of your organization is under scrutiny," Acheron said, "the best way to justify your existence is to create a need for your services."

"Unleashed demons means we need Black Cleavers?" I asked. "That seems way too methodical, too forward thinking, for them. They don't come across as this clever. Some of them barely survive dispatching the demons."

"Some may be stumbling fools, but not all. The gravest error would be to underestimate them."

"I don't underestimate anyone or anything that presents a threat. It's just been my experience that most Black Cleavers are about as bright as a sack of bricks," I said, sneezing because of the demonflame. "Put that thing out already."

"Some of their leaders are quite cunning," Acheron said, dousing the flames with a motion of his hand. "Don't let the foot soldiers deceive you; Flint is brilliant."

"Still, it's a risky move," I said. "Flint wouldn't risk this kind of exposure. The OSA would stomp on the Cleavers if they felt they were consolidating power."

"He would take the risk…if it couldn't be traced back to them," Acheron said. "The sigil is part of a larger set and…is something that would get lost in the larger design of the circle. I didn't see it. It's very likely no one else would have either."

"Unless you knew what to look for," I said. "What are you saying?"

"This was a test of sorts," Acheron said, looking around. "It's possible this was a dry run. Imagine inserting a sigil like that in a major summons."

"That wouldn't be murder by proxy…"

"No, it would be murder on a massive scale," Acheron answered. "You need to report this."

"No," I said. "We still don't know enough. Why was I able to see it?"

"We know enough to know that this is dangerous. You *need* to inform The Seven."

"Not yet," I said, looking at the unconscious sorcerer. "He may know more. Who was he trying to attack? Who gave him the sigil and that incantation?"

"None of that will matter if Victoria finds out you withheld this information from her," Acheron said. "Especially if she finds out you can see this sigil when a *Demon Lord* couldn't. That would bring up all sorts of questions...uncomfortable questions."

"You will not tell her about that," I said, my voice hard. "By your bond. Say it."

"By my bond I will not tell her you could read that sigil when I couldn't," he said, his voice strained by the compulsion. "You could have just asked, you know."

"Sorry," I said. "Last thing I need is for The Seven to examine me again."

"A simple request would have sufficed."

"Can't take that chance," I said. "What if they get their hands on you and try to get information?"

"Kidnap me for interrogation?" Acheron mocked. "You do realize I'm a Demon Lord?"

"I'll tell her...eventually," I said. "You know how The Seven get: it gets classified, and immediately, we're off it."

"The Seven will not be pleased," he answered with a head shake. "Especially Victoria."

"You say that like I should care."

"You should. She only happens to lead one of the most powerful sorcerous organizations on the planet," Acheron said. "I'd say that bears some consideration."

The Seven were a different entity altogether. Even though they were called The Seven, no one really knew how many they numbered. Some said the hundreds, others said there were thousands of them. However many they were, they had an excellent PR team.

This was a group of secret sorcerers operating worldwide outside of the OSA, answering to a different set of authorities. They were an ancient, sorcerous black ops group that managed to convince the world they didn't exist.

It was the group that let me become an Otherkin.

"I don't," I said. "It didn't matter when I was human, and it certainly doesn't matter now."

"It wasn't their fault you became Otherkin," Acheron reminded me. "That was an error. Mostly *your* error if I recall."

"An error?" I said, feeling the heat of anger flush my face. "Oh, you mean like a slip of the tongue?"

"I meant..."

"Like an oversight? Something overlooked? Forgotten?"

"What I meant to say was...nevermind," he said, choosing the wiser path tonight. This wasn't a battle he could win, and it wasn't worth dying on this hill. "You're right, they could have acted, placed you in stasis, or tried to reverse the transformation."

"Yes, they could have," I snapped. "They could have prevented what happened...but they didn't. They *let* it happen, encouraged it even, so they could have a pet Otherkin."

"Otherkin are rare," Acheron answered. "Rare enough for them to let the transformation run its course."

"They didn't ask *me*."

"She taught and trained you."

"She forged me into a weapon."

"The rest of The Seven wanted you eliminated," Acheron said. "You do realize that the alternative was death...yours? She convinced them."

"I'm aware," I said, my voice soft as marble. "That's why when the time comes...she'll live. I'll repay her kindness...a life for a life."

"The rest of The Seven may have a difference of opinion," he said. "Something you may want to consider in that future massacre."

I looked into Acheron's eyes and let my rage seethe until he looked away.

"They...let...it...happen. Just to see what I would become. Like I was some experiment. All of them."

"Except Victoria."

I nodded.

"Except her," I said. "She gets a choice. Walk away or die."

"It's so nice to see you mellowing with age," Acheron said with a grin. "At least it wasn't worse. You only became an Otherkin."

"Only became?" I asked, exasperated. "What would've been worse?"

"At least you didn't become a demon," Acheron said with a small shrug, trying to diffuse my anger. It worked. "That would have been...awkward, not to mention a serious blow to the reputations of demons everywhere."

"Screw you."

"No thanks, pass," He said. "If I ever find an interested, hunky Otherkin, I'll pass him your number."

I smiled and he nodded. That was his plan all along, bringing me back from the edge of rage. I let out a long breath and composed myself. None of it was Acheron's fault. The anger I carried had a specific target: The Seven.

"We need to find out how Clueless here found out about this summons," I said, ignoring Acheron's hunky comment. "We start there and work backwards."

"If you use that sigil, you're going to get us banished," Acheron said with a chuckle. "Or worse."

"What's worse than hell?"

"You mean besides being on this plane stuck with you?"

"I didn't realize you were suffering so," I said, feigning concern. "Is it bad?"

"You have no idea," Acheron replied, milking the moment. "The indignities I'm forced to bear."

"If it's really that bad, I could always attempt a free-cast and send you back," I offered. "I haven't attempted one on a *Demon Lord* of your stature, but how hard could it be?"

"Let's refrain from any casting attempts...free or otherwise," Acheron said quickly. "The last time you cast, you nearly obliterated yourself, along with a ten-block radius of this city."

"I was angry."

He raised an eyebrow

"Are you inferring that there are times you aren't angry?"

"The last time I cast, I ended up with you."

"Which nearly killed you. I rest my case."

"I've been practicing since then. I think I can do it—I'm at least forty-five percent sure."

"You think?" he asked. "I will not be experimented on, thank you very much. Keep your 'practice' to yourself."

"No one likes to be the guinea pig," I said. "Everyone wants to conduct the experiment. Are you sure?"

"Absolutely certain."

"Your loss," I said with a shrug. "You could be home right now, back in a cell, tortured every hour on the hour."

He glared at me, uncomfortable that I knew what he had been going through while imprisoned in Hell. What I didn't know was *why* he had been imprisoned. How bad do you have to be to get imprisoned...in *Hell*?

"I strongly suggest you brief The Seven," Acheron added after a moment of silence. "At least inform Victoria. She seems to tolerate your outbursts of rage."

"Victoria will tell me to come in and drop it," I said. "You know that."

"Not a bad idea," Acheron said with a nod. "This seems deeper than we can see right now. What we need is some perspective."

"Your job is to help *me*, not worry if we're going to get into trouble with The Seven."

"*We* don't get in trouble," Acheron said, pushing up the glasses on the bridge of his nose. "*You* do that well on your own."

Two figures clomped through the bushes and approached us. They were about as stealthy as rhinos charging through a field. OSA field agents defined the term 'blunt instrument'.

"OSA," the one on the left said, showing me a softly glowing, intricate sigil on his palm, before looking down at the unconscious sorcerer. "This the suspect?"

The field agents wore a uniform of black on black. Black suits with black long coats over them, with no distinguishing marks or insignias. It was like a Goth convention on steroids.

Get a group of them together and you had a ready-made funeral procession. These two were rank and file agents, above average sorcerers with measurable ability, but nothing overly impressive. Their superiors were the real force behind the OSA. They were some of the most powerful sorcerers on the planet. These two were grunts, and about as smart as dirt.

"I need a full background check on him," I said. "He was casting way above his skill level."

"And you are?" the agent on the right asked, giving Acheron a serious case of stink-eye. "What's your designation?"

They knew who I was, everyone in the OSA did, but they enjoyed driving the point home. I wasn't one of them. I was an outsider and didn't belong. It was a tired pointless jab, but like I said, smart as dirt.

"How many Otherkin do you know that roam the streets with a demon partner?" I asked, my voice laced with irritation. "Should I inform Victoria you're confused about who I am?"

If the OSA was the magical police, The Seven were closer

to a sorcerer black-ops group of elite practitioners. The Seven were feared and disliked, but respected. Especially Victoria. Pissing her off could guarantee an agent, OSA or otherwise, outpost duty...on Antarctica.

"No need to get bent out of shape," Agent Left said. "We're just verifying ID. We're not aware of many freaks who would partner with filthy demon scum, but hey, maybe there's more than one of you."

I was used to the insults by now. That didn't mean they could just sling them without consequence. My wrath was one of those cold dishes, and I was in no hurry to serve it.

Agent Right crouched down and began a full-body scan on the sorcerer. It was standard procedure to make sure there were no hidden sigils or glyphs that could unleash death and destruction on an unsuspecting OSA agent.

"I need a full background check run," I repeated, ignoring the slur. "He summoned a *Minoras*."

"Bullshit," Agent Right said, getting to his feet after he completed the scan on the unconscious sorcerer. "He barely has enough energy to summon a clue, much less a *Minoras*,"—he glanced at me—"you've been sniffing your partners demonflame?"

"Smells like it," Agent Left said, sniffing the air. "Or maybe this demon just needs to be sent back where it belongs?"

"You intend to banish me?" Acheron asked, his question laced with a gentle undercurrent of menace. "All by yourself?"

"As much as I would like to dive into the OSA brain trust you two represent, I know what he summoned and have the bruises to prove it," I said. "Get me a full background check. I need to know who he is and why he was casting."

They both eyed me cautiously. Going up against a *Minoras* wasn't something to take lightly. I knew they believed me, and that was the problem.

I scared them.

"We'll get right on that," Agent Left added with a snicker. "Right after hell freezes over."

I sighed and glanced at Acheron who nodded.

"Don't fry their brains," I said, silently through our bond as he stepped close. *"Just freak them out a little."*

"One low-level freak out on the way," Acheron said, approaching the OSA agents. *"You may want to turn away for this."*

I turned to the field agents.

"You brought this on yourself," I said. "Enjoy."

FOUR

"Holy hell!" Agent Right screamed, right before turning away into the brush and throwing up. The retching sounds went on for a few minutes, followed by some more cursing.

"Shit," Agent Left muttered as he shuddered and turned away. "That was uncalled for."

"What the royal hell, Nyx," Agent Right said, wiping his mouth after a few more dry heaves. "You actually spend time with this...this *thing* as your partner? You're more twisted than I thought."

"For your information," Acheron said matter-of-factly, "the temperature of hell would melt the skin off your bones. It's in no danger of freezing over, not now, or *ever*."

"It was a damn joke," Agent Right said, looking at me, but keeping his distance. "What the hell are you?"

I gave him a sweet smile.

"My *partner* expects that background report before the sun rises, understood?" Acheron asked. "Oh, and if you ever call me filthy again...I'll make sure you live to regret it...over and over."

"We'll get right on it," Agent Left muttered, still shaken. "We'll head back right now."

Agent Left cast a mild weightless spell on the unconscious sorcerer, and his body floated gently off the ground. Agent Right pushed the body back the way they had come, as they retraced their steps back to their vehicle.

I had once asked Acheron to reveal his true-self to me, but he had refused. According to him, my body had fundamentally transformed, rendering the fear effects of a true-self ineffective. Apparently, my becoming an Otherkin had made me immune.

It sounded like a lie.

"I said freak them out," I watched the shaken OSA agents leave the park, nearly tripping over each other to get away from Acheron. "Not melt their brains."

"That *was* a tiny freakout," Acheron replied. "Did you notice they left of their own volition? No bowels were evacuated and—"

"Stop, I got it," I said, cutting him off, to prevent getting into a conversation about bowels evacuating. "Next time, dial it down."

"All I ever do is reveal what is in the viewer's true nature," Acheron said, quietly. "What they see is what is within their own hearts and souls. Most don't take it well."

"Well... the last thing I...*we* need is the OSA coming after you for field agents ending up in psych wards, because you were helping them attain enlightenment."

"They wouldn't dare...would they?"

"Victoria makes sure they don't...officially," I said. "Doesn't mean they won't come after you—"

"*Us,*" Acheron corrected with a smile. "If they come after me, you can rest assured they are coming after the *freak* who is my partner."

"Right," I said, realizing he was correct. "Doesn't mean

they won't come after *us*...unofficially. It's not like Vic is watching over us twenty-four seven."

"She could be our unofficial guardian angel...Saint Victoria," Acheron said as we headed out of the park. "You could call her Saint Vic. I'm sure she'd love that."

"I will do no such thing," I said, absentmindedly, as I thought about the sigil from the circle. "She'd probably blast me if I did."

Acheron looked up at the sky.

"It will take the OSA a few hours before we get the information on the sorcerer," he said, "even with the motivational dose of fear I shared with them. Where to?"

"We need to find out more about that sigil," I said. "Let's go see Liv. She may know more."

"You're serious about this sigil?" Acheron asked warily. "I think we should leave it alone. Forget it."

"No. We need answers," I said. "Plus, we get to see Liv." I knew she was his weakness. She could easily be anyone's weakness. "You always want to see *Liv*."

"Ahh, Liv," Acheron said, wistfully. "This day is shaping up considerably. Fine, you drive a hard bargain, but I agree...we must go see Liv."

I rolled my eyes.

"We are going to see her on *business*," I said. "Keep it in your pants."

"I am the very definition of propriety," Acheron answered. "I can't help that Liv is staggeringly attractive. How am I supposed to resist?"

"I'm sure the fact that she's a succubus has absolutely nothing to do with it...right?"

"That's just a pleasant happenstance," Acheron assured me. "You do realize I'm a Demon Lord? I'm not affected by her demon power."

"You're a *male* Demon Lord," I corrected. "I'm going to

repeat myself: we are going there *on business*. Keep it together."

We stepped outside of the park and there, waiting by the entrance, was my Mantis NFN-8. It was a gift from The Seven after the two previous vehicles they provided me were blown apart or totaled. In my defense, it was their fault for giving me sigil-free, commercial vehicles to conduct demon hunting work. Regular vehicles and demons don't mix.

Eight, as I called her, was a military APC with all the bells, whistles, and firepower I could need. One of The Seven, Rodrigo the Sigilsmith, even created the sigils that protected it from destruction. She was the only vehicle I knew that could take a direct blast of demonflame, without melting into abstract art.

I loved my ride.

She wasn't pretty, but she was virtually indestructible. Rumor was that the original manufacturer used enhanced metal to create the body, which allowed for the sigils to operate as intended. Whatever they did, it was perfect.

I placed my hand on the door handle. The engine roared to life as the door unlocked and the headlights illuminated the street around us.

"I hate it when it does that," Acheron mumbled, getting in the back. "Why couldn't they have given you something more sensible...like an M1 Abrams?"

"Don't hate on Eight," I said, tapping the dashboard as I jumped into my seat. "She's a good girl, and even lets your demon ass ride in her."

"It's not my fault if your conventional vehicles are affected by demon physiology," Acheron answered, strapping into his seat. "Do you think you can manage to drive like we aren't being pursued by a horde of angry Brood?"

"I'll give it a shot," I said, revving the engine with a roar.

The sound brought a grin to my face, and I saw Acheron wince. "Probably not."

"Why do I even bother?" he asked as I stepped on the gas and launched Eight down the street with a yell.

FIVE

Liv Rei owned a bookstore downtown.

Calling it a bookstore was slightly misleading. The Grimoire was what was known as a repository of reliquaries. Liv collected rare books and items from all over the world. She didn't sell them.

If she did, it would be like selling magical nukes. The OSA, The Seven and any other number of three letter agencies would line up to take her down and put her away. It would be a nightmare because Liv was dangerous and powerful.

As long as she remained neutral and refused to sell the contents of her shop, everyone left her alone. Access to The Grimoire was limited and Liv vetted each and every visitor personally. If she said you weren't welcome...no access.

The artifacts in her shop were dangerous. In the wrong hands, they could wreak untold havoc and destruction. It meant she had to be careful about who was allowed access to her collection.

The service she provided was closer to a research reference library. If you made it through her vetting process, you could study the items she housed in her shop, but she wouldn't lend them out, much less sell them.

The Grimoire was located in the Village at 221A Bleecker. It was a squat, two-story building, sitting catty-corner to 6th Avenue, sandwiched between Winston Churchill Square and Molly's Cupcakes. The ground floor was a Sweetgreen—the eco-chic salad chain, with The Grimoire taking up the entire top floor. The only access to The Grimoire was through the lower-level, Sweetgreen.

I pulled up in front of the Sweetgreen and parked Eight with a low rumble.

Eight had OSA plates, courtesy of Victoria. This meant local police wouldn't touch her, much less try to ticket and tow. The sigils all over her chassis gave off a subtle 'keep away' vibe, just in case an overzealous traffic officer got too close.

I had tried to convince Rodrigo to create some 'run away screaming' sigils for Eight, and he just shook his head. I remembered his words:

"The last thing I need is to hunt down innocents sitting in a corner gibbering madness because of my sigils, mija," he chastised me when I asked. "You get keep away sigils and be smart about where you park that thing."

The sun was peeking over the horizon as I killed the engine. Visiting Liv during the day only minimized the chances of dealing with creatures out to *borrow* her collection by force. Contrary to popular belief, not all monsters kept their activities to the night hours. The real scary dangerous creatures roamed during the day.

I took a deep breath and prepared myself mentally for the conversation I needed to have. I had to give Acheron 'the talk', or he would be impossible to manage inside of five minutes. I swear he had the hormones of a teenage boy discovering girls for the first time.

"We are here on official business," I said, my voice firm.

"I'm serious."

"Whoa, are you using the 'bad cop' voice?" Acheron asked. "I haven't done anything...yet."

"Official business," I repeated, staring into his eyes. A feat very few could do while keeping their sanity. "Are we clear?"

"I'm officially in lust," he replied, ignoring me and looking out the window before running his fingers through his hair. "Absolutely clear. How do I look?"

I sighed. This was a losing battle.

"If you can't keep it together, you can wait in Eight," I said, my tone still serious. "Last thing I need is you flirting with Liv. Did you forget what happened the last time you tried to flirt with her?"

"How could I?" Acheron replied with a grin. "It hurt so good."

"I don't know why you insist on pushing this with her," I said with a sigh. "You know she's taken a vow."

"Please explain it to me," Acheron said. "How can a succubus take a vow of celibacy? It's practically criminal... especially when the succubus in question is one inhumanly spectacular Liv Rei."

"We've been over this," I said, letting the anger creep into my voice. "The vow makes sure she keeps The Grimoire. We need The Grimoire and we need her guarding it. Why is this complicated for you?"

"I understand it," Acheron answered. "I just don't like it."

"Celibacy and neutrality," I said. "She stays clear of all OSA affairs, they leave her alone."

"Beautiful and smart," Acheron answered wistfully. "I need to convince her to break this vow, at least for me."

"Will never happen," I said with a small smile. "You just gave the perfect reason."

"I did?"

"She's smart, practically a genius," I answered. "Why

would she risk that for some scruffy Demon Lord who's all hormones and no brain?"

"Ouch," Acheron said with a grin. "That was uncalled for."

"It's her choice, so drop it," I answered. "Tell me you understand."

"A vow like that should be illegal."

"Do I need to *compel* you?"

Acheron's face darkened at my words.

"You wouldn't."

"Watch me," I assured him. "You stop the blood flow to the head on your shoulders, and you'll find yourself crawling back to Eight so fast, it'll give you whiplash."

"Mmmm...whips and lashes. Can you make sure Liv is doing the lashing?"

"You are a lost cause, did you know that? Do not make me compel you. I'm serious."

The bond we shared, through the summons that went wrong, bound Acheron to me...completely. We didn't like to talk about it...well, *he* didn't and I avoided bringing it up. Mostly, because we both made errors that day. Errors that had long-lasting consequences for the both of us.

"Threats...are beneath you," he said, tugging on his vest indignantly and straightening the glasses on his face. "A simple request would have sufficed."

I bit my tongue and took a deep breath, counting to ten to restrain myself from driving a fist upside his head...repeatedly.

"Just...get out," I said, unstrapping my harness. "She should be expecting us."

"She always is," he purred. "One of the things I love about Liv."

I shook my head.

"Holy hell," I muttered under my breath. "You can be a total pain in my ass."

"There's nothing holy about hell," he answered with a grin. "I should know."

"Out...now."

"I can hardly wait," he said, jumping out of Eight. "Let's not keep her waiting."

We stepped into the Sweetgreen, and Acheron scrunched his face.

"Behave," I said under my breath, adding an elbow in his ribs for good measure. "We're not here to critique the place. Leave Becca alone and head to the back."

He peered into the containers holding different kinds of food.

"Do humans really eat this...? Does it even qualify as food?" he asked, his face still scrunched up. "This is food for rodents. Really, this can't be a food of choice. This is some sort of torture...yes?"

"People like to eat it and keep your voice down."

I nodded to the counter person who stood behind the large glass panel. She gave me a short nod in return, moving on to take care of the next customer—who was giving Acheron a serious case of side eye. Acheron smiled and winked at her. The customer blushed and quickly looked away. There were days he was impossible.

Today was one of those days.

The counter person standing behind the large glass panel observed this brief interaction and slowly shook her head with a small smile. Her name badge said Becca, but I knew she was really one of Liv's guardians. She gave me another subtle nod, directing me to the back.

Becca stood at least six feet tall, her gymnast's physique easily clearing the tall, glass panel. Her black hair was pulled back in a long, tight braid, contrasting starkly against her pale skin. Her violet eyes shone with latent power, her gaze following us for a few feet as we walked past.

If anyone tried to get to Liv or The Grimoire upstairs, Becca was the first line of defense. To my knowledge, The Grimoire housed five guardians on the premises. I'd only ever seen Becca. The other four were either a myth or invisible.

Not that Liv needed guardians. She wasn't some helpless waif waiting to be rescued. I'd never faced a succubus in combat, but the rumors around Liv made me glad I was on her good side.

"Did you ever find out what she was?" Acheron asked, returning an elbow shot to my ribs, and knocking me out of my reverie as we headed to the storeroom. "Becca is not part of the Brood."

"Do you *really* want to know?" I asked and slowed down. "I could always go back and ask her."

"No, thank you," Acheron said with a sniff. "I just wanted to know if you knew. Who's being crass now?"

"She's a guardian...a powerful one," I said after a moment of thought. "Not someone or something I want to face without serious backup."

"That was my assessment as well," Acheron said, his face serious. "I just thought you would know what kind of guardian. The subject is broad."

"It never really crossed my mind to get into detail with Becca. I don't plan to ever launch an offensive against The Grimoire, do you?"

"Not The Grimoire, but that poor excuse for an eatery? Possibly."

"If you *really* want to know what she is," I answered, picking up the pace again, "you could always ask Liv."

"Ignorance is not bliss in my world," he replied. "In my world, ignorance is one step away from oblivion. What you don't know can kill you."

He did have a point.

"Know yourself and know your enemy?"

"Sun Tzu knew what he was talking about," Acheron said. "I don't like facing unknown entities in battle."

"We aren't facing her in battle, we're walking past her and upstairs to see Liv."

"She's an unknown quantity and that makes me uneasy."

"Whatever she is, I don't want to tangle with her," I answered, heading to a black, unmarked door at the rear of the storeroom. "If Liv trusts her to protect The Grimoire, she's capable and dangerous."

"*I'm* capable and dangerous," Acheron said, looking back over his shoulder to the front area. "Becca is something more...something old...something worse."

"Something worse than you? I seriously doubt that."

"There are many things out there worse than me...deep unknowable things in an abyss of mystery."

I snapped my fingers to get his attention.

"Abyss and gazing...don't," I said, refocusing his attention on the door in front of us. "Do you want to open the door, or should I?"

"Allow me," Acheron said, tracing a sigil on the door. It gave off a faint hint of demonflame, and instantly disappeared in a small puff of red flame and smoke. The door opened slightly a few seconds later. Acheron gestured with a small bow and a flourish. "After you."

"Show off," I said, pushing the door open. "Remember: this is official business."

"Sweet, sweet business," he sing-songed as he followed me upstairs. "It's like automatic gunfire...a stairway to heav—"

"Knock it off," I said, stopping on the stairs. "Game face, now."

"Now, I'm confused," he answered with a mischievous smile. "Is this business or a game?"

"It's always a game...with deadly outcomes if we screw up. Let's go."

SIX

We reached the top of the stairs, and at the end of a short hallway sat the door to The Grimoire.

Each stair was covered in a specific set of sigils designed to prevent entry if Liv wished it. They were hard for the untrained eye to see, but I had had plenty of painful training in uncovering them.

The short hallway at the top of the stairs seemed innocent enough. This was an illusion. Every surface of the hallway was also covered in barely perceptible sigils. These were more along the lines of 'end your life in agony'. The kinds of sigils I stayed away from. Liv valued her privacy and protected it with applied lethality.

I guess Liv felt that if the uninvited guests could get past the stairs, they needed to die in the hallway. The sigils we walked past were, thankfully, dormant, but could easily turn lethal. If Liv was having a bad day, it guaranteed anyone in the hallway was going to have an excruciating one.

"Liv takes her security seriously," Acheron said with a hint of admiration, stopping to peer at one of the sigils on the wall. "This one here is new. It will"—he pointed at the symbol

—"turn your insides out. I do so love a connoisseur of the classic maneuvers."

"So glad you're a fan," I said. "Let's not do anything to make her activate them."

"And this one," he said, pointing to another. "Will literally boil your blood...Delicious."

"There's something wrong with you, you know that?"

"Nothing like warm blood on a cold winter night."

"It's summer."

"Warm blood on a hot night is good, too."

"How about you don't give me the fine details on the sigils I'm currently surrounded by?" I asked, feeling queasy. "I'd rather not hear about having my insides ripped out or my blood boiled."

"No, not ripped out," Acheron corrected. "You would be turned inside out...literally. Quite effective as a method of stopping an attack, I would think."

"No shit," I said. "Let's get to the door. Leave the walls alone, thank you."

We approached the large, intimidating door. It was the kind of door that made you regret leaving your RPG at home. I placed a hand against the cool steel, feeling the power thrumming beneath the surface.

"This is an impressive door," Acheron said. "She's recently modified it."

"Can't imagine the amount of firepower needed to bring this thing down," I said, admiring the door. "Did she borrow it from Fort Knox?"

Acheron stepped close and licked the door, stepping back with nod.

"Just as I suspected," he said as if what he had just done was the most normal thing ever. "Tartarus steel. How she ever managed to get this in place is astounding. Liv is a demon of many talents, not all of them titillating."

"Tartarus the prison?"

"Do you know of a different Tartarus?"

"Only the one that's in the depths...Scary prison. The 'no escape ever' type of place."

"The one and the same," he nodded. "This would be a... cell door, I think...for something particularly powerful, but yes, this door came from Tartarus."

"How did she get it?" I asked, wondering. "Were they renovating and changing doors?"

"I would say Liv is a lot stronger than she lets on...If Becca the Guardian is any indication of her power and standing, Liv is beyond even my level."

"Stronger than a Demon Lord? What's stronger than a Demon Lord?"

"There are many levels. King James said it best: principalities, powers, rulers, and wickedness in high places," Acheron said. "To get this door here, Liv has to be among the first two."

"Where are you in that group?" I asked. "Are you more like wickedness in low places?"

"I'm one of a kind, my dear," he said. "I can't be classified."

I turned back to the door of The Grimoire.

It was the kind of door that made bank vaults jealous. Blue sigils covered the grey surface and pulsed to a gentle rhythm. There were no locks or handles. It was just a large piece of metal designed to be slid into the wall, allowing entry into the space beyond it.

Tartarus steel was reinforced and alloyed with some impenetrable metal I didn't recognize. For all intents and purposes, it could've been adamantium. All I knew was that no one got through this door unless Liv wanted them to.

Someone or something had tried not too long ago.

Before the guardians, Liv had operated The Grimoire

alone. She had, at that time, a rare artifact designed to enhance the amount of power a sorcerer could control—basically a turbocharged leveling up device.

Whoever it was had gotten past the outer defenses of The Grimoire unchallenged, until they had gotten to this door and wall. The metal made up the door was also part of the walls that encased the entire second floor of the building.

Rumor was that Liv had just kept the door closed and called the OSA, who disposed of the remains. Ever since that day, guardians had appeared at The Grimoire and no one ever showed up unannounced...except me.

Somehow, Liv always knew when I was on my way, much to Acheron's delight. He considered it a point of personal pride that she would be aware of his presence to such a degree.

I suspected it had more to do with the threat he posed. A Demon Lord bound to an Otherkin could be seen as a security issue and threat, not only to The Grimoire but to the city and, if powerful enough, to the world.

What was to stop me from compelling him to breach The Grimoire?

Not much. We didn't know what the guardians were, but I would bet on Acheron being able to deal with them; same for the walls on the second floor. It would take some time and maybe insane amounts of power and explosives, but I was certain that with enough time, and maybe a missile or two, he could get through.

The only thing that could stop him after all that would be Liv herself. If I were her, I would keep tabs on us too.

Liv opened the door before we knocked, and smiled.

"Hello, Nyx, Acheron," she said, her voice a husky blanket that wrapped itself warmly around me. "Please, come in."

Liv was beautiful in a 1920's femme fatale kind of way, emphasis on the fatale.

Auburn hair framed her pale face and was pulled back in a loose ponytail. Her eyes, similar to Becca's, radiated a soft violet light, with the only difference being that Liv's pupils were actually violet—a rare trait.

With humans, it was known as Alexandria's Genesis; in demons, it denoted power...Arch Demon level of power. It meant Liv was beyond a heavyweight. She was a succubus at the top of the food chain, and everyone and everything else beneath her could easily be a snack. I reinforced my a mental note to never piss her off...again.

Liv wore a loose-fitting pair of jeans and an old, oversized black T-shirt that did little to hide her curvy figure. She was at least as tall as Acheron, and the wiry muscles in her arms were an indicator of the strength she possessed.

Liv was no one to trifle with, which made this path she chose an odd one. She seemed to enjoy the quiet life of librarian-demon. Maybe one day I'd ask her why she took her vow... but not today.

Acheron nearly tripped over himself trying to step inside Liv's sanctum.

"Take a breath," I said under my breath. "She's not going anywhere."

"I keep forgetting how breathtaking she is...every single time."

I had to agree.

Liv was beyond beautiful. She was nearly perfect, which, if you were paying attention, was the first indicator that you should be running in the opposite direction. The truth was that by the time your brain got the memo, it was too late. Liv was dangerous, and I was doubly glad for her vow of celibacy and neutrality.

She was, literally, deathly beautiful.

"She is beautiful and...*unavailable*," I almost whispered. "Remember we are here on *business*."

"Yes, yes, business," Acheron said, waving my words away without taking his eyes off Liv. "I'm all *business*."

"Right," I said, rolling my eyes. "C'mon."

I stepped farther into The Grimoire.

The space was laid out in a wheel fashion: one main room acted as the hub, with smaller connected rooms acting as the spokes. The main room was for general research, with glass display cases, and tables were covered with books.

The walls around the main area were covered in bookcases filled with books. The smaller rooms allowed for some privacy and quiet reading away from the main room.

We stepped in, past the initial entrance. To the side was a large reception area, with a wide desk acting as the boundary between the entrance and the main room proper. The desk was made of ebony wood and shimmered with subtle sigils of power. Liv walked around the desk, and made a waving gesture with one hand. I heard the door slide shut behind us. Several metallic noises rang out through the space. We were effectively locked in.

Liv sat in the large chair behind the desk, grabbed a mug of dark liquid I really hoped was coffee, and looked at us.

"How can I help you, Nyxia?"

SEVEN

I stepped up to the desk, picked up a pen, and one of the small note pads.

"I need to show you a sigil," I said. "Can I use the room?"

"Is that really necessary?" Liv asked. "Why not just show me here?"

"Something about this one feels off," I answered. "I'd feel safer in there."

"Indulge her," Acheron said. "This sigil is...different."

"Of course," Liv said, pointing to the room off to my right. "It's currently unoccupied. Help yourself."

The room, officially known as the safe room, was designed as a vault within a vault. It was used only for the most dangerous or volatile texts and sigils. The pulsing, orange sigils carved into the surface of the walls of the room acted like one large dampener, neutralizing the power of sigils and rendering them inert.

Some of Liv's books were housed permanently within the safe room, behind secure steel cases, and only viewed with Liv present. The one time I asked to look at one of the tomes in the cases, she laughed and shook her head no, mentioning how she enjoyed breathing. I wasn't that dangerous.

Despite what my history said.

Liv waved a hand in the direction of the safe room, and the sigils on the door glowed red for a second before disappearing. Acheron made a move to come in with me, but I waved him off.

"Are you sure?" he asked. "You don't know what that thing can do outside of the circle."

"If there's one place I'll be safe, it's in here," I said. "Besides, if something goes sideways you could always break down the door."

Acheron stepped to the side and examined the safe room door.

"That one would be easier than the entrance, but not by much,' he said. "Try not to let anything go sideways."

"I'll be fine," I said, reassuring him. "I'm just going to draw the sigil, I'm not in a circle and the safe room is right here in complete view."

"True," he said, tapping his chin, "and the view is much better out here."

"Stop being a lech and focus," I said, heading to the safe room. "Focus."

Acheron glanced at Liv.

"I *am* focusing," he replied, still looking at Liv. "You go do your demon doodles, and I will focus on what's important. Don't worry, I am *totally* focused."

I almost did whack him upside the head just then, but opted not to. Strong emotions affected Liv. Just because she took a vow, didn't mean she was immune to the emotions around her. It would be like an alcoholic working in a bar. Sure she could handle it, but why invite the temptation?

Despite all of his flirting, Liv could easily handle Acheron. If I introduced anger, or some other strong emotion, she could accidentally use her powers. That would trigger Acheron. He was mostly harmless, but he was still a Demon Lord. If she unleashed her succubi powers, the outcome was anything but predictable.

I didn't want to find out what could happen with Acheron under the effect of Liv's influence. I shuddered at the thought.

"Behave," I said, stepping into the safe room. "Business."

"Of course," he said and I could tell he meant it. "Don't tarry too long in there."

He actually sounded concerned, which set off my radar. Acheron rarely sounded worried, and when he did, it was with good reason.

"What is this sigil she wants to show me?" Liv said. "Is this something new she learned?"

"It's something old she learned...watch," he said. "The room *is* secure, yes?"

"Absolutely," Liv said. "No sigil can activate in there. The room is inert."

The acoustics of the interior of The Grimoire, and the safe room in particular, allowed for sounds to travel easily where there shouldn't have been any, considering the thickness of the doors and walls. I figured it was part of the safe room design to allow sound to travel without having to open the door.

The top half of the door to the safe room was made of sigil-inscribed glass. It allowed Liv to keep track of what occurred in the room without having to open the door or break any seals.

In the center of the safe room sat a small desk and chair, similar to the ones in the main room. Around me on the walls were the locked steel cases holding the most volatile or dangerous books in The Grimoire.

The walls and floors were covered with softly glowing

sigils. They cast a soft light as I sat at the table. I closed my eyes, bringing the sigil to my mind's eye. I saw the symbol clearly and began replicating it on the pad without opening my eyes.

"What is she doing?" I heard Liv's voice as if she were some distance away. "The room is reacting to what she is writing. What is she writing, Acheron?"

"You said the room was inert," Acheron shot back. "What is going on?"

"The room *is* inert...she is not," Liv answered crisply. "What is this sigil?"

"Liv...I'm going to need you to open the door," Acheron said as I opened my eyes. "Now."

Around me, black flames were slowly rising.

"Acheron...are you seeing these flames too?" I asked as I backed up from the wall of dark energy. "This isn't supposed to happen."

The flames, which were blocking the only exit, were increasing in size and fluctuating in color between a black and dark orange. It was starting to get hot in the safe room.

"Now!" yelled Acheron as he approached the safe room door. "Open it, or I will."

Liv waved her hand and—judging from Acheron's expression—nothing happened.

"The door sigils are gone," Liv said in awe. "How could that be? What is going on?"

"Move back," Acheron said as he grabbed the door handle and looked in my eyes. "Stop writing."

"I...I...did," I said, holding up the pad. The sigil lifted off the paper and floated into the center of the room. "That can't possibly be good...Acheron?"

"That sigil," Liv said, her voice tight with fear. "Impossible."

"You recognize it?" Acheron said, whirling on Liv. "You know it?"

Liv nodded and set her jaw.

"You need to get her out of there...now. Those flames will kill her."

"Nyx, I'm on my way," Acheron said, his voice dropping a few octaves. "Liv, take cover."

"No," Liv said. "You need help."

EIGHT

Demon Lords are powerful.

Demon Lords assisted by whatever Liv was, were mind-blowing on the scale of power. I kept moving back from the flames as the heat increased. My brain rebelled at the fact that the flames were burning without consumption...until I started to feel weak.

Soulflames.

The flames were consuming my life force...Shit.

Otherkin were tough, nearly invulnerable beings of destructive force, but we had one major weakness... soulflames. They could stop us in our tracks, literally. From what I had researched, soulflames were the answer to the Otherkin, created specifically to stop and kill my kind. I'd like to find the clever idiot who thought soulflames were a good idea and pound him.

Someone was gunning for me. This was personal.

"Acheron," I said, trying to remain calm and failing. "These are...soulflames."

"Soulflames?" Acheron asked, surprised and then looked at Liv. "Liv?"

"I heard her," Liv snapped. "We're going to need a tether. I need a moment."

"Are you sure?" Acheron asked as I saw him brace himself. "I hate those things."

"Unless you have another way to get through that door in the next few seconds?"

"We're going to need the tether," Acheron said with finality. "Even I'm not carrying that much power."

"Didn't think so…Get ready," Liv replied. "These things are unmanageable in the best of circumstances."

"Hold tight," he said, looking at me. "We're coming in. Move back."

I saw Liv place a hand on Acheron's shoulder as she extended her other arm behind her. She said something I couldn't understand, and the temperature dropped noticeably.

A black stream of energy erupted in the center of the main room, connecting the floor to the ceiling. Liv opened her hand and leaned closer to the black energy. She said some more words I couldn't understand, and the stream began vibrating.

"Acheron, prepare," she said, her voice tight. "This is going to be…unpleasant."

A tendril shot out from the column of energy, raced into her outstretched arm, crept across her body, and into the other arm. It kept moving, sliding over into Acheron with an audible crack, mimicking the sound of a whip.

Acheron gritted his teeth as the energy slammed into him. Black lines of power traveled down his shoulder criss-crossing his body. A lattice of dark power created a fractal pattern that slowly crawled across his face.

His face transformed briefly into an expression of pain, but he quickly got it under control. There were few things that could hurt Acheron on this plane, if he was feeling pain, even for a moment, this tether Liv was using was devastating.

"Liv, when I pictured...joining with you," Acheron said, his voice strained, "this is not...what I had in...mind."

"Careful...what you wish for," she answered, her voice just as strained. "Always...read the fine print, especially with demons."

Acheron smiled and nodded. Liv answered his nod, her expression serious.

"Open it," she said. "Now, while the tether is intact. I can't hold this power for much longer without causing serious damage."

Acheron began pulling on the door as I sank to the floor, the feeling of exhaustion overwhelming me. With a final scream, Acheron wrenched open the door, and rushed inside as my vision tunneled.

He scooped me up and barreled through the exit, slamming the door behind him. I saw the flames flicker and then surge in intensity as the sigil glowed brighter for a few moments, before winking out completely. The flames dissipated a few seconds later.

The black energy that had filled the main room seconds before was gone. Becca stood in the center of the room, a long dark sword in one hand, and some kind of gun in the other.

"Is everything secure, Mistress?" Becca asked, looking around. Her gaze hovered over Acheron and me for a few seconds longer than was comfortable, as she swept the main room. "We sensed a large surge of energy in here. Are you safe?"

"The threat has been neutralized," Liv answered. "They are blameless for this. The source is elsewhere."

"Do they need to be removed?" Becca said, staring mostly at Acheron. "Is the demon a threat?"

"Everything is under control," Liv said as she moved to her desk. "Please return to your station. I will handle this."

Becca nodded and vanished.

"Are you implying I'm not a threat?" I said, offended. "I can be plenty threatening."

"Credible threats rarely have to announce themselves," Liv said, moving to her desk. "However, if you like, I can call Becca back, and you can show her just how threatening you can be."

"That sounds like a real bad idea," Acheron said quietly. "Maybe you can get skewered by Becca next time we visit?"

"I think you're probably right," I said as a wave of nausea gripped me. "Next time."

Liv slumped in her chair, as Acheron placed me gently on the floor. The room did a quick spin and then tilted a few times before settling into place.

"That's a neat disappearing trick," I said when the room and my stomach settled down. "She doesn't need to use the door?"

"Becca is a guardian," Liv said. "The position comes with certain...perks. Let's forget Becca for the moment. I need you to focus on what just happened."

"You mean how I almost got flambéed?"

"Technically, the term is seared," Acheron corrected, "since no liquor was used in the process."

Liv and I both stared at him.

"Can we not do that again...ever?" I said with a groan as my stomach heaved again. "I feel like freshly stomped dirt."

"You look pretty bad too," Acheron added. "You also smell positively hellish. I think a shower or two would benefit the general environment—at least those of us with a sense of smell—and maybe burn those clothes?"

"Stop trying to cheer me up," I said, slowly sitting up. "Liv, what happened?"

Liv had a faraway look in her eyes.

"I've not seen a reaction like that in many years," Liv said. "Especially from a secondary sigil transcription. The power it takes to do that is formidable."

"Are you saying it was *meant* for me?" I asked. "This was a targeted attack?"

"Where did you find that sigil?"

I told Liv about the sorcerer, the summoning circle and the Minoras.

"A *Minoras*?" she asked. "From a low-level summoner? It was a deflection."

"What do you mean?"

"Who saw the sigil?" Liv asked. "Was it both of you or just Nyx?"

"Just me," I said as Acheron nodded. "I had to show it to him. It was buried in the symbols of the summoning circle."

"This sigil you discovered, did it look like this?" Liv traced the sigil on a piece of paper sitting on the desk. "This one?"

"Yes, except the bottom part was curled up, not straight like that one."

"This was meant for you," Liv answered slowly. "You have a powerful enemy. Who did you anger?"

"Are you referring to today or in general?" Acheron asked. "The list is extensive. She has a particular gift for this."

"Shut it," I snapped as I slowly got to my feet and sat in one of the large chairs. "Who can do this?"

Liv shook her head.

"Only Otherkin and certain demons can see this sigil," Liv said. "Someone knew you would find it...or wanted you to find it."

"If only Otherkin could see it, weren't they taking a chance someone else would discover the sigil?" I asked. "Another Otherkin?"

"There are more of your kind, but most of them are reclusive and remain hidden."

"Whoever did this knew we would intercept the sorcerer."

"The *Minoras* was bait," Acheron said. "Black Cleavers?"

"If it's them, they've gone from minor irritant to major threat," I said. "I still don't see it. They're a bunch of clueless wannabes."

"Don't underestimate Flint," Acheron warned. "He's intelligent and skilled. A dangerous combination."

"This was meant for you and Acheron," Liv replied. "How many Otherkin-Demon Lord partners do you know who are working for The Seven, fighting against demons?"

The odds of someone else discovering this particular sigil were non-existent.

"Are there any other Demon-Otherkin teams working the streets against rogue sorcery?" Acheron asked. "It seems unlikely."

"I haven't heard of any," I said. "I doubt there's another Otherkin crazy enough or suicidal enough to partner with a demon."

"Their loss," Acheron said with a huff. "I'm what's called a catch."

"I have a few names I could call you," I said. "A *catch* isn't one of them."

"There aren't any others," Liv answered. "This was meant to attack...to kill you. There was a clear indicator."

"The soulflames."

"They aren't exactly common knowledge," I said. "Who do we know could put that much power into a sigil that would cause it to trigger soulflames when I replicated it?"

"I don't have that information," Liv said. "Even if I did, I would be reluctant to share it with you."

"Why?" I asked, suddenly upset. "Whoever it was, tried to kill me. I think they deserve some pain in return."

"That's why," Liv answered with a sigh. "You think this was some novice sorcerer targeting you? No, this is someone with resources, power, and most of all patience. Whoever this is, they're playing a long game."

"I'm inclined to agree with Nyx on this one," Acheron said. "This person needs to be stopped...with extreme prejudice."

"By who? You two?" Liv asked. "If this had happened anywhere else, how were you going to put out the soulflames, Acheron?"

Acheron remained silent and looked away.

"I thought so," Liv said. "Neither of you are nearly powerful enough to deal with this on your own."

"Who is?" I asked. "Who do *you* think can deal with this?"

"Go see Victoria," Liv said. "This is more her league of power. Besides, as a repository of rare artifacts, I have to call this in. I can give you an hour before I have to make the call."

"Shit, you're serious?"

"I'm a demon, not a sorcerer," Liv answered. "While I study and collect arcane work, it doesn't mean I understand all of the deeper aspects of sorcery. For that, you need..."

"A sorcerer," Acheron finished. "Victoria will not be pleased we didn't come to her first."

"It's a risk you will have to take," Liv said. "She should have the answers you need."

"If she shares them, that is," I said, displeased. "I can't believe this is the only option."

"No, it isn't," Liv said. "You can wait until you encounter some other hapless, novice sorcerer who summons something more powerful than a *Minoras*, something even more lethal. It's only a matter of time, but it will happen. These traps are being planted for the both of you."

Acheron pointed at me.

"This sounds like your fan club," he said. "I don't anger people to this level of intensity."

"Your confidence in me is overwhelming."

"I have complete confidence in your ability to anger dangerous individuals."

"We need to go see her," I said. "I don't want some clueless sorcerer getting killed because someone wants to erase me."

"That is your best course of action," Liv insisted. "Act as if your life depended on it…because it does."

NINE

The Seven were headquartered on what was considered sacred ground. This wasn't to say that The Seven were holy. If anything, they were the furthest thing from holy I knew. Last I checked, sorcery was a non-starter in the holiness department. Same went for being an unnatural creature, or associating with Demon Lords.

The temple above the Basilica Headquarters had been considered holy ground long ago. Underground, it contained one of the only remaining catacombs in the country.

There was a huge difference between sacred and holy.

The catacombs were sacred, but not holy. They held an ancient, primal power tied to death. The temple above them, which was considered holy, celebrated life on the surface, yet hinged one of its core tenets on death and resurrection.

Seemed pretty much like the same thing to me.

The Seven didn't use the catacombs proper. They were headquartered several levels below the catacombs, in an underground state-of-the-art base of operations. No one entered the Basilica without clearance. Those who tried, only tried once.

We left Liv in her office and headed downstairs to Eight. Becca gave us a large dose of stink-eye as we exited the Sweetgreen. Her gaze followed us until we got in Eight and started the engine.

"What is her issue?" I asked, once we pulled away. "Did you spit in her high-end kale or something?"

"She's a guardian," Acheron said. "They are a twitchy bunch when it comes to protecting those in their care. They usually err on the side of hack, slash, and shoot first. Ask questions never."

"Well, at least now we have an idea of what she is."

"Dangerous, is what she is." Acheron said. "Well armed, too."

"I don't think I ever want to fight her."

"Guardians are notoriously difficult to kill," Acheron said. "They aren't exactly immortal, but they are close. Makes perfect sense to have one at The Grimoire."

"One that we can see," I said, speeding down the street. "She said '*we* sensed a surge of energy in here'—plural. Means Becca is the one we can see, but maybe there are others on the premises?"

"Possible," Acheron said. "Guardians have been known to gather in trinities."

"In what?"

"Imagine Becca, three times as deadly," Acheron said. "They serve in groups of three."

"Seems like a fun bunch," I said, swerving around traffic. I jumped on 6th Avenue and pulled onto West Houston. "Did you see how she just—*bamf*—appeared in The Grimoire?"

"*Bamf?*" Acheron asked. "What is a *bamf?*"

"*Bamf*. The sound of teleportation? Everyone knows this. Anyway that's not the important part."

"Since when do teleports make a *bamf* sound?" Acheron

asked. "I think we have different definitions for this word. I thought *bamf* meant, bad ass motherfu—"

"Focus," I said, heading down Houston until it intersected Mulberry Street. "She appeared there, without having to worry about any of the defenses. She just *bamfed* in. Can you do that?"

I made a right on Mulberry and drove down the street until I was behind the Basilica. The main entrance was located on the opposite side of the block, on Mott Street. The entrance to The Seven HQ was located in the catacombs. They could be accessed through a little private garden on Mulberry, which was walled off from the public.

The wall closing off the garden extended from the temple to a small building farther down the block, making the garden inaccessible to the general public. Sigils decorated the old doors to the garden. They gave off a subtle 'keep away' vibe that dissuaded anyone from examining the doors too closely.

Scaling the wall—if you could get past the sigils—would be met with excruciating pain. The kind that felt like iron spikes driving into your soft skin at odd angles as you bled out.

The Seven took their security seriously.

"Can I do what? Be a badass motherfu...?"

"Teleport," I said, approaching the doors to the garden. "Can you teleport like that?"

"Why would I want to?" Acheron said, pulling down on his vest. "I'm a Demon Lord. I don't need to *bamf* anywhere. Besides, Demon Lords probably don't *bamf*. I'm sure if I teleported, it would sound closer to a heavily Christopher Nolan influenced *BRAAAM*, with plenty of bass and earthshaking."

"Right, sure, *bram*," I said. "Sounds just like you. Are you prepared?"

"Yes, proceed when ready," he said, shaking his arms out. "I hate this part."

"Just focus and move fast," I said. "The entrance is only forty feet in."

"Forty feet may as well be forty miles," he said, waving me on. "Let's get this over with."

I pressed a series of the door sigils in sequence and opened the doors.

A wave of power spilled out onto the sidewalk where we stood. Acheron braced himself as we headed into the garden. Long ago, the Basilica had been attacked by demons. Ever since that incident, The Seven took measures to prevent another demon attack on their premises—ever.

"You...would think...Victoria...would make...a...concession...for me," Acheron said as he walked, leaning forward as if struggling against hurricane force winds. "This...is quite uncomfortable."

"You know she can't," I said as the large exterior doors closed behind us. "Just a little farther. You can make it."

"Do not patronize me, Nyx. It's bad enough I'm even setting foot in this place."

"See? If you could *bram* your way in, this wouldn't be an issue."

Acheron glared at me and kept moving forward.

I moved ahead and stood before a large, white marble mausoleum which took up one quarter of the garden. It always reminded me of a small Roman temple. Another set of sigil-covered doors waited. I placed my hands on them. They gave off a soft blue glow as energy traced the outline of the symbols. A few seconds later, they opened silently.

"The things I do for you," Acheron said when he reached the threshold of the mausoleum. "At least this part is tolerable."

We stepped inside the cool building and sat on one of the stone benches. The fail-safes in this building weren't as overt as the ones outside, but they were no less deadly. I gave Acheron a moment to catch his breath and mentally prepare.

"Ready?" I said. "I'm not hurrying you, but I'd rather tell Vic first, before Liv calls her about The Grimoire."

"If you had gone to Victoria first, like I advised, you wouldn't be rushing me now."

"I'm not rushing you," I said, "but you can't get down there on your own. You know that."

"I'm aware of the defenses employed by The Seven to protect their precious Headquarters from my kind," Acheron replied, with thinly veiled venom. "They used our own defenses against us."

"Can you blame them?" I asked. "Demons breaking in here would be a disaster. The artifacts and tomes of knowledge they could acquire—"

"Artifacts and tomes that were stolen from us in the first place," Acheron added, his anger increasing by several levels. "Let's not forget *that* little fact. The Seven *appropriated* power that didn't rightfully belong to them."

"Winners and spoils," I said. "You know how that goes and why."

"We never should have trusted them in the first place. That was our downfall."

I nodded.

"I'm not arguing with you," I said. "I'm stating facts. We still have to navigate the labyrinth. Ready?"

"Bloody hell, I hate this."

"Me, too," I said, taking his arm and heading to the stairs leading down. "Let's go, old demon. I got you."

TEN

"The blindness should set in momentarily," Acheron said, reaching out with his other hand as we stepped downstairs. "Ah, there it is. Right on cue."

The dimly lit, eternal labyrinth was a devious defense created by Rodrigo the Sigilsmith. In simple terms, it was a labyrinth with endless permutations. The corridors shifted and changed each time you entered it and on every turn.

To spice things up even more, Rodrigo had embedded, into the stone, sigils that caused blindness to the uninitiated, or to demons. These sigils didn't work on Otherkin—which made me a threat.

Most of the time, I felt Vic tolerated me under the whole 'keep your friends close, but your enemies closer' policy. I certainly never felt like her friend, which, in my mind, only left one alternative—enemy.

Getting lost in here was easy if you used normal senses. Even though the sigils barely affected me as a hybrid, I still had to move slow. If Acheron and I got separated, there would be no way for me to find him, even with our bond.

That sorcery was ancient and powerful enough to block even my abilities in these passageways.

The irony wasn't lost on me. Having this labyrinth under a catacomb was about as subtle as a brick to the head. The Seven were sending a message. Any demon that made it this far would wander here endlessly…forever.

We walked down the passageways, waiting at the intersections for the configuration to change. Being an Otherkin gave me the uncanny ability of never getting lost. I had an internal compass and eidetic memory that allowed me to navigate any labyrinth without losing my bearings.

Acheron, on the other hand, hated this place. With good reason.

The blindness was only the first layer. Any and all demon abilities were immediately nullified. In this place, he was about as vulnerable as demons could be. My attention was completely focused on keeping Acheron close and on the permutations of the labyrinth…I missed the shift in energy until it was too late.

"Hello, freak," a voice said behind me. "Your demon can't save you in here."

"What the—?" I managed as I turned in time to catch a bright red orb to the face.

It blasted me off my feet, but I managed to hold onto Acheron, dragging him back with me. Being an Otherkin meant I was naturally resistant to attack magic. That didn't mean it didn't hurt like hell.

"Nyx," Acheron hissed as we fell backward. "Who is it?"

"Fuck, I don't know," I hissed back, rubbing my face. "I didn't get a good look due to the orb punching me in the face."

"I can't help you in here," Acheron said quietly. "Seems like whoever this is, counted on that fact."

"That would mean they are informed about your kind."

"And my weaknesses," Acheron added grimly. "Which also means whoever it is, is dangerous."

"I just said that," I snapped. "Shit, that hurt."

"Calm down," Acheron said. "They're counting on the attack unsettling you. Are you damaged?"

"Only my ego," I said. "I don't enjoy being sucker punched. I didn't expect an attack down here."

"What have I always told you?"

"Always expect an attack—"

"It's how you stay alive." he finished. "Now, get your bearings."

"I got this," I said, keeping my anger in check and moving down the corridor. "Whoever it is, they're going to regret waking up today."

"Don't let them bait you," Acheron said, gripping my wrist. "They'll want to separate us. Divide and conquer. It's what I would do."

"You're right," I said, stepping back until I was next to Acheron. "How did they even get in here? We're in a literal labyrinth."

"Excellent question—perhaps one you want to ask Victoria, if we get to have a word."

Another red orb raced down the passageway. I pushed Acheron down and deflected the orb with my arm.

"Dammit," I said with a grunt of pain. "That one hurt less."

"What happened?" Acheron asked, trying to orient himself and failing. "Can you see them?"

"They're sniping," I said. "Trying to pick us off."

"We need to move," Acheron said. "Before they—"

A low rumble filled the passageway as I barely made out the silhouette of a *Minoras* in the dim light of the corridor. Dragondogs and tight spaces usually meant instant, gruesome death.

They were fast and agile. Indoors, they could scale walls with ease, which meant I had to be ready for several different angles of attack. Facing a Minoras was bad. Facing one in a cramped corridor was suicidal.

"Before they do something like that?" I asked warily. "That sounds—"

"Sounds like the growl of a *Minoras*," Acheron said, getting to his feet. "It will be hindered, but still deadly in here."

"No shit," I said, letting my claws grow. "This is the last place I want to face a Dragondog. There's no room to maneuver."

"For either of you," Acheron answered, reaching into his coat. "How close are we to Victoria?"

I closed my eyes for a few seconds, reoriented myself, and got my bearings.

"About two permutations behind us," I said, getting a feel for the labyrinth again. "The first one is just a few feet away."

"Lead me to the next permutation," Acheron said. "Are we close?"

"Yes," I said, stepping a few meters to the next intersection. "Here. We can make it."

"No, we can't, but *you* can," Acheron said, feeling for the wall. "I'll only slow you down."

"No," I said, my voice final, grabbing him by the wrist. "I'm not leaving you here. That thing will shred you."

He twisted his hand around toward my thumb, using the move to break free of my grip. As he stepped back, he used the sudden momentum to send me down the corridor, and past the intersection.

"It's touching that you care," Acheron said, feeling the wall and heading back down the corridor. "You need to go...now."

"Don't do this," I yelled. "I can help you, what are you doing?"

"Saving your life...again," he said. "Find Victoria, tell her it's time to give you the Darkin."

"Darkin? What the hell is a Darkin?"

"She'll know what I mean," Acheron said, moving back toward the *Minoras*. "Get moving before they decide to take matters..."

A barrage of red orbs filled the passageway. There was no way we could avoid all of them in time. Several of the orbs slammed into Acheron, bouncing him off the wall and spinning him into another assault of orbs. A second group of orbs missed Acheron completely and zeroed in on me.

I raised my arms as the orbs crashed into me.

ELEVEN

I landed in a roll and stopped my momentum with my claws. The permutation kicked in, and the corridor shifted, separating me completely from Acheron.

I was alone.

Acheron was out there, blind and defenseless. I tried to sense him through our bond.

Nothing.

"Sniping orbs. The cowards," I said, shaking out my arms. "Acheron?"

I punched a wall in fury, cracking the stone, and screamed my frustration. It was no use—I couldn't go back and find him, not this deep in the labyrinth. The only way out now was forward.

I ran down the next corridor and waited at the intersection, cursing The Seven and Rodrigo for his sigils. The permutation kicked in a few seconds later, shifting the corridor again. When it finished, I saw the door that led to The Seven HQ.

I ran down the corridor and came to a stop before the door.

Emotions were tugging at me in different directions. Fear for Acheron, anger at the defenses, all layered with the mistrust I always kept warmly stoked for The Seven. If I didn't get myself under control, I was going to enter and attempt to shred everyone in sight. That would last all of five seconds, as one of The Seven—or even Victoria herself—blasted my rampage to a screeching halt.

I took several deep breaths and placed my hand on the door, activating the security sigil. The door slid to the side and into the wall. It was a setup very much like the door at The Grimoire.

I stepped into a cavernous reception area that would have made more sense in an office building downtown. Plush, brown carpet covered the floor. Sconces hung on both walls to either side, providing pools of warm light at even intervals. At the other end of the floor, behind a massive desk, sat Mura the Receptionist.

Mura was, in many respects, the first line of active defense for anyone unlucky enough to make it this far. As far as I knew, she wasn't a sorcerer, and no one had made it past her for as long as The Seven had had their HQ on this site.

She sat behind an immense desk, easily ten feet across and half as tall. The desk was one large slab of granite. I didn't know how they got it down here, and frankly I didn't want to know. I was sure it involved some kind of earth sorcery.

Behind the desk, embedded into the wall I saw the large copper VII that graced every one of The Seven's base of operations and main offices. They were subtle at not being subtle.

Mura was currently proportional to the desk. She sat behind it, peering down at me, like I had stepped in mud and was tracking it all over her clean carpet.

We weren't exactly friendly with each other.

Mura looked like an oversized human, until you got close.

Then you could see that her skin was actually brown stone. She was dressed in business attire—if that business happened to be obliterating large groups of enemies. The combat armor she wore was almost as intimidating as the enormous hammer that sat next to her desk.

The first time I had seen it, I had thought it was some kind of abstract office sculpture. It wasn't until I had seen her relocate it one day that I realized it was her weapon—as if her fists weren't enough. Her short black hair was cut in a bob which was stylish and offset her features nicely. Rumor was: she was a stone giant Victoria had saved. I never had the opportunity or inclination to ask Mura the truth.

Mura wasn't the chatty type. Creatures that were extra-human didn't readily divulge their origins. In some cases, it could give away weaknesses. This meant most of them had poor social skills or just didn't play well with others.

Some creatures were just cranky, angry asses. I was a combination of poor social skills and angry crankiness. This didn't mean I wanted to tangle with Mura—angry didn't mean suicidal.

Mura always treated me politely but her priority was always The Seven.

"Nyxia White," Mura said, as the sound of my name filled the entire reception area.

"State your business."

"You have a breach," I said. "Someone jumped me and Acheron in the labyrinth."

"Yet, here you stand," Mura answered, still looking at me like an annoying ant. "Did you see who it was?"

"No, an orb to the face prevented me from a positive ID."

"Are you saying a sorcerer infiltrated the eternal labyrinth?"

"And took my partner...or worse," I said, tamping down my anxiety over Acheron. "I need to go find him."

"That is not your business; that is a series of situations that have recently occurred," Mura said. "Why are you here?"

"Did you just not hear what I said? Acheron is gone."

"Yes, I heard," Mura answered, pressing some buttons on her desk as she disappeared from view, shrinking down to normal human size. She stepped around the desk and faced me. "That doesn't tell me *why* you are here, Otherkin."

"I need to see Victoria," I said, "right after we find Acheron."

"The search for a demon will not take precedence over a meeting with Victoria," Mura said, staring at me. "Does she know you're coming?"

"She's expecting me," I said. "She's always expecting me."

Mura answered with a silent nod.

"I have sent agents out to the labyrinth to locate the demon or his remains," she said. "Follow me, please."

"He's not dead."

"Irrelevant," Mura answered. "He's a demon in the labyrinth. He knew the risks. If he's alive, he will be escorted to Victoria's office. If not, his remains will."

We walked down the enormous corridors. I always felt small in Seven HQ. I figured the corridors were extra-large to accommodate Mura when she was in her industrial-sized mode. No point in having a giant security person who can't navigate the area she was securing.

I knew Mura wouldn't react to Acheron going missing. To The Seven, demons were the enemy or sources of information and power to exploit. The fact that one of them was lost, trapped, or worse, in the labyrinth, meant nothing to them. Acheron was expendable. He didn't matter in the larger scheme of things.

He mattered to me.

Acheron was my friend and partner. I would ask Vic for help. If she refused, I would find Acheron on my own. It was familiar territory for me. The only person who ever stood by my side was now trapped in an eternal labyrinth, defenseless.

Mura walked off to a side corridor; her footfalls were surprisingly silent for someone made of stone. I didn't expect her to go clomping around, but I didn't expect her to be ninja-silent either. I filed that away for future reference.

She opened a door at the other end of the last corridor.

"Wait here, please," she said like I had a choice. "I will inform Victoria of your presence."

"Sure thing," I said, pointing to the floor. "I'll just wait right here."

Mura raised an eyebrow at me, nodded and went inside.

TWELVE

The door opened a few seconds later.

"She will see you now," Mura said. "Do I need to remind you that comportment befitting an agent of The Seven is expected of you?"

"You just did," I said, walking past her. "I'll behave...mostly."

"See that you do," Mura answered and started increasing in size as she walked away. "I would hate to have to collect you."

"Me too," I said under my breath as she rounded a corner. "Not now or ever."

I closed the door, turning to face the short corridor that led to another door.

This corridor looked empty, but I knew it was the most secure corridor in all of The Seven HQ. The defenses in this sigil-covered corridor were beyond anything I had ever seen. The one time I had tried to 'see' what they were, I nearly fried myself on the spot.

I learned that day. Some secrets are better left undiscovered.

This corridor was the same height as the others I had just walked with Mura, but the stone was slightly darker, with a reddish hue. There were no overt design elements; it was a short, barren corridor with a door at the end.

The dim lighting originated in the stone itself, light enough to see where you were going, dark enough to hide the lethal sigils covering every surface.

I reached the door and knocked.

The door opened, inviting me in further. I kept my emotions in check. Victoria was a significant threat. I needed to approach her calmly. I stepped into the room, beyond the door.

Victoria's office was an understated space but still impressive. Two walls held floor-to-ceiling bookcases, requiring one of those rolling ladders to reach the top shelves.

An undercurrent of power, originating from Victoria, filled the room. I could see the softly pulsing sigils on the walls and floor, indicating this room was as—if not more—secure than the corridor outside. Behind a large wooden desk sat Victoria, going over several piles of papers.

Three computer monitors, one on each corner, and one in the center dominated her desk space. On the wall directly behind her, I could see a large, amber holographic image of the world map in a Mercator projection, with red blips flashing on every continent.

A few feet to the side of her desk, in front of the bookcases, sat a large, leather chaise. Opposite that, on the other side of the room, were three large chairs arranged in semicircular fashion, which I assumed were for visitors to her office. The space directly in front of her desk was empty of all furniture or obstruction. I figured she wanted a clear line of sight in case she needed to blast someone.

On the other side of the space, near the entrance, sat a medium-sized, circular conference table covered with folders.

Seven chairs were situated around it, with a monitor sitting in front of each chair. No one was currently occupying any of the chairs at the table.

I wondered if there were really seven Directors, or if it was a myth to give the impression of a group of sorcerers running the organization. My money was on Vic being the head sorceress and the *only* sorceress in charge of The Seven.

Victoria wore a slate gray suit with a white blouse. She looked more like a CEO than a powerful sorceress heading a secret society. Her hair, peppered with gray, was cut short, in an almost severe hairstyle with the sides shaved close and the top fairly long.

"Liv called me," Victoria said, placing a sheet of paper down without looking at me. "Show me the sigil you found."

"Acheron—"

"Can wait," she said, cutting me off. She looked up and gave me a stare. "Liv tells me this sigil almost killed you."

"She was exaggerating," I said. "It's just a—"

"Liv has never, to my knowledge, exaggerated anything," Victoria answered. "If I'm going to start my day speaking to a demon, even one that is currently allied to us, I want to know why. Show me the sigil."

She pushed a piece of paper forward across her desk.

"Are you sure?" I asked. "The last time I did this, things went sideways...dramatically."

"I'm certain," Victoria answered. "Draw it."

I drew the sigil, held my breath and passed the paper back.

"That's it," I said, exhaling when the office didn't go up in flames. "It nearly barbecued me with soulflames."

She picked up the sheet of paper, examined the sigil and typed something on her keyboard. She looked at the center monitor for a few seconds, nodded, and then focused on me again.

"Soulflames?" Victoria asked. "Where did you learn this sigil?"

"It was buried in a summoning circle of some third-rate sorcerer who nearly killed himself when he summoned a *Minoras*."

"What happened to the *Minoras*?"

"I ended it."

She raised an eyebrow.

"Alone?"

"Acheron helped," I said, "but I did the heavy lifting."

"This is an ancient, *forbidden* sigil," Victoria said, pointing to the paper on her desk. "One designed to eradicate your kind. Who was the sorcerer?"

"Don't know," I said, losing my patience. "He was picked up by the OSA. Can you have Rodrigo disable the labyrinth so I can go find—?"

"Your demon partner is no longer on the premises," Victoria said, leaning back in her chair. "He was removed shortly after you two were separated."

"What?" I asked as my anxiety and anger mixed into a volatile cocktail. "Why didn't you say something?"

"I just did."

I did my best to keep my anger in check, but my claws were slowly extending.

"I could've used a hand in the labyrinth, you know. Someone blindsided us."

"Really, *you* could have used a hand?" Victoria asked. "I seem to recall you not needing anyone's help. You were very vocal when you expressed this sentiment to me the last time we spoke."

"I was pissed."

"When aren't you?"

"I need to go," I said. "He needs my help."

"Sit down," Victoria said, looking at my hands. "Are you in

a rush to get yourself killed? Retract your claws. I don't need holes in the chairs...again."

I pulled my claws in and sat.

"I need to go find Acheron. I don't know who has him or why they took him."

"This has the Black Cleavers written all over it," Victoria said. "Few know who and what you are."

"It doesn't make sense," I said, confused. "They don't have the firepower to banish Acheron. Especially if they removed him from the labyrinth."

"The reason is simple. You're just too close to see it."

"Reason? This makes no sense," I answered. "I mean if it's the Cleavers, I can see it on principle; but this seems personal."

"They want you and are using Acheron as bait."

"Me?" I asked. "Why would they want me?"

"That is the real question," Victoria said. "Why would they want *you*?"

Acheron's words came back to me.

"What is a Darkin?"

"Excuse me?"

Victoria was visibly surprised—which was rare. Her expression usually varied between serious, displeased, and seriously displeased. I had never seen her surprised by anything.

"A Darkin. What is it?"

"*Where* did you hear that term?" she asked. "*Who* said this to you?"

"Acheron did, right before we split up in the labyrinth," I answered, wondering why this was getting her worked up. "He said you needed to give me the Darkin."

"Those were his exact words?"

"Yes," I answered. "*Tell Victoria it's time to give you the Darkin*. Care to elaborate?"

"Not particularly," she said, resting both hands on top of the desk. "It seems your partner knows more than I anticipated."

"What is the Darkin?"

"A Darkin cannot be 'given'—it can only be coaxed out, with great risk for everyone involved."

"That explains a large amount of nothing," I said, tired of the deflections. "What exactly is a Darkin?"

"A weapon catalyst. One designed to be used only by Otherkin," Victoria answered, after a pause. "It causes an altered state in your kind."

"Altered state? What kind of altered state?"

"The actual weapon can be traced back to the chakram in history," Victoria said. "This particular weapon, when wielded by Otherkin, has the potential to make them Darkin. It makes them incredibly lethal and highly...*dangerous*."

I didn't like how she said that last word.

"I'm *already* dangerous."

"Not like this," Victoria answered. "How did Acheron know we possessed it?"

"I'd like to ask him that, too," I said. "As soon as I locate him. Why didn't you tell me you had a weapon designed specifically for me?"

"Because it's deadly."

"It's a weapon; they're supposed to be deadly."

"Deadly for *you*," Victoria answered slowly. "Every Otherkin who tried to wield it, perished...horribly."

"They weren't me," I said. "What kind of weapon is it?"

"The kind you don't get to use," Victoria said. "You can barely control your claws. You think you can control an ensorcelled weapon?"

"I won't know until I try."

"Or die in the process. You need to let this go."

"I will, as soon as you let me try *my* weapon," I said, my voice harder than my claws. "Where is it?"

"The Vault."

"You placed a weapon meant for me in the Vault?"

"Yes, I prefer to see you breathing," she said. "This weapon is dangerous. Rodrigo placed it in the vault, for safekeeping."

"And you let him?" I said, letting my anger get away from me. "Without telling me?"

"I didn't *let* him. I *instructed* him," she said with a small sigh. "I don't require your approval to conduct Seven affairs, contrary to your over-inflated opinion."

I stood and glared at her.

"Tell Rodrigo I'm on my way. I expect him to release the weapon," I said. "Is this going to be a problem?"

"Yes," Victoria answered. "There is a very real chance of it killing you when you try to use it."

"I'll take my chances," I said. "It's not like you or The Seven are tripping over yourselves to help me find Acheron. If the Cleavers have him—"

"He's just a demon, Nyx," Victoria answered. "It's time you dissolve that partnership. Grow up. Associating with a demon will only shorten your life expectancy."

"Someone wants me dead, and your advice is to cut off the only person that has my back?" I asked. "That's just twisted."

"It's pragmatic," Victoria said, giving me a hard look. "If someone is after you, giving you that weapon and having a demon partner will only make matters worse."

"Let them come," I said, heading for the door. "Tell Rodrigo to open the vault, or I'll open it myself."

"You're strong, but not that strong," Victoria said. "Wait." She picked up the phone. "If you insist on this course of action, I'll call Gryn."

"I can do this without Gryn."

"No, you can't, and you won't," Victoria answered her voice as soft as iron. "You want the Darkin? It comes with Gryn. No Gryn, no weapon. You wanted a choice? Choose."

"Tell Gryn to meet me at the vault," I said as I opened the door. "Anything else you're keeping from me?"

"Plenty," Victoria answered with a smile. "When I deem you to be ready for the information, I will share it with you."

"This is why I love The Seven so, it's the transparency."

"It's to keep you safe."

"No"—I turned to face her—"don't insult my intelligence by lying to me," I said. "It's to give you plausible deniability in case I go psychotic and you need to shut me down."

Victoria gave me a hard look, then a tight smile.

"You are a clear and present danger, Nyx," Victoria said, steepling her fingers. "When you turned, everyone wanted you exterminated on the spot. Everyone, except me."

"Are you saying I should be grateful?" I asked with venom. "The Seven let this happen to me."

"I'm saying you should tread carefully," Victoria answered. "The Seven is not a charitable organization. You either have a use, or you don't. You're either an asset or a liability."

"What are you trying to say?" I asked, knowing what she was trying to say. "Are you saying I'm a liability?"

"Partnering with a demon can be viewed as such. They are our enemies."

"Might have something to do with the banishing and killing of their kind."

"They do worse to us," Victoria answered. "Don't be fooled. Acheron is not your friend. He is bound to you. There is a difference."

"Keep your friends close and your enemies closer?"

"Precisely. Every contingency is planned for, Nyx," she said. "This is The Seven. We don't like or entertain surprises. You do good work, in spite of a demon partner, which we, which *I*, tolerate—within reason. I'd suggest you don't become a liability."

"Liabilities are removed," I said. "Right?"

"Like the cancer that they are," Victoria said with a slight nod. "You want the weapon? Go meet with Gryn. Otherwise, we have nothing more to discuss."

"I'm guessing that's a 'no' on the assist to locate Acheron?"

"I just provided you with a weapon and a trainer," Victoria said, picking up another sheet of paper. "I'd say that's plenty of help—if you want it."

I glared at her and left the office, trying my best to shatter the door as I slammed it closed. I took a few steps and got my breathing under control. Somehow, I managed to avoid putting my fist through the corridor wall in rage.

I was going to find Acheron; then we needed an exit strategy from The Seven.

Before I tried to kill everyone.

THIRTEEN

I drove Eight uptown until I reached the Vault.

Located on 14th Street and Eighth Avenue, the Vault was situated inside the building that housed the Museum of Illusions. With locations in most major cities, the MOI buildings made it easy to hide artifacts in plain sight. More of the subtlety The Seven excelled at.

To the general public, the building was an old bank converted into a museum. For The Seven, the museum was the perfect cover to house artifacts of power. This was going to be a difficult meeting. Rodrigo and I didn't really see eye to eye on things.

He thought I was a menace to The Seven, and I thought he was an arrogant ass. It was only going to become more complicated by having Gryn there. Gryn Dell was a cranky, ancient sorcerer and weapons master. He worked with The Seven in what he liked to call a 'freelance' capacity.

He *was* free to do as he pleased, and they were welcome to shove a lance up their nether regions if they didn't agree. Rodrigo didn't like Gryn either, but he couldn't challenge him. Rumor was that Gryn was as powerful as Victoria and as proficient in attack magic. I had only seen Gryn in action once.

Rodrigo wouldn't last long against an angry Gryn.

To make matters worse, Gryn disliked Rodrigo, and called him the famous 'paper tiger' of The Seven. In Gryn's defense, he was mostly antisocial, unless he was training someone; then he thoroughly enjoyed pounding on his victims.

To get the Darkin weapon, I needed to convince Rodrigo —who thought I was a menace—to release it to me, as long as Gryn, who he couldn't stand, trained me in its use. What could possibly go wrong?

I exited Eight and stood outside the building.

"You think the weapon is going to float out to you?" a voice growled next to me. "What are you waiting for?"

I turned to look up at Gryn who towered over me. He stood an easy six and a half feet tall, and looked like a renegade Gandalf. He was dressed in a long coat, which covered a dark gray suit.

"Hello, Gryn," I said, eyeing his clothing. "You have an interview somewhere today? Or did you dress up special for me?"

"Victoria requested I appear in this getup"—he motioned to his clothing—"and present myself here professionally. As your trainer."

"It's a nice change from your scruffy Gandalf look," I said with a smile. "You almost look decent."

"No one will ever accuse me of being decent, Claws," he said with a scowl. "Tori"—as far as I knew, he was the only living being allowed to call Victoria by that name, and survive —"tells me you lost your demon? Cleavers?"

"I didn't *lose* him," I said. "We were attacked in the labyrinth."

"Best place for it, if facing a demon," he answered. "Are you sure it was The Cleavers?"

"No, I'm not. The list of people who could pull off that attack is short though," I said. "I'll find them."

"Or they'll find you."

"They're going to wish they never attacked me or Acheron."

"I see," he said, heading up the stairs to the museum. "Are you surveying the building? I'm told you need a weapon...let's go get it."

"Rodrigo is not going to be happy to see you," I said, climbing the stairs two at time to keep up with him. "You do recall last time?"

Gryn smiled wickedly.

"I'm not here for a popularity contest," he said, growing serious. "Besides, it's not like he's going to be ecstatic to see you either."

"True," I said as we reached the door. "But I'm not a threat to him. You, on the other hand, are."

Gryn held the door for me as we stepped inside the museum.

"He's just going to have to get over his insecurities," Gryn said as the door closed behind us. "My purpose here is to secure the weapon for *you*. I'm not here for a duel."

The interior of the museum was a large, open plan with exhibits designed to fool and trick the mind into seeing or believing something other than what they presented. It was a sleight of hand that mimicked the subterfuge The Seven pulled on the world.

The building consisted of stone and marble, heavy on the Roman influence. Gryn and I walked past the exhibits to a small alcove at the rear of the museum. A young woman stood in the alcove. She wore a museum uniform and a small badge that said 'Information'. Beneath that it read, 'Lydia'.

To the regular patrons she appeared to be an employee of the museum. She was actually one of the Vault security detail, a sorceress working under Rodrigo to keep the artifacts safe. Gryn approached and extended a hand revealing a sigil. She nodded and turned, walking down a small corridor to the right of the alcove.

"Right this way, please," Lydia said. "The exhibit you are looking for is this way."

We followed her down the narrow corridor. When we reached the end, she placed her hand on the smooth marble wall. A section of the wall in front of us opened inward.

"Thank you," Gryn said. "Is he in?"

"He's always in," Lydia answered crisply. "Will there be anything else?"

"No, thank you," Gryn answered. "I know the way."

Lydia nodded and left us alone. A few seconds later, the massive door whispered shut behind us as we stood in the Vault. In contrast to the outer museum area, the Vault space was a mix of hi-tech security and minimalism.

This wasn't exactly the Vault, but more like the vault reception. If you didn't make it past this area, you didn't belong in the building.

We stood in a large, empty atrium. I saw cameras mounted in every corner, covering the entire floor space. Under each of the cameras were nasty-looking mini-Gatling guns with oversized magazines. They appeared to be capable of significant damage.

"Those look painful," I said, glancing at the guns. "Conventional weapons? Really? I expected something a little more—"

"Esoteric?" Gryn asked as he pointed to the marble floor. "Pay attention. Have you been keeping up with your sigil study?"

"Not really," I confessed. "Things have been a bit hectic lately. Why?"

"We have to get to the other side of this floor. If you step on the wrong sigil, it's the last step you'll take in your life. Step where I step, precisely. Do not deviate from the path I take, clear?"

"Completely, follow in your footsteps like a good padawan, or in this case, a dark apprentice," I said with half a smile as I examined the blue sigils glowing softly in the marble. "Lead the way, Emperor."

"Otherkin humor," Gryn said, shaking his head. "Still atrocious."

He started walking across the floor. I made sure to follow him exactly.

"Couldn't someone just memorize these to get across?" I asked as we made our way across. "This doesn't seem like much of a deterrent."

"The path changes every few seconds," Gryn said, looking down. "You don't know the next sigil until you are on the current one. Oh, and those guns are manually controlled, not automatic."

"Oh," I said. "That could be bad. But still, regular bullets? I know a few things that would laugh at regular bullets."

"Who said anything about normal ordnance?" Gryn asked. "Those guns are equipped with Gorgon rounds."

"No way," I said, looking at the guns again quickly. "Gorgons, really?"

"Yes way, really. Now, watch your step. Let's go."

Gorgon rounds were officially known as Desiccators. Anything they hit would immediately begin to dehydrate. Within seconds, a few Gorgon rounds could turn a target into a statue and then a dried-out husk. Didn't matter how powerful you were—if all your bodily fluids stopped being fluid, it was the end.

Someone into Greek mythos nicknamed them Gorgons, and it stuck. They were incredibly dangerous and impossible to acquire—unless you were the sigilsmith of The Seven, it seemed.

"How did Rodrigo get his hands on Gorgons?" I asked. "Those things are banned worldwide."

"Yes, they are," Gryn said. "Then again, The Seven doesn't exist. Who is going to tell them they can't procure or use them? Who will tell The Seven, 'no'? They operate with impunity and answer only to themselves."

"That's a bad idea," I said. "No one is watching the warden."

"Correct," Gryn said as we reached the other side of the room without incident and faced another alcove. This one was larger than the first one Lydia had stood in. "The general populace is oblivious, and the guards have no oversight. A recipe for disaster."

"*I'll* tell them no," I said. "No one organization should have that much power."

Gryn laughed and then grew serious.

"Watch your words in here, Claws. Let's discuss that after you get what you're here for."

I nodded.

We stepped into the alcove, and a wall of blue energy descended behind us, enclosing us in the space. The floor shifted slightly and we began dropping down into the Vault proper.

FOURTEEN

We arrived at the lower level to a glowering Rodrigo.

This level was similar to the one above. It was a wide-open space minus the Gatling guns and tiles of death. Two large doors sat at opposite ends of the room. The rest of the room was filled with small cases holding various artifacts.

I knew from previous experience that the artifacts in this room were low-lethality items. The dangerous artifacts were kept in a separate area, which only Rodrigo could access.

"We're here to—" Gryn started.

"I know why you're here," Rodrigo answered. "I just got off the phone with Victoria. The answer is no."

Rodrigo was dressed casually in a black dress shirt and dark jeans. His sleeves were rolled up and I could see some of the sigils inscribed on his arms. His brown hair was cut short, making him look younger than his years.

"Acheron was taken," I said. "I need to get him back."

"So, go get him," Rodrigo answered, standing in front of us with his arms crossed. "He's a demon. Shouldn't be too hard to locate him. Or even better, maybe he's dead by now?"

I refrained from driving my claws into his chest and

removing his heart. It would've been futile—I seriously doubted he possessed one. I took a breath and calmed myself.

"It's not the locating, it's the extraction," I said, measuring my words. "Are you planning to help me?"

"To rescue a *demon*?" he scoffed. "Have you smashed your head into a wall recently? Why would I help you—period?"

"Didn't think so," I answered. "Since I'm doing this solo, I'm going to need the weapon."

"No, absolutely not," Rodrigo said, shaking his head. "This is the worst idea I've heard. How can Victoria be serious?"

He was going to agree…eventually.

Denying my request meant he would have to deal directly with Victoria and Gryn. As a sigilsmith, the vault was his sphere of control. Few people had more authority regarding artifacts than Rodrigo.

I just happened to be sent here by the one person who outranked Rodrigo in The Seven when it came to vault contents, and he was being all pissy about it.

"Are you questioning her judgement?" Gryn asked. "If you like, I could give her a call. I'm sure we could—"

"This Vault is *my* responsibility," Rodrigo seethed. "Giving her"—he glanced at me—"an ensorcelled weapon is a recipe for disaster. No, not happening."

"Thanks for the vote of confidence," I said. "I promise not to break your vault."

"The Vault? It's not the vault I'm worried about; it's the innocent lives that will die by you handling this weapon, before you kill yourself."

"That's why I'm here," Gryn said. "If she can't handle the weapon, I will make sure she leaves here without it."

"Victoria may have sent you," Rodrigo asked, turning to Gryn, "but I trust *you* less than I trust the Otherkin."

"If I gave your feelings any consideration, I'd be insulted," Gryn replied. "I don't need your trust. Just your compliance."

"Because this hybrid isn't dangerous enough?" Rodrigo asked, looking at me with contempt. "All offense intended. Now we need to arm her so she can go rescue a demon? I don't know what Victoria is thinking, but this...this is wrong."

"Should I call Victoria so she can tell you what's on her mind regarding this situation?" Gryn asked. "Or would you prefer an old-fashioned brawl? You seem a little tightly wound. Are you getting out enough? I hear fresh air does wonders for the disposition."

"You think you can take me?" Rodrigo asked. "You're not as strong as you think you are, not by a long shot."

"I never claimed to be strong," Gryn answered. "What I am, is old, crafty, and devious. That makes me dangerous, especially to scholars who would rather bury their noses in books than face real threats."

"You know what, Gryn?" Rodrigo snapped, pointing a finger in Gryn's face. "Fuck you."

"Is that a proposition or a threat?" Gryn answered with a smile. "I'm unclear as to your intent."

Black energy crackled around Rodrigo's body. For a few seconds, I thought he was actually going to attack Gryn.

"Rodrigo..." I warned.

Gryn raised a hand, cutting me off.

"Are you certain you want to choose that path?" Gryn said with a smile that never reached his eyes. "Last time, I restrained myself out of courtesy for Victoria. This time, I won't."

Rodrigo paused and the energy around his body slowly dissipated. The last time they had faced each other in combat, Rodrigo had nearly died. It had taken him months to recover.

If that was Gryn holding back, I didn't want to see him

cut loose. I was pretty sure Rodrigo wouldn't survive a no-holds-barred Gryn on the attack.

"Victoria authorized this," I said, trying to get us back to subtle hostility instead of open warfare. "She knows I'm here. I need your help."

"Fine," Rodrigo said, turning away from us. "Victoria wants to give the mutant creature the equivalent of a nuke, so she can unleash death on the streets of the city? This disaster is on her. I'm not cleaning up the mess."

Rodrigo started walking away to the rear of the floor. He was headed to one of the large sigil-covered doors. This door made the one at the Grimoire look about as secure as wet cardboard.

"Do you want us to join you?" Gryn called out as Rodrigo opened the door and stepped through. "Do you need assistance?"

"Do I look like I need your assistance?" Rodrigo shot back. "Wait here and touch nothing."

Rodrigo stepped into the space behind the door as it closed silently, leaving us in the large space alone.

"Mutant creature?" I asked. "I'm the mutant creature?"

"It would appear so," Gryn answered. "You're like that character with the metal claws...what's the name?"

"Wolverine?"

"No, the other one. The female. Is it Lady Deathsprite something or another?"

"You mean Lady Deathstrike?"

"Exactly," Gryn said with a snap of his fingers. "You two have that similar fingernails-to-claws thing happening. Maybe Rodrigo doesn't like your claws?"

"I think he just doesn't like me."

"More like he doesn't accept what you represent," Gryn said. "You're not human. Not anymore. On some level, that frightens him. Humans kill what they fear."

"And now Victoria is telling him to give me some weapon that may alter me into a Darkin," I said. "Wonderful. All that's going to do is trigger him further."

"Correct," Gryn said, removing his long coat. "I would expect the sigilsmith to be soiling his undergarments at this turn of events—hence the near suicidal outburst earlier. Fear is the only thing I can attribute his lack of self-preservation in challenging me."

"Were you really holding back last time? He nearly died."

Gryn glanced at me for a few seconds and then smiled.

"If I was serious, he'd be dead before he traced his first sigil," he answered, still smiling. "Then I'd have to explain to an upset Victoria why I eliminated her favorite Sigilsmith."

"She would be so pissed at you," I said, looking at the door. "She likes Rodrigo, or at least likes him more than most of The Seven."

"Exactly. His death would only lead to complications," Gryn said, waving a hand. "Angry agents, then dead angry agents, followed by more angry agents. The cycle would get boring, fast."

"I thought Victoria called him?" I asked. "Is this weapon that powerful? He's acting worse than usual, and usually he's a colossal ass."

"Must be something you said or did," Gryn said, looking around the floor. "They really need to get some housekeeping in this place."

"Something I did? Are you serious?" I asked. "I barely deal with him, or The Seven for that matter."

"Well it's not like he's releasing the weapon to *me*. Aside from bruising his ego, there's no reason for him to be upset with me. Logic dictates that you must be the target of his animosity. Makes perfect sense."

"No, it doesn't," I said, following Gryn's gaze. "Plenty of sorcerers are thin-skinned egomaniacs."

"You've just described two-thirds of The Seven."

"Two-thirds? What about the remaining third?"

"Those are the real danger: thin-skinned egomaniacs, with power."

"Still, I don't understand why he would react like this," I stared at Gryn. "I mean aside from your insults."

"I did no such thing," Gryn said, raising his hands in surrender. "I merely pointed out the flaws in his thinking. Attacking me would be fatal—for him. Questioning and disregarding a direct request from Victoria is also ill-advised. I think he just needed to flex his sigilsmith muscles."

"This was a horrible idea," I said. "What *was* Victoria thinking? She knows Rodrigo can't stand us."

Gryn nodded.

"Could be she wants to see how determined you are to get this weapon," Gryn said, turning to face the rear door as it opened and Rodrigo re-appeared in the doorway. "If this minor obstacle can deter you, then you don't deserve to wield it."

"I wouldn't exactly call Rodrigo a 'minor obstacle.' He is a sigilsmith."

"I wasn't referring to him, but rather what he represents."

"I don't understand," I said, keeping my voice low as Rodrigo approached. "What are you talking about?"

"Another time, Claws," Gryn said, focusing on Rodrigo. "Now, that wasn't so hard now, was it?"

"I'm going to assume you need the Room," Rodrigo said, handing Gryn a small flat box. "Is it just the two of you?"

"The Room would be excellent, yes. Just the two of us. Why?"

"It'll be easy to fill out the report and identify the bodies when she messes up and kills you both," Rodrigo answered, glancing at me warily. "Just so you know—partnering with a demon is wrong."

"For you, maybe," I said, letting the anger seep into my words.

"Not just for me, for any human."

"He's my friend and he needs help. *My* help."

"He needs your help?" Rodrigo mocked. "Of course; I forgot, you stopped being human long ago, *hybrid*." He turned to Gryn. "You know where the Room is. I'll swing by once she fails to align with the weapon."

"I'll align with it," I said. "It's meant for me."

"That's what every Otherkin said, right before we carried out what was left of them," Rodrigo answered. "Try not to kill yourself. My schedule is packed, and I don't have time to clean up after you."

"You are a complete assh—"

"I will inform you of her progress," Gryn interrupted. "Thank you for your assistance, Sigilsmith."

Rodrigo stormed off.

FIFTEEN

We headed over to the door opposite the one Rodrigo used earlier.

"You would do well to learn some diplomacy," Gryn said, heading to the other door. "At the very least, work on being less antagonistic."

"I don't do diplomacy," I said. "I prefer to act from a position of strength. Diplomacy always seems like giving away your power. No, thanks."

"It only seems that way because you don't know how to use it," Gryn said, placing a hand on the surface of the door. "Being diplomatic is akin to being powerful, not powerless."

"That hasn't been my experience," I said. "The things I face only respect immediate, bone-crushing power."

"Only the truly powerful embrace diplomacy. Weakness resorts to immediate violence and shredding. Having a position of strength doesn't mean you have to use it. It's enough that your adversary knows you *can* use it, if need be."

"The potentiality of pain?" I asked. "It should be enough that they know I have claws. That way I don't need to use them?"

"Precisely."

"I'll make sure to use diplomacy on the next demon I face," I said. "Should go well."

The sigils on the door pulsed red for a few seconds and the door opened slightly.

"After you," Gryn said, holding the door open for me. "Are you sure you want to do this?"

"You asking me that now?"

"Just making certain," Gryn said, stepping in behind me. "Once this door is closed, you either align to this"—he hefted the small box—"or I carry your body out of here. Yes or no?"

"Yes," I said, certain. "If I don't do this, no one is going to help Acheron."

"If you do this, no one is going to help you. If you think they fear you now, just wait."

"They don't fear me. They can't stand me."

"Don't be fooled, Claws. Their behavior is rooted in fear."

"The Seven are powerful," I said, looking around at the empty room. "They only associate with me because it's convenient for them."

"No one will associate with a Darkin," Gryn said with a crooked smile. "Well, no one reputable."

"I can live with that," I said. "Let's get started."

"Very well," Gryn said and turned to close the door behind him. "Live or die."

"Truth or lie." I said, remembering the phrase reflexively.

"First to strike."

"Last to yield."

"Strong when soft."

"Weak when hard," I answered. "I can't believe you still remember that."

Gryn nodded in approval.

"Let's see if you understand it now," Gryn said as the door closed, "or if you're still taking it literally."

He opened the small box as the light grew dimmer in the room. Sigils around the walls and floors flickered to life. I looked down at the box and saw a circular throwing weapon about a foot wide. The outer edge looked sharp enough to cut me from a distance.

The center was a hollowed-out dual teardrop design, reminding me of a yin-yang symbol. The blade area was a thin band of metal about an inch wide, inscribed with indecipherable golden sigils.

"What *is* that? A death frisbee?"

"This is what will make you a Darkin, if you can control it."

"You sure it won't just make me a warrior princess?"

"Are you quite finished?" Gryn asked, irritated. "Pick it up. From the inside, please, if you want to keep your fingers attached. Be careful."

The metal was warm to the touch.

"It's warm," I said, grabbing the center of the circle of metal. I grazed a finger along the edge, drawing blood as it cut into me. "Damn, this thing is sharp."

"You aren't attuned to it yet," Gryn said, stepping to the other side of the room. "That will change, if you attune to it."

"*When* I attune to it," I corrected. "So what now? We play catch and try not to slice each other's fingers off?"

"Remember the phrase?"

"You ingrained it into me, how could I forget?"

"Good, you will need it now. Get ready."

"We're standing in an empty room," I said, glancing around. "What am I supposed to get ready for?"

I turned to face him, but Gryn was gone.

The room shimmered and transformed around me. Instead of an empty room, I was standing in a deserted street, complete with parked cars and buildings. I was about to call out Gryn's name again when I heard the growl.

"Another morsel to snack on," a voice said from above me. "I'm certain the marrow of your bones will be sweet on my tongue."

"Not funny, Gryn," I called out. "And for the record, gross and sort of pervy."

A crash, like a truck colliding with the street as it fell from orbit, enveloped me. Dust, debris and chunks of street kicked up into the air as something moved in the center of the devastation.

"What the fu—?"

"Hello, little morsel," the voice came from inside the dust cloud. "I promise to end you quick. No pain, just death."

I took several steps back and bumped into Gryn who was leaning against a car.

"Nice illusion," I said as I kept moving back. "What is that thing?"

"That is a Darkin, a real one," Gryn said, pointing a finger. "It's the beast of the weapon. Cute, isn't it?"

"Not exactly the word I was going for," I said. "More like grotesque."

"It's not an illusion," Gryn said, his voice serious. "You beat it, you get to live and control the weapon. You lose, you die. Simple."

"Simple? That thing is the size of a truck. How am I supposed to beat it?"

"Only one thing can hurt it," Gryn said and pointed at my hand. "You have the means. Do you have the will? Use the phrase and good luck."

I was certain the Darkin was some kind of demon. It made a *Minoras* look harmless in comparison. It came from the same mold: six legs, scales for skin, enormous fangs to gore me with, and an evil intelligence lurking behind its glowing eyes.

That was where the comparison ended. Saying that the

Darkin was a demon like the *Minoras,* was like stating that great white sharks and guppies are fish. Technically correct, but a guppie won't chomp on your bone marrow, while a great white could chew you in half.

This was not some Dragondog, this was closer to a Dragon*demon*.

I hefted the weapon in my hand. I still had no clue what to do with it. If I threw it, I would lose my only means to do damage. If I held onto it, and fought close-quarters, one blow from that thing meant catastrophic damage.

Use the phrase.

Live or die.

I wasn't dying here to this creature. I raced forward as it roared. Fear gripped my stomach as I closed the distance. I could swear I saw it smile as I charged at it.

"Finally," it rasped, "one worthy to die by my hand. Come, little one. Race to your death."

I pumped my legs harder and extended the claws of one hand. Five feet from the creature I dropped into a slide, using my claws in the pavement as an anchor to change direction. I managed to slide next to the Darkin and open a gash in its side with the weapon.

First to strike.

It roared in anger, lashing out with a leg, connecting with my side. The force of the kick launched me into a wall. I impacted with enough force to see spots dancing in my vision. It turned to crush me into the wall.

Truth or lie.

The pain I currently felt was real. If this thing pounded on me, I was dead. I got my bearings and rolled away as it crashed into the building in an effort to turn me into paste.

"Stand still and die, little one," it said as it shook off the debris from the wall. "I'll make this quick."

"No thanks, ugly," I shot back as I tried to catch my

breath. "Why don't you roll over, like a good boy, so I can just end you?"

The Darkin laughed and extended its tail, shaking it like a rattlesnake. It jingled, making a metallic sound, and I realized the top third of the tail consisted of metal circles of death, like the one I held in my hand.

"Hey, no fair," I said, leaping over the hood of a car as death donuts sliced through the air. "I only have one."

Some of the circles buried themselves in the car. The others bounced off the walls, nearly shredding me with the rebounds. I kept moving as more death circles filled the air. Rather than run away, I moved to close the distance. Next to the Darkin was the safest place to be, if I avoided the claws and fangs, that is.

Last to yield.

That's when the solution came to me. It was a risk, but it was the only chance I had. Somehow, I needed to get close enough to its neck without getting shredded in the process. I needed to last long enough to yield.

"Fine," I yelled out from behind a car. "You win!"

"You yield?" it roared, clearly disappointed. "Come and face your fate, coward!"

I stepped out from behind the car and into the middle of the street.

"There's no way I can beat you," I said and felt the weapon shift in my hand. The center had become disengaged and separated. I kept it as one piece as I stepped closer. "I don't deserve to wield you."

It roared again, towering over me.

"You will die with honor," it said. "You have earned that much."

I stood in front of its massive head and looked into its eyes. It stared back intensely, and for a split-second I thought about running.

I cowered instead, getting to my knees.

It reared up on its hind legs, prepared to pounce on me.

Strong when soft.

The weapon separated in my hands with a burst of golden light. I shifted the weapon in my hands. I now held two half-circles, one in each hand. Demonflame covered the blades as the Darkin descended on me.

Weak when hard.

The Darkin was committed to its trajectory, and descended right onto the blades as I buried them into its neck—the only vulnerable spot I could think of. I lost my grip on the weapons as the Darkin thrashed away from me. As it rolled away, it whipped its tail around. I tried to dodge, but it was like trying to dodge a redwood. It was too large, too fast, and I was too slow.

The tail slammed into me, launching me down the street. I bounced several times before rolling to a painful stop. I turned in time to see the Darkin go up in a massive fireball of demonflame, illuminating the entire street around me.

Covered in flame, it walked slowly toward me.

I staggered to my feet and extended my claws. If I was going to die here, I was going down swinging, causing as much damage as possible. It stepped close and bent its forelegs, kneeling in front of me. In its mouth, it held the weapon. The Darkin extended its head and offered me the weapon. It was covered in demonflame. I took it, but it didn't feel hot. I felt the same slight warmth as before.

"You have risen where others have fallen," the Darkin said. "This is rightfully yours, as is my power. This weapon is forged in both fear and demonflame. Its edge will not cut you, nor will its flame burn you. In your hands and by your will, you have become Darkin."

The flames enveloping the weapon raced up my arms and

engulfed me. A few seconds later, the weapon vanished. The Darkin crouched, still covered in flame, and jumped at me.

The flames around my body absorbed it with a *whump* before they were extinguished.

"As within, so without," I heard the Darkin say. "As above, so below. It is done."

I stood on the empty street as everything shimmered around me. Gryn walked toward me with a smile on his face. I took a step in his direction as he started to tilt sideways. I was about to ask him why he was tilting that way, when I introduced my face to the floor of the Room.

Everything blurred into a gray cloud after that.

SIXTEEN

"Where is it?" I heard Rodrigo demand. "Where did you put it?"

I kept my eyes closed. I knew he wasn't talking to me and I preferred to sit this one out.

"You can stop pretending," Gryn said. "We know you're awake."

"I'm not awake," I said as my body ached everywhere. "This is part of a nightmare I can't escape."

"Where is the weapon?" Rodrigo asked, clearly not amused by my blazing wit. "What did you do with it?"

"It's in the Room, I'm guessing," I said, looking around. "Right?"

I was sitting in a large hospital bed. I knew the Vault contained emergency medical facilities; I just had never had the need to use them. It made sense having them on the premises. If something went wrong with an artifact, they wouldn't have time to race to the nearest hospital, much less be able to explain that the patient was handling some ensorcelled artifact filled with arcane power.

"Tell him what it said," Gryn said. "At the end. What did you hear?"

"It was hard to hear anything over the roaring flames," I said. "I don't really remember—"

"Try," Gryn coaxed. "Focus and recall the last words."

I closed my eyes and went back to my last moments facing the Darkin.

"*As within, so without*," I said, with my eyes still closed. "*As above, so below. It is done.*"

"Impossible," Rodrigo said with a look of shock and anger. "There's no way you attuned with it. How?"

"I suggest you go inform Victoria, while my student and I discuss her training," Gryn said, glancing at me. "I'd hate for this nuke to go off and atomize the city. Don't you agree?"

"I can't believe this," Rodrigo said as he backed away. "Victoria is going to lose her shit."

Rodrigo left the room in a hurry.

"What the hell is he scared of? It's me."

"Precisely," Gryn said with a smile. "It's you."

"I need to go," I said, sitting up and throwing my feet over the side of the bed. "Acheron."

"Not yet," Gryn said, pushing me back into the bed as the world swayed. "Rodrigo is right about one thing: sending you out into the world with power and no training is a recipe for disaster. You need to be able to handle the Darkin first."

"Acheron. He's in trouble."

"When you are ready, and I promise it will be soon," Gryn answered, "I will help you get your demon back."

"Promise," I said. "I need to...I need to..."

"Yes, I know," Gryn said, tracing a sigil in the air, as my vision tunneled and the grayness returned. "I promise. You're going to need all of the help you can get."

"Thank...thank you, Gryn."

I couldn't keep my eyes open and my body suddenly felt heavy.

"Get some rest," Gryn said, sounding far away. "The promise of pain awaits, Darkin."

THE END

THEY REND
BOOK TWO

ABOUT THE STORY

Sometimes to fight monsters...you must become one.

When Nyxia White transforms, she realizes she possesses a fearsome weapon and power of the Darkin.

There's only one problem, she doesn't know how to use them...yet.

Gryn, an old sorcerer, has just the solution—intense training bordering on torture.

Now, with little time, Nyx must survive Gryn's training, harness her new power and hunt down whoever kidnapped Acheron, before they rend him to ash—a demon extermination.

In order to save her friend, she must become the monster other monsters fear.

"Therefore I will be unto them as a lion: as a leopard by the way will I observe them. I will meet them as a bear that is bereaved of her whelps, and will rend the caul of their heart, and there will I devour them like a lion: the wild beast shall tear them."
Hosea 13:8

temet nosce-know thyself

ONE

"Temet nosce," Gryn said, staring down at me. "Do you know what that means?"

We were in an old warehouse Gryn used, to *train* his victims. I say *train*, but what I really mean is unrelenting torture. I could tell it was designed to cause me agony, because he was enjoying himself and actually smiling.

That only happened during *training*.

I made a mental note to pay Victoria back for this little gift of pain she had made possible. Agreeing to this training facilitated my rescue of Acheron. I stared across the floor at my immediate source of discomfort.

Gryn wore his usual: black loose-fitting pants and a burnt ochre T-shirt with long sleeves. He looked like a rebellious Shaolin monk hiding out in the city. His long hair hung loose around his head and his bare feet lightly grazed the floor, as he floated lazily in place. We had been drilling movement exercises, where he did the drilling and I did the movement.

So far, it had been an utter disaster.

Several hours of getting pummeled by his orbs had put me

in a foul and homicidal mood. He, on the other hand, was irritatingly cheerful.

"Of course I know what it means," I said in-between gasps. "It means 'reckless harm'. *Temet* is the root of temerity, which means rash or reckless, and *nosce* is latin for noisome, which means harmful. I mean, really Gryn. Don't you know Latin?"

He continued staring at me for a few seconds more before shaking his head.

"That is totally and unequivocally...incorrect. Your lack of knowledge is a glaring chink in your defenses."

"Excuse me, your professorship, I spent most of my time after turning fighting for my life," I shot back. "Somehow, I never made time for those university classes I wanted to take."

"Don't mistake education for knowledge," he said. "Formal education has its place, but I acquired my knowledge in more, shall we say, unconventional ways."

"So, what you're really trying to say is that you don't know either?"

"Did one of my orbs impact that thick skull of yours?" he asked. "Of course I know what it means. It *does not* mean reckless harm, even though that would be a perfect definition for a certain Otherkin I know."

"That's total BS," I said, raising a hand to catch my breath. "You can admit I'm right, you know. It won't kill you."

"You are so wrong, on so many levels, I can't even begin to describe the depth of your wrongness. It staggers the imagination."

"You probably need to get out more, give that imagination a workout. Let it roam free."

"Is that what you're going to say to whomever kidnapped your demon?" he scoffed with an evil smile. "*Let him free. He's my friend and you need to let him go.*"

"This is a waste of time," I said, my voice dark. "There will be no words for whoever took Acheron. Only pain and death. I know myself well enough to know that."

He stared at me again, searching my face.

Of course, I knew what *temet nosce* meant, know thyself. I didn't last this long by revealing my strengths. I made it a point to capitalize on perceived weaknesses. You underestimated me at your own peril, and I made sure it only happened once.

"If you go in there unprepared, you will die," Gryn answered. "Your demon will be banished or worse, they will rend him."

"I won't let them."

"If you can't stop me, they will rip you, and your demon, to shreds," he answered. "Didn't you say you wanted to get your demon back?"

"You know the answer to that question," I said, glaring at him.

"Do you?" Gryn asked. "Because a half-assed attempt will only get you dead. For that matter, I may as well put you out of your misery now."

"You could try," I said, my voice low. "You won't find it so easy."

"Why are you here?" he asked. "I mean, besides testing my patience."

"The only reason I'm here is to get Acheron back."

"Then act like it. Focus and do it again."

I extended my claws and raced at him.

Gryn was a merciless, implacable taskmaster, but he was the best at what he did—attack magic. The only thing that made his training sessions bearable was the knowledge that he had suffered worse at the hands of his teacher—Circe.

Yes, *that* Circe.

He was one of a handful of apprentices that had not only

survived her training, but actually thrived in the midst of it. It made him powerful, and dangerous. The stories of the suffering were gruesome. Many of those who apprenticed alongside Gryn died in the initial training. The rest became his enemies.

When Circe said life-or-death training, it was heavily weighted to the death side of the equation.

That small nugget of knowledge always made me smile, at least until training started. Then Gryn would become a world-class anal cavity of immense depth—a real Marianal Trench. If I was going to face a group of sorcerers insane enough to kidnap a Demon Lord, I needed to be ready.

Gryn would make sure I could face them and walk away alive.

I slid forward, using the claws on one hand as a rudder along the floor to control my direction. My claws dug deep grooves into the stone warehouse floor as I approached. Halfway through the slide, I changed direction, moving perpendicular to his position. I lunged at his leg, planning to slice through it.

He tracked my approach and moved to the side at the last possible moment, avoiding my attack entirely, while unleashing a fist to the the side of my head which sent me sprawling across the floor. I rolled for several feet before sliding to a stop.

I shook my head as the constellations dancing before my eyes calmed down and slowly vanished. He raised a fist, smiling as he showed me his glyphed knuckle-duster.

I returned the smile. The old bastard fought in my preferred style—dirty.

"It would have been easier if you had emailed me that attack beforehand. I could have saved you the energy you wasted in that amateurish attempt."

"Fuck you, Gryn," I growled, rubbing the side of my head. "That hurt."

"It was supposed to hurt," he said. "That's why I wear these. Maximum damage, minimum effort. Besides, I'm not going to bare knuckle that thick skull of yours and break my hand."

"You...are a proper bastard," I said, getting slowly to my feet.

"Cursing at me, while entertaining, will not change the outcome of your demise when you fail," he said. "You need to use the weapon. Bring it out."

"I barely know how to control the thing," I said, frustrated, "how am I going to use it?"

"I think I understand," Gryn said, rolling up his sleeves. "You need to feel like you're in *actual* danger. It's apparent I've been taking this matter too lightly. My apologies. Allow me to rectify the situation."

He extended his hands, palms up, and formed two nasty-looking orbs of black energy.

"Gryn?" I said, taking a few steps back. "That's not funny. Those things look dangerous. Put them away."

"I have never been accused of having a sense of humor," he said, his voice grim. "These orbs are some of my favorites. I affectionately call them 'obliterators'."

"You are one sick puppy," I said, putting more distance between us as the orbs crackled with energy in his hands. "What the hell kind of training is this?"

"Someone has taken your partner—a Demon Lord, I might add," he answered. "Do you think they will deal gently with you? My training will prepare you for what you face."

"Your training is going to kill me before I rescue Acheron."

"If it does, then you don't deserve to rescue him, or to wield the power of the Darkin. Training is over."

"Excuse me?" I asked. "What are you saying?"

"The training portion of this session is over. We have now entered the survival portion," he said with a self-satisfied nod. "These orbs are sufficiently powerful to erase your irritating presence from my life—permanently. Don't get hit."

He casually launched the orbs in my direction. They floated in the air for a few seconds before homing in on my position.

"Shit, you're serious?" I yelled out, as the orbs raced at me. "You crazy fuck."

"Deadly serious," he said, pointing towards the orbs. "Watch."

One of the obliterators slammed through an iron column, converting the iron to rust in seconds as it left a gaping hole in its wake. I did the most strategic maneuver I knew.

I turned and ran.

Gryn's laughter chased me as I picked up the pace, trying to put some distance between me and his death orbs. I had managed to leave the first room and make it to an adjacent space, as the odor of sulphur reached my nose. The hairs on the back of my neck stood on end as I lunged forward.

I dropped into a roll as an orb raced past above me. I scrambled to the side without looking back as the other orb punched into the floor next to me.

"Not funny, Gryn!" I yelled out again. "You totally suck."

The orb that hit the floor had disappeared, leaving a large crater in its wake. That left one orb to deal with. Well, one orb and one psycho sorcerer, as I saw Gryn float into the room.

"You know what I was thinking?" he asked as he approached. "It may be better if I kill you here. It's not like anyone cares about you or your kind. I doubt one less Otherkin will be missed."

He extended a hand to his side and formed a black blade of pure energy.

"If you kill me—" I warned.

"The world will be a better place without you in it," he finished. "Trust me. Besides, who's going to complain? The Seven? OSA? No one cares about you or Otherkin. I know I certainly don't. Killing you is my way of doing you a favor, Nyx. You should thank me."

"You know what? First, no thank you," I said, letting the rage inside me free. "Second, fuck you very much. Don't do me any favors, especially not the lethal kind."

My weapon formed in my hand a moment later, as my body transformed, unleashing the Darkin within. The circle of metal in my hand gleamed in the low light as it pulsed with energy. I could feel the presence of the Darkin inside, a ravenous hunger willing to devour everything. Thick scales covered my skin as a low growl escaped my lips.

Gryn smiled.

"Now we're serious," he said. "Time to die, demon."

"*As within, so without,*" I heard the voice of the Darkin in my thoughts. "*As above, so below. Destroy this enemy...now.*"

"Come," I said, with a beckoning finger, "come and face your death, old sorcerer."

My low laugh filled the space as Gryn closed in on me.

TWO

Gryn moved fast.

I moved faster. The power of the Darkin inside me roared with bloodlust. I wanted, needed, to kill and destroy. Gryn lunged forward with a thrust, his blade of energy humming with power.

I parried the thrust with the chakram and raked across his chest with my free hand. Gryn dodged and just barely managed to avoid being shredded. His shirt wasn't so lucky. When he looked down, he was wearing a tattered mess.

"I liked this shirt," he said, ripping off the pieces that remained. "You owe me a new shirt."

I laughed.

"That's going to be the least of your concerns when I'm done, old sorcerer," I said my voice blending with the Darkin. "Come closer, so I can sink my claws into you."

That's when I saw the look. It was only there for a fleeting moment, but I saw it in his gaze as I circled him, looking for an opening.

Fear.

"Don't think so," Gryn said, forming a group of orbs. "I

like my skin claw-free. Here, let me help you calm down. It's clear you're getting agitated."

He released the orbs in my direction. Part of my brain defaulted to my previous strategy. *Run!* Another, stronger part refused. *Darkin do not run from opponents or threats. We run toward them.*

Great, my own brain was conducting a mutiny while impending death raced at me.

Embrace me, little one, and I will show you true power.

I didn't have much of a choice. The orbs were too close to evade, and Gryn was ready to slice and dice me the moment I tried. Damned if I did, damned if I didn't.

I surrendered to the power within.

The Darkin roared inside my head. It sounded like shoving my head in a raging ocean. The scales rippled along my body as I grew. I didn't exactly become immense, but my arms looked like I had just spent a few years in the gym getting swole. My entire body felt heavier, thicker, and stronger. Everything was just...denser.

I raced toward the orbs.

The chakram split in my hand. I threw one half at Gryn, using the other to bisect the closest orbs. Gryn raised his energy sword to parry my weapon. The chakram phased through the energy blade and sliced into his shoulder while sailing past him.

He grunted in pain and immediately created a wall of energy in front of him. A wall of energy I was running toward. I slammed into and through the wall, shattering it into nothing.

Gryn looked as surprised as I felt.

I drove a fist forward, aimed at his chest.

I never reached him.

He had cast a second defensive barrier behind the first one. I impacted a small shield of energy in front of his body that bounced me back across the floor at speed. I slammed into the far wall, cracking it.

"I truly hope that wasn't the best you could do," Gryn said, placing a glowing hand on his wound to stop the flow of blood. "Brute force has its place, but a blunt instrument is easily countered. By the way, I didn't expect the negation properties of your weapon. That has been rectified."

I glanced down at the half of the chakram I held.

"We'll see," I said, getting slowly to my feet. "I noticed you couldn't negate my weapon cutting through your arm."

"Like I said, that issue has been rectified," Gryn answered, his tone angry. "I can adapt to a situation. Can you?"

"I'm still here, aren't I?"

"With half a weapon," Gryn pointed to the wall behind him, where the other half of my weapon rested, partially buried. "Shame there's no automatic retrieval on that thing. Or maybe there is, and you just don't know how to activate it?"

I growled in disgust at my amateur move. Throwing the chakram had been careless but not stupid. I managed to wound him, which meant I just needed to close the gap between us—not throw my weapon away.

"I'm going to hurt you now," I said, raking my claws across a column and leaving deep gouges in the iron as I approached him. "You don't know what you're facing."

"Oh?" he answered. "I particularly enjoyed the column rake as you threatened me. I'd say you have Darkin theatrics down to a science. Fighting skill? Not so much. All you've done is murder my shirt and scratch my arm. Not very fear-inducing, if you ask me. But please"—he materialized another black blade of energy—"don't let me dissuade you. Things were just getting interesting. I might even let you live."

"That's not your call."

"Prove it," he said, approaching me. "You said I don't know what I'm facing. Come show me, Darkin."

I closed the distance and slid to the side, lashing out with my claws. It was a feint to open his side to a weapon attack. He ignored my claws and parried my weapon, deflecting it to the side. There was no phasing this time. He followed the parry with an uppercut designed to remove my jaw.

I stepped back, tucking my chin as the knuckleduster grazed my nose, filling my nostrils with the scent of sulphur and burning meat. The sigils he had inscribed on them were absolutely hellish. The pungent odor of demonflame surrounded me. I backed up, putting distance between us.

The scent triggered my memory—something the Darkin had said to me when I earned the right to wield the weapon.

This weapon is forged in both fear and demonflame. Its edge will not cut you, nor will its flame burn you.

I had the weapon part, but where was the flame?

I need your flame. Like now.

You need to surrender. My flame is not for those who pretend. You must be prepared to wield its power.

Does it look like I'm playing here? He's trying to kill me.

That is exactly what you are doing. I could have killed this old man ten times over, had I been untethered. Yet here you are exchanging blows. Surrender and free my flame.

Somehow, that sounded like an incredibly bad idea.

I will not surrender my will to you. You serve me, not the other way around.

Your choice and your death. It has been an honor.

Shit. Gryn was circling in on me, looking determined to skewer me with his blade. We really had entered survival mode, and there was no way I was going to die here. Not without rescuing Acheron first.

"Fine," I said, looking at Gryn. "Don't say I didn't warn you."

"Can you feel my fear?" Gryn scoffed. "I'm nearly petrified with fright."

Do it. We are not killing him. Just getting close. Understood?

Like you said, I serve you.

I trust you about as far as I can throw you. On your bond. Say it, demon.

I felt the internal struggle of the compulsion. Its will was strong. Mine was stronger.

On my bond, the old sorcerer will survive this encounter.

Unleash the kraken!

The Kraken is a being of the ocean. I possess no power over the ocean and its denizens. Have your faculties for thought been compromised?

My brain is fine. Release the flame!

THREE

My body became engulfed in flame.

My first reaction was to stop, drop and roll. Then I realized that while I was covered in flame, I wasn't burning. Not even my clothes were being consumed, to my relief. Facing Gryn naked while my clothes burned to ash would've been awkward.

The flames burned bright orange at first, and then settled into a reddish-pink color, similar to the flames Acheron materialized when he used demonflame. I made a mental note to ask the Darkin about that later.

Right now, I had an old sorcerer to beat silly.

"Demonflame?" Gryn asked as he backed up. "That's new. Are you getting in touch with your inner demon?"

"Why don't you let me reach out and touch you, old man?"

I closed the distance.

"Do you even know how to control the flames?" Gryn asked as he parried my first thrust. "It's not a fashion statement, you know. The flames actually serve a purpose."

"I know," I said, extending a hand. "Charbroiling you, for starters."

Nothing happened.

I stood there waiting for a blast of flame to launch out at him. I just looked like a demonic traffic officer ordering him to stop with my arm outstretched. It was a fatal error and gave him plenty of openings.

By the time I realized this, it was too late.

Gryn whirled under my arm and swiped upward with his sword in a move designed to remove it. The sword slammed into my arm and lifted me off my feet.

Amazingly, my arm remained attached to the rest of me.

I looked down, surprised at the fact that my arm was still part of my body. Gryn rotated his body and unleashed a vicious sidekick into my side. I flew across the floor and landed with a crash.

I laid immobile for a few seconds.

"Still alive?" he called out from the other side of the floor. "Are you ready to quit now?"

I remained silent.

The fact that he wasn't rushing at me spoke volumes. He could move me around, but he couldn't actually hurt me. At least that's what it seemed like. The flames and scales stopped his blade, and his kick was a blunt impact, but it didn't actually hurt. It was more like a dull pressure across my side.

I felt pretty tanky, but the problem was getting close enough to him to inflict damage. He wasn't going to just stand there and let me hit him. If I could fling fireballs, that would make life much easier.

Let me hurt him, the Darkin said.

Hurt him, yes. Kill him, no.

I leapt to my feet and moved. I want to say I ran, but it was faster than that. It wasn't quite teleporting, but I closed the distance faster than I anticipated. More importantly, it was faster than Gryn anticipated.

One moment I was across the floor, the next we were face to face. He recovered faster than I expected and slashed at my neck. I raised an arm and blocked his blade with my forearm. His other hand had formed a black orb covered with crackling red energy.

An obliterator on steroids.

I moved fast.

I drove a fist into his stomach, causing him to double over and fall back. He collapsed into a backwards roll and unleashed the orb. I threw the remaining half of the chakram at it and regretted it instantly. My weapon bounced off the obliterator and sailed across the room as the orb closed on me.

"No weapon and no clue," Gryn said with a smile from the floor. "Why not try and see if your flames—?"

I leaped forward and embraced him, rotating my body as the orb homed in on me. The obliterator punched Gryn in the chest with a *thwomp,* sending us both flying. I landed in a roll. Gryn landed with a crunch as he slammed into the nearest wall back first, before collapsing to the floor. I ran to where he lay, my claws extended, when an orb smacked me in the face, launching me straight into and through the ceiling.

I landed on the floor above, in pain.

My flames were extinguished and I was missing most of the scales on my torso. Gryn floated up gently through the hole I had made with my body. I was on all fours and gasping for breath.

"I'm not finished...not finished with you," I managed through the pain. "Give me a moment and I'll shred you."

"You're done," Gryn said, shaking his head. "The message just hasn't gotten through that thick skull of yours. If you doubt me, allow me to prove it to you. Attack me."

"What?"

"I'll just stand here while you attack. I won't even defend against your next attack, no matter what it is."

"Are you insane? I'll kill you."

"You're welcome to try," he answered with a smile. "I'm waiting."

I got slowly to my feet and extended my claws. I saw him raise an eyebrow in approval and then what appeared to be concern. I let out a low growl and took three steps before the floor shifted sideways from under me and the world started rotating. The floor mercilessly stopped my fall as my body stopped responding.

I was still conscious as I saw Gryn's feet approach. I couldn't even move my head in his direction.

"What the—?" I started.

"Temet nosce," Gryn said. "You don't know yourself. Not yet. If I were your enemy, this would be the part where the Darkin dies, defenseless against a blade of pure energy."

He formed a black blade of energy and brought it close to my face. I couldn't even move my head away.

"Do it then," I said through clenched teeth. "Don't be a bitch about it. Make it quick."

"I'm going to give you strength," he said, letting the blade cut into my skin. "The same way I was given strength."

I felt the blade cut from my jaw, down my neck and stop at my clavicle. It burned as I screamed. I reached up and grabbed the blade, my vision clouded by rage. My other hand grabbed him by the neck, but true to his word he put up no resistance.

"Do it then," he said, using my words defiantly. "Don't be a bitch, Darkin. Be the mindless demon you know you are. Make it quick."

For a split second, the voice of the Darkin roared in my mind.

KILL HIM.

No. He's right. If he was my enemy, I'd be dead by now.

I released his neck and the blade.

Gryn nodded.

"Now we can start."

FOUR

The next few days were a blur.

Each day my anxiety about Acheron increased. Gryn, being the evil bastard that he was, used that against me. He'd discuss Acheron and then launch another attack, hoping to catch me off-guard and distracted.

It worked the first few times.

Painfully.

When that stopped working, he tried to undermine my confidence by planting seeds of doubt in my ability and lethality.

He was still in the middle of that phase when I realized the purpose of it all.

Preparation.

"You know, at this point, it's probably an exercise in futility trying to rescue your demon," Gryn said. "Do you even know where to look?"

"I know what you're doing now, you old bastard."

"I'm trying to save your life," Gryn answered. "Acheron is dead or worse at this point. If you don't get this, you're wasting time. Do you think you have all the time in the world to learn how not to die?"

"Banishing a Demon Lord isn't entry-level sorcery," I answered. "It's going to take time and a heavy duty cast. They're going to need some serious firepower. I would know it if they tried."

"Oh excuse me, I didn't realize I was in the presence of such greatness," Gryn scoffed. "Time is not your ally in this. Demon Lord or not, he can be destroyed."

"He's a Demon Lord," I said. "If they managed to banish him, he was weaker than I thought, and deserved it. What self-respecting Demon Lord lets himself get banished by a bunch of third-rate sorcerers?"

"True," Gryn said with a nod as he formed half a dozen obliterators. "Or they were stronger than you anticipated. It's possible he lied to you. Maybe he was only a Demon Lord's assistant?"

"You seem to forget that I'm the one that summoned him in the first place," I said, bracing myself as I stood in the center of the warehouse floor. "I know what level demon I summoned. It nearly killed me."

"Technically, it did. That was the last day you were a human."

"I was blinded with rage and burdened by immense amounts of stupid," I admitted. "I summoned a demon way beyond my power level and paid for it."

"Are you saying Victoria should have let you die?"

"Maybe, I don't know," I said. "All I know is that it wasn't pretty and I wished for death a few times in the process."

"Despite all that, she saved you."

"If you call me becoming an Otherkin saving...then sure, she *saved* me."

"I'm sensing some pent-up anger in you," Gryn said.

"Blind rage can cloud your vision. You need to get that under control...channel it."

"Who knew you were so perceptive?" I asked. "Blind rage is where I'm at. At least on a good day. Most days it's irrational fury, but thanks for the tip. I'll work on it."

"Perhaps it would help if you knew why she did it?" Gryn asked. "I could always ask her."

"What for? It's not going to change anything. I don't pretend to know why she does anything, anymore," I said. "I stopped trying to figure her out long ago."

"Yet, you do owe her your life," Gryn said. "You do realize this, yes? She controlled the transformation. Without her intervention, you would have become something"—he waved a hand at me—"not this."

"I know. That's why when I deal with the Seven, she gets to live."

"You're playing a dangerous game," Gryn answered. "Even this state you're in is preferable to death."

"You make it sound like being an Otherkin is all unicorns and pretty green fields of flowers with a rainbow shooting out of my ass."

"Is that one of your abilities? Rectal Rainbows?" Gryn asked. "I've never really studied Otherkin extensively. Most of them were too aggravating to spend any real time around. I found myself wanting to blast them to dust. Seems to be the consensus about all Otherkin, from what I've learned."

"We aren't known for being cheery and jubilant, no."

"Yet, Victoria seems to have steered your transformation in this direction," Gryn said, pensively. "I wonder why? I mean, aside from the fact that your summoning was a colossal failure. What *were* you thinking summoning a Demon Lord?"

"Death, that's what I was thinking," I answered. "I just didn't figure it would start with mine."

"Your lack of preparation was astounding, but the fact

that you managed to summon a Demon Lord was...is impressive," Gryn said. "You couldn't have possibly expected a demon of that level."

"I didn't," I growled. "This"—I extended my arms—"all of this, is the price I paid, willingly, for what I did."

"There is always a cost...always," Gryn said. "You know this. It's an immutable law of energy manipulation. To wield power, you must pay the cost. You wanted a powerful demon; the cost was astronomically high."

"This is why I no longer summon," I said. "Aside from the fact that I can't anymore."

"Right," Gryn said with a short nod. "That ability has been transformed in you. Part of the 'price' you paid. Have you tried?"

"Once, afterwards," I said, keeping my focus on the gently floating orbs. This was one of his tactics. Lull me into dropping my guard with conversation, and then unleash an attack. "The process nearly melted my brain. No more summoning for me. My body has been fundamentally changed. The energy involved in a summons directly affects me."

"Must be that the demonization of your body is reacting to the catalytic properties of the summons," Gryn said with a fascinated tone. "It would feel like part of you is trying to split from the other. Almost like a—"

"Rending," I finished. "That's exactly why I don't even think about it now, and part of why I do what I do. No one else should go through this...should feel like this."

"These things happen, but now you understand the depth of your choice. The question is, what will you do now?"

He released the orbs with a flick of his wrist. The old sorcerer nearly caught me off-guard.

Nearly.

I braced myself and controlled my breath, accessing the power of the Darkin within. I felt the energy race through me, starting at my neck with a bloom of heat and pain, then radiating outward from there.

The orbs moved slowly at first, spreading out. A half-dozen spheres of potential death and guaranteed pain. I made a point to keep them all in my line of sight.

My new scar throbbed with a dull pain. It had healed completely, and was only visible when my skin wasn't covered in scales. At first, I thought it was just a jagged wound and that Gryn was some kind of twisted sadistic sorcerer.

After a few days, I discovered the wound wasn't a random attack.

I still thought he was a twisted sadistic bastard, but the wound he gave me was more than just a wound. After he carved it into my skin, I found I could control the ability of the Darkin with less effort and with greater expression of power.

I soon realized that Gryn had etched a sigil of power into my skin, an ancient lost symbol that he refused to decipher. He would only say that he had given me power, the same way it had been given to him—through pain and blood.

What he said was true. He had given me power. More than I had possessed in my life. The questions that nagged in the back of my mind were: Why, and at what cost?

When I asked him, he would answer with: *"Adjust, adapt, or die. What has been given cannot be taken. In time, I would know the reasons, but not now."*

The words were a small comfort when my scar flared with breath-stealing agony. At times, it felt like someone was holding a blowtorch to my neck and gently melting the skin away. The last time I complained, he wordlessly removed his shirt and showed me his back. A much larger, gruesome, angry and deeper version of my scar covered his entire back.

It must have taken him months to recover from the inscribing. I honestly didn't comprehend how he had survived. It held the same grisly fascination of a large scar. You realized the scar was bad, then after a few moments, your brain processed that the wound must have been horrendous.

I stopped complaining about my scar after that.

"Focus," he said. "Or they will help you focus...painfully."

The orbs hung in the air, floating and bobbing slowly for a few more seconds. They formed a large circular formation, and froze for moment, as if sniffing me out. Black energy crackled around each orb as they raced at my location. With a thought, and minor use of energy, scales and flame covered my skin.

I dodged the first orb, sidestepping it, while materializing my weapon. It gave off a dull orange glow as I separated the halves and sliced through the next two orbs, destroying them. I launched the two halves, intercepting the next two orbs as I rolled to the side, dodging the first and last orbs as they criss-crossed above me.

The two weapon halves boomeranged back to me as I extended my claws. I had finally managed—after much pain—to throw the chakram so it would return to me on the trajectory I wanted. I slashed through the nearest orb and backpedaled from the other as the chakram halves raced back at me.

Once my back hit the wall, I waited. The orb closed in fast, but my chakram halves were faster. I ducked at the last possible moment. The chakram impacted with the orb right before it slammed into the wall where I stood a moment earlier, destroying it.

I removed the halves of the chakram from the wall, absorbed the weapon, and doused the flames covering my body. I kept the scales up, just in case Gryn was feeling medieval and launched a surprise attack.

He was devious that way.

"Not a complete disaster," he said, nodding. "At the very

least, you've learned some of the mobility required to harness this new power. How's the scar?"

The dull, familiar pain throbbed along the side of my face and neck. It felt like a hot poker being shoved under my skin, threatening to burn my entire left side.

"Excruciating, but nothing I'm not used to by now," I said. "Will the pain go away?"

"Eventually, yes."

"Eventually isn't a timeframe," I said. "Am I just supposed to deal with the pain?"

"Yes," Gryn said. "Pain is good for you. It focuses the mind and gives you purpose. Don't you feel focused now?"

"Oh? That's what this is?" I asked, pointing to the scar along my neck. "Focusing purpose? I thought it was you being a sadistic fuck."

Gryn smiled.

"You have no idea what a sadistic fuck is," he answered. "I'll introduce you to *my* teacher one day when I'm feeling exceptionally cruel and homicidal. She redefines and elevates the concept of sadistic fuckery to new heights."

"Pass," I said. "I have enough psychopathic sadists in my life, present company included."

"It would seem you are ready to not die," Gryn said. "I won't say you've attained mastery, but your skill should suffice to liberate your demon without rushing to your immediate demise."

"That almost sounded like a compliment," I said, raising an eyebrow in surprise. "Are you feeling okay?"

"It wasn't," he snapped, waving my words away. "Your timing was horrendous, at best. Your techniques were overly showy and unnecessary. Do you think you're auditioning for Cirque du Soleil?"

"No, I was just trying—"

"I'm not finished," Gryn interrupted with a glare. "It was

a rhetorical question. You should be focusing on economy of motion, not flashy maneuvers. The first dodge was barely passable. Everything after that was showboating. You must use minimum energy expenditure. Express your movements in precision and economy of motion."

"I wasn't—"

"Showboating will get you *dead*," Gryn said, his expression dark. "Precision of execution. Use exactly how much you need. No more, no less. The flames, however, were a nice touch, but unneeded."

"You just said no showboating, but now the flames are a 'nice touch'?" I asked, confused. "I don't understand."

"Showboating is executing unnecessary acrobatics and flips when taking a step will do. The weapon is tethered to you. There was no need to wait for the halves to return to your location, you know this. You were just showing off with that move."

"But the flames are okay?"

Gryn sighed and pinched the bridge of his nose before continuing.

"Aside from making you nearly indestructible, the fire you summon is a primal force. It activates the limbic system in your opponents. Most people…creatures…fear fire, fear being burned. When you encase yourself in flame, you trigger the instinctual response of fear. People react badly when scared; you can use that to your advantage when facing enemies."

"Also, the fire is completely badass," I added. "Admit it."

"Also, the fire is completely badass," Gryn admitted with a small smile. "Let's get you prepped. Your demon won't wait forever."

FIVE

"How many days have I burned in this warehouse?" I asked, concerned I would be too late to save Acheron. "I completely understand why, but maybe you're right. Maybe it's too late to save him?"

"Days?" Gryn asked. "What are you talking about?"

"What?" I replied, confused. "By my calculations we've been here for at least two weeks, if not more. Are you losing track of time? I mean, I get it—old sorcerers tend to lose track of time, I'm sure. All that sorcery must affect the few remaining brain cells you have left."

"Oh, there's that famous Otherkin humor I keep hearing about," Gryn answered dryly. "We've been here longer than that, my brain cells are in tip top shape and I never lose track of time…ever."

"More than two weeks? What the hell, Gryn!"

"I thought you said that if he succumbed to their attacks he deserved it?" Gryn said. "Something about third-rate sorcerers and the like."

"That doesn't mean I wanted to waste time," I said. "Yes, he's a Demon Lord, but he's not invincible."

"You are a peculiar person," Gryn said, staring at me. "You actually care about a demon?"

"He's not just a demon, he's my friend," I said. "Probably my *only* friend."

"I don't know what's sadder," Gryn said with a slow head shake. "That you care about the demon, or that he's your only friend."

"He has my back when it matters...always."

"Because he has to; the bond compels him," Gryn answered. "He is *not* your friend. He is a demon. He is your slave. If you don't believe me, release him and see how fast he turns on you."

"Don't you think I tried?" I said. "I don't know *how* to release him. I barely survived summoning him."

"It's actually quite simple," Gryn said, lowering his voice. "Do you want to know?"

"Yes."

"Are you certain?" Gryn asked. "If you break the bond, he will be free of your compulsion, and able to do as he wishes."

"That's kind of the point, isn't it?"

"The Seven will consider him a real and present threat. They will hunt him down, and you too, for unleashing a Demon Lord on the world. Think this through."

"Yes," I said, my voice firm. "I don't want anyone in my life who feels forced to be there. I will release him, and if he wants to leave he's free to do so."

"And if he attacks you?" Gryn asked. "A Demon Lord compelled to serve an Otherkin is quite a slight in his world. You are considered a lesser being, inferior to his status. He may even *need* to kill you to remove the stain of his bond to you."

"If he attacks me, then only one of us is walking away from that fight," I said. "I'll feel like shit for having to kill my friend, but there's no way I'm picking him over my life. Not happening."

Gryn laughed.

"I like you, Nyx," he said. "You remind me of me when I was young and stupid, minus the young part. I will show you the sigil."

"Why?" I asked, wary. "Why are you doing this? Helping me? Showing me how to break Acheron's bond?"

"Because, like you said, you don't have many friends," Gryn said, looking in my eyes. "I know that feeling intimately. I also know what it feels like to be used, to be a pawn in someone else's game. I think it's time you had some agency over your life. Perhaps, even change the rules of the game."

He traced the sigil in my hand several times, and had me repeat it until he was satisfied I knew it.

"That's it?" I asked. "Doesn't seem so complicated."

"It isn't...if you ignore the blood component," Gryn said. "That is a blood sigil."

"A blood sigil? I thought those were banned?"

"So is summoning a Demon Lord," Gryn replied with a tight smile. "It will require blood from both of you to break the bond."

"Shit, how much blood?"

"Enough to make it dangerous."

"Enough to make it dangerous?" I scoffed. "Well gee, thanks, that sounds accurate. Should I slit one vein or two?"

"I'd go with two, just to be on the safe side," he answered. "In this case, it's better to err on the side of caution...more is more. You will need to convince your demon to do the same... good luck with that. I hear most demons are reluctant to part with their blood."

"Are you fucking serious?"

"Did it sound like I was joking?" he asked. "You cast the sigil and you both must pay the blood cost. That will break the bond and maybe kill you in the process. Nothing ventured, nothing gained. Don't say I didn't warn you."

"You are a real piece of work, old man."

"Thank you," he said with a mock bow. "I do try."

"In the meantime, you had me waste time in your rundown warehouse of pain and punishment," I snapped. "You really are a sadistic bastard."

"I won't refute my sadistic streak. I find pain is quite the motivator. My warehouse is in no way, shape, or form rundown. I prefer to think of it as gently aged."

"Gently aged, my ass," I said, looking around. "This place is a dump, you bastard."

"You keep using that word," he said. "I don't think it means what you think it means. My conception was quite legitimate."

"Yay for you," I growled. "Still doesn't change the fact you had me waste weeks in this dump."

"Time is an elastic concept in this place," Gryn said, gesturing to the space around us. "If you were paying attention, you'd realize it."

"Realize what?"

"Haven't you felt it? The odd passage of the hours? You don't get hungry or tired. What did you think caused that? Your excellent Otherkin constitution? Even immense pains in the ass, like you, require sustenance and rest. When was the last time you slept?"

"I slept the other day," I said, confident in my tracking of time. "I mean I'm sure I did *some* sleeping."

"I didn't notice," Gryn answered. "When exactly did you manage to sleep? Was it between my pummeling of you? Or when you were dodging my obliterators?"

"I'm sure I slept. I mean, how could I go for weeks without sleep?"

"You can't. Use some deductive reasoning. I know there's a functioning brain in there...somewhere."

"If I didn't sleep, then the only other, alternative is that you must have done something to time."

"Not the only other, but *one* of the other alternatives."

"Then I did sleep," I said, certain. "I'm positive of it."

"Really? What day was it?" Gryn asked. "In fact, what day is it today?"

"What do you mean what day is it today? It's—"

As much as I tried, I couldn't recall what day it was.

"Can't recall?" he asked. "Makes sense. Time isn't flowing in any fashion you are familiar with. It's to be expected."

He was right. Ever since I stepped into the warehouse, time felt strange. The minutes dragged, feeling like hours.

"What did you do?" I asked, suddenly aware of the stasis around me. "You froze time?"

I looked around the warehouse as if noticing it for the first time. The details of the space were fuzzy. At certain points, they would be in focus, but the moment I looked away, they would become blurry, like a hazy memory.

"I facilitated your training with a temporal pocket."

"A temporal what?"

"In this place, time has *almost* stopped," Gryn answered. "Once you step out of the door, your demon will have been kidnapped for approximately three hours from the moment you left the Seven HQ, give or take a few minutes. I merely compressed a week into each hour."

"What? You compressed what?" I asked, now completely confused. "How?"

"The process is too involved to get into, requiring an immense expenditure of power. You wouldn't understand me even if I tried to explain it to you," Gryn said, shaking his head. "Suffice to say, I'm not strong enough to stop the flow of time entirely—few are—but with the right sigils and location"—he gestured to the space around us—"I can slow it down considerably."

"Only three hours have passed?" I asked, still trying to wrap my brain around the concept of slowed time. "That's it?"

"Give or take a few minutes, yes," Gryn replied. "Once you leave, this location will cease to exist on this timeline until I summon it again."

"What about you?"

"What about me?"

"Are you going to poof out too?"

"I have never, and will never, *poof* anywhere," he answered. "I will make sure my warehouse is shunted to an adjacent timeline until I need it again."

"Then what? Off to torture other victims—I mean, trainees."

"I can't assist you in recovering your demon if that's what you're asking," he said. "I'm sorry. That would create an untenable situation between myself and the Seven."

"Untenable?"

"Are you unfamiliar with the word?" Gryn asked. "Assisting you overtly would necessitate the spilling of blood, none of it mine."

"I understand. There must be a high demand for sadistic sorcerers in the world," I said with a tight smile. "Besides, I don't want you to get into trouble with Vic."

"Does she know you call her that?" he asked.

"Does she know you call her Tori?"

"Of course," he said. "I'm the *only* one who does."

"Same here," I said. "Vic suits her. It's not like she can stop me."

He shook his head and looked off to the side, as if gazing through the wall and into the distance. For a moment, his gaze became soft and unfocused.

"I do have other matters to attend to besides training aggravating Otherkin," Gryn answered with a slight nod. "Victoria wanted you prepped, consider yourself prepped. She may not approve entirely of my methods"—he pointed to my scar—"but she doesn't get to dictate the how, just the what."

"Victoria knew you were going to do this?"

"Do what?"

"The power," I said, tracing a finger along my scar. "Did she know you were going to increase my power?"

"Now, how would she know that?" Gryn said with a slight smile. "Besides, I think life is more interesting when you have some surprises in it. You being a more powerful Darkin than expected, will be quite surprising to anyone who encounters you. I have to say, you certainly surprised me."

"She's going to be so pissed at you," I said with a smile that matched his. "I doubt she wants me stronger. She already sees me as a threat."

"Now she will respect the threat you pose, rather than dismissing it, as others are prone to do upon first viewing you."

"Or, she will go full force and try to take me out, thanks."

"Are you saying you're scared of the Seven or Victoria?"

"Neither," I said, my expression dark. "I'll deal with them when the time comes."

"It's refreshing to hear such determination, even in the face of suicidal odds," Gryn said. "Such boldness is inspiring, even if it's short-lived."

"Well, I have you to thank for putting me in this position now."

"My pleasure," he said with a tip of his head. "You have few allies; I figured I would even the scales somewhat. With my gift, you being a Darkin now, and your demon, you may even stand a chance against the Seven."

"Or she will be even more pissed and put out a kill order on me and Acheron."

"What makes you think one doesn't exist now?" Gryn asked, his voice serious. "Assume you have no friends, only enemies and opportunists. You'll live longer."

"Acheron is my friend," I said, defiantly. "He is my friend."

"He is your demon. There is a difference. You two share a bond."

"He would still be my friend, bond or no bond."

"That remains to be seen," Gryn answered. "The fact of the matter is that he *is* bound to you, compelled by your summons. Let's see what happens when he is no longer under that compulsion."

"Are you saying he would turn on me?"

"I'm saying you'll find out if and when the bond is dissolved. It's not unheard of, demons befriending humans or in your case, almost humans. Rare, but not impossible."

"Why? Why did you do all this? You didn't have to help me."

He waved my words away.

"Victoria had one explicit instruction regarding you and this weapon: the training was not to kill you. Everything else was left to my discretion. I have to say I fulfilled my end of this contract."

"And this scar, the increase in power?"

"Consider that *my* gift," he said. "Be wary of the Seven. *They* are not your friends, Victoria included."

"I will."

"I'll stay in touch," he said, reaching into his jacket, removing an envelope and handing it to me. "You still have much to learn, but what you have acquired in this accelerated, or rather, decelerated time, is enough to get you started."

"What's this?" I said, holding the envelope. "Your bill?"

"Child, you can't afford me," Gryn said with a laugh. "The

price I would extract from you, would kill you many times over. That cost has been covered by Victoria. That"—he pointed to the envelope—"is something else."

"What is it?"

"Vengeance and death," he said, quietly. "That is the location of your demon. Use the information wisely."

"You knew? All this time?"

"No, it took some tracking, but his trail wasn't difficult to pick up."

"How? You were here with me."

"I'm an accomplished sorcerer," Gryn said, mocking offense. "I can even manage to walk and chew gum at the same time. Locating your demon and dealing with you barely required any effort on my part."

"Where are they?" I asked. "Where is Acheron?"

"It's all in there"—he pointed to the envelope. "Be careful, Nyx. Yes, you're stronger now, but you're not invincible. Remember what I said earlier: focus on precision of execution."

"Thank you," I said, suddenly realizing how much he had helped me. "I mean it."

"You're welcome. Everything you need is in there," he said, looking down at the envelope. "May you find your demon, and rain down pain and death on your enemies."

"I will," I said with a grin, as I looked down at the envelope. "You are one wily old bast—"

I felt the charge of energy around me.

When I looked up, Gryn was gone.

SIX

I tore open the large manila envelope.

It contained a map, an address, a set of blueprints and a small slip of parchment-colored paper covered in dark red sigils. On the back of the small slip of paper, written in what I assumed was Gryn's handwriting, I saw six words neatly arranged: *For Emergency Circle Destruction Use Only.*

I turned the paper over again, and examined the set of complicated sigils interlocked to make one large design. I didn't recognize it, and wondered how it would help me in an emergency if I couldn't even make out what it meant or how to use it.

Crazy old sorcerer.

I folded it and placed the small slip of paper in my pocket, opening the map and stretching it out on a nearby table. It was a map of lower Manhattan, below 14th Street.

One area was circled in red. The address was written on the side of the map, and there was a large arrow pointing to the circle. Gryn wasn't being subtle. The circle was located in what used to be an area of warehouses, but was now known as the Triangle Below Canal Street—or 'Tribeca' for those in the know.

The city was full of these new names for old neighborhoods. Noho, Soho and Dumbo. The last one, located in Brooklyn, really was a stretch. DUMBO stood for Down Under the Manhattan Bridge Overpass. Basically, what it meant was: we need a new upscale name for this old area so we can charge exorbitant prices to the new transplants that move into this area—the Dumbos.

Actually, giving it some more thought, I realized the name fit.

The address was located farther downtown—74 Laight Street. It was an area that used to be mostly industrial spaces, but had been converted to upscale apartments and restaurants in recent years, in an effort to attract money to a forgotten neighborhood.

It worked.

Tribeca was now considered upscale, with money pouring in to finance new construction and a massive wave of gentrification. The old lofts, which used to be populated by artists and creatives, were now renovated spaces priced in the stratosphere.

Attached to the back of the map, were the plans of a large warehouse with an extensive complex of tunnels beneath it. Tunnels that, upon further investigation, made no sense in that part of the city. I studied the plans for a few minutes, memorizing points of entry and egress, before heading out of the warehouse.

I took one last look around the warehouse of pain before stepping out of the door and into the early night. Gryn was right. Time snapped back into place the moment I stepped on the sidewalk outside the warehouse. I looked back to find the entrance, but the door I had just used was gone.

Parked on the street, directly in front of me was Eight.

I placed my hand on her side and she purred to life with a roar of her engine. The door flashed orange as the sigils inscribed on her bloomed to life.

I patted the steering wheel as I strapped in. Eight gave another, louder roar, and then settled into a throaty rumble.

"I missed you too," I said, adjusting my straps. "Let's go get Acheron."

I raced down the street and drove downtown, avoiding most of the traffic.

I parked a few blocks away from my target location. Eight was many things, but subtle wasn't one of them. She didn't pull off stealthy well. Her engine's idle could be louder than some cars in full rev. I loved that sound, but tonight I needed a silent approach.

I fully expected to run into Black Cleavers. Only they were crazy enough to try and kidnap a Demon Lord. There was only one problem with that scenario though. Black Cleavers were mostly unhinged fanatics, few of them had the capacity to banish, much less rend a demon of Acheron's level.

Kidnapping and containing Acheron would've required sorcerers of considerable skill—something I knew the Cleavers lacked. It was possible the Cleavers were foot soldiers in this, but someone else was pulling the strings—someone powerful.

I took one last look at the plans, and stepped out of Eight, placing a hand on her side to lock her tight. I walked down Washington Street, keeping to the shadows and pausing in my approach several times to flush out any tails.

A block away, I partially extended my claws, and used them as crampons to scale the building adjacent to the one I needed to infiltrate. No one would be expecting a top-down approach, especially if they were using the tunnels below the warehouse to contain Acheron.

The Cleavers weren't smart, but they made up for that with sheer numbers. Never underestimate what a group of easily manipulated sorcerers, with the collective IQ of a brick, could accomplish if directed with skill.

It was actually scary to see them in action.

I scaled over the edge of the building and looked across. At first, the image didn't register. On the roof across from mine, I saw four Agents from the Order of Supernatural Affairs, one stationed in each of the corners.

What the hell was the OSA doing here?

It didn't make sense. The OSA stationed on the roof was the last thing I expected. Cleavers were one thing, but OSA Agents were somewhat competent. This changed everything. I couldn't count on collective stupidity now.

It started to make some kind of sense though; the attack at the Seven HQ was too coordinated. The way they managed to get the jump on us, knowing to attack while we were in the labyrinth and Acheron was at a disadvantage, was too clever for the Cleavers by half.

I still didn't have the entire picture, but it was coming into focus. How did they know we were in the labyrinth? Someone inside the Seven must have let them know. It didn't surprise me that had been attacked. What pissed me off was that they thought we were low hanging fruit. Did they think they could do this without consequences?

If I wanted answers, I'd have to ask questions...violently.

Gryn's words came back to me: *Adjust, adapt, or die.*

"Adjust and adapt it is," I said to myself, as I made my way silently to the edge of the roof. "Time for pain."

I leaped across the gap between the buildings and landed noiselessly on the roof, surrounded by oblivious OSA Agents. This night had just gone horribly wrong for them.

They just didn't know it yet.

SEVEN

I made my way to the first OSA Agent.

I had options. If I pushed him off the roof, it would look like an accident, but it would get everyone's attention.

The roof had several air conditioning units and electrical boxes situated in the center of the space and provided adequate cover. The corners of the building were mostly bare, except for large cellphone signal boosters that dominated most of the real estate on the buildings in the city.

Attention was the last thing I wanted right now. The voice of the Darkin echoed in my head.

"Destroy him where he stands. He is an enemy and deserves no less."

"You need to dial it back...way back. I have too much baggage in my head to add your bloodlust."

"You are now Darkin. You must destroy. It is your purpose."

"My purpose is to rescue my friend. Then we can discuss wholesale destruction."

"After the rescue?" It asked hopefully. *"Then you will unleash pain and death?"*

"If you can manage to keep it down while I figure out how to get to Acheron and get out of here alive...then yes, we'll go to town."

"We are destroying an entire town? I approve."

"Not an entire town...never mind. Keep quiet."

The voice died down as I crouched down behind Agent One. I extended the claws on one hand and was about to slit his throat, effectively silencing him, when one of the other OSA Agents spoke.

"Do you think she'll come?"

I slipped back into the cover provided by the HVAC ducts as I pinpointed who spoke. It was the Agent adjacent to my initial target, Agent Two. The conversation seemed relevant. I figured they were waiting for me, considering my connection to Acheron.

I was somewhat insulted there were only four of them. Clearly, I needed to work on my threat rep. Four OSA agents as a deterrent hardly seemed appropriate for an Otherkin of my skill. There should have been at least ten agents on the roof.

"Doesn't matter," Agent One, my initial target answered. "We end that filthy demon tomorrow at sunrise. If she comes before then, we detain until sunrise. Instructions are to hold until dawn, and then we rend them both."

Last I checked, I wasn't susceptible to sunlight. Maybe these rocket scientists had me confused with a vampire. Demons weren't affected by the sun or any dawn rituals. They didn't grow weaker in sunlight, and I was curious if a rending increased in strength during the day as opposed to the night. I would have to do some research on the rending ritual—right after I dealt with these OSA Agents.

"I've never done a rending, never even seen one, have you?" Agent Two asked. "I hear it's agony for them."

"It's what they deserve, goddamn demons," Agent One answered. "They don't belong here. They belong in hell."

"No, they deserve to be destroyed, period," Agent Three said from across the roof. "I just want to be there when it happens."

Great, a fan club. Righteous, clueless and sadistic. I was going to enjoy eliminating those three. They were the typical OSA type: full of themselves and empty of all sense. They usually realized the error of their ways when gasping their last breath at the hands of an angry demon. Tonight, I would be playing the part of angry demon.

It was the last agent that gave me pause.

The fourth Agent had remained quiet. He was the one I deemed most dangerous. He kept his eyes scanning. Not only would he observe his quadrant out over the side of the building, but he would turn back and look at the roof behind him at regular intervals.

"What do you think, Carter?" Agent Three asked the silent Agent Four. "You think she'll show?"

"I think you should all keep your mouths shut and focus on why we're up here in the first place," Carter answered with a quiet menace. "None of you have faced something like her. If she does show, most of you will piss your pants, right before she shreds you. Now, eyes up and focus."

"Shit," Agent Two scoffed. "I saw her in the labyrinth. She was five foot nothing of half-demon and ran her ass off after a few orbs slapped her in the face. I'm not feeling the threat. I'll take her on alone if you're too scared, Carter."

Agent One and Three laughed.

"Damn straight, I'm scared," Carter shot back. "If you had any sense, you'd be scared too. She bonded to a demon, and not just a regular one, but a Demon Lord."

"Big deal," Agent One said. "It's still a demon and it can still be destroyed."

"You really are clueless," Carter said. "Did you even read the mission brief?"

"What's to read?" Agent One replied with a chuckle. "She's a demon. Her buddy downstairs is a big demon. Tomorrow he burns. If she shows up, she burns with him."

Carter looked around the roof for a few seconds before answering.

"A Demon Lord shouldn't be able to be bound," Carter answered, still scanning the roof. "The fact that she managed it means she presents a real threat. But since you're going to take her on alone... well, now I feel all secure."

"I heard she was human once, before she made a blood pact with the demon downstairs," Agent One said, becoming serious. "You think she'll survive the rending? I mean she *is* half-human."

"She's not human anymore," Agent Two answered. "She's a demon bitch now. What? You feeling sorry for her?"

"Me?" Agent One said. "Hell no. I was just curious what would happen after the rending."

"No one assigned you to this post because of your curiosity," Carter answered. "You're here because there's a good chance she will try this approach first."

"Wait a min," Agent Three said. "They think she might come up here first?"

"Yes," Carter said, "and they put us here in case she did. What does that tell you?"

"It tells me I need more hazard pay. What the fuck?" Agent One said. "Whose idea was that?"

"We're fucking expendables," Agent Two said. "Shit, we got redshirt duty. Seriously?"

"Doesn't mean anything," Agent One said. "If she comes here, we'll blast her. I don't know how she survived in the labyrinth, but she shows her face here, I'll make sure to rip—"

Agent One never got to finish his sentence. I had crouched behind him again, drawn my claws and severed his Achilles tendons, compromising his balance. He teetered near the edge for a second, before I assisted him forward with a gentle push, sending him out over the edge and into space.

The look of surprise on his face as he plummeted was almost as satisfying as the wet thud his body made when it impacted the street below. I slid back into the cover of darkness and moved away from the edge.

"Holy fuck!" Agent Two yelled, moving away from his post and backing into the HVAC ducts. The same ducts where I waited, crouched. "Brenner fell off!"

"Keep it together," Agent Three hissed, looking around and drawing a gun. "He was clumsy. Don't you be stupid. If he fell, fine, we'll fill out a report. In the meantime, we sweep the roof."

"You think she's—" Agent Two began, his words dying with him as I slit his throat and dropped him quietly behind the ducts.

"Louis?" Agent Three asked. "Stop fucking around...this is no time for games."

Agent Three made his way to where Louis had made his last stand and looked around. I stepped silently around him, crawled under the ducts, and approached from his side. The best way to a man's heart is through the third and fourth rib, at least from my angle of attack. I let my claws shred his heart with one silent strike. He crumpled to the ground, falling on Louis.

He was dead before he hit the floor.

"You did this," I said, stepping out into the open. "You set them up."

"I did," Carter admitted. "I had to see what we were facing. I have to say, I'm impressed."

"Where's Acheron?"

"Your demon pet? Downstairs, but you won't make it to him alive. Trust me."

"Trust you? I'm here to end you."

He formed an orb of red energy in his hand as I closed the distance.

EIGHT

Carter was good.

Just not as good as he thought he was. I could smell the fear coming off of him. Acrid sweat with an undercurrent of putrid locker room wafted over to my nose. He was scared shitless and putting on a brave face to hide it.

Too bad he couldn't mask the stench that was punching me in the nose.

"That was clever," I said, trying to put some of the duct work between us. "Is that a new strategy at the Order of Supernatural Asses? How to use your team as bait?"

I had a feeling the OSA had no idea I wasn't just a regular Otherkin—if there was anything regular about Otherkin in the first place. I wasn't going to reveal my transformation.

Not yet.

The orb of red energy sailed at me. It looked and felt potent at first glance, but I had been dodging Gryn's obliterators for the better part of three weeks. I was almost tempted to let the orb hit me. I figured evasion would be the better option.

Gryn's words came back to me: *Economy of motion. Efficiency of execution.*

I sidestepped the orb at the last moment, letting it sail past me and into the night. I glanced over my shoulder just to make sure it wasn't coming back to bite me in the ass...literally. Gryn would've had it return and blast me in the back. Carter was nowhere near the skill level of Gryn, but I wasn't taking any chances.

The look on Carter's face spoke volumes. In his mind, I shouldn't have been able to dodge his orb. In that brief moment, everything he thought he knew about the world had just been upheaved and shattered.

"How...how did you—?" he stammered.

"How did I dodge your orb?"

"You weren't supposed to be able to do that," he said, his voice betraying his anger. "They briefed us on you and your abilities. You may have heightened reflexes, but that won't save you."

I realized in that moment that Carter was just like the three agents—he was being used to gauge my skill level. Someone wanted to know how strong I was. I almost felt sorry for him.

Almost.

He did try to blast me with an orb, and frankly, the smell coming off of him was becoming an environmental hazard. Despite all of that, I was willing to postpone his termination to a date that didn't conflict with the rescue of Acheron.

I'm thoughtful that way.

"Listen," I said as he formed another orb of red energy. "Why don't we put a pin in this? I can always kill you later, if you want."

"Kill me later?" Carter asked, his voice dark now as the rage surfaced. I could still hear—and smell—the undercur rent of fear, but he was determined to take me out. "I'm going to kill you now."

"You don't get it," I said. "You're as much a redshirt as your three dead friends. Someone is playing you."

"Fuck you, demon," Carter said and unleashed the orb. "Die."

I really was willing to kill him later, but the insult sealed his fate. Well, the insult and the second orb he threw at me. One orb? Fine, I can cut some slack. Two orbs and a curse? I have to draw the line somewhere.

I sidestepped the second, third and fourth orbs, getting closer with each evasion. By the time he missed with the fourth orb, I had buried my claws in his neck and watched him bleed out on the roof.

I turned to the sound of soft clapping.

A tall figure stood at the other end of the roof, right on the edge. I felt the energy coming off him and realized this was the real threat.

"Impressive," he said after he finished clapping. "I underestimated you, Otherkin."

His bass voice echoed across the roof. He wore a dark suit with a blood red shirt and a black tie. I took in his scent and noticed the absence of fear coming from him. This was no amateur. He wasn't as strong as Gryn, but he wasn't a pushover either.

"Who are you?" I asked, shifting my body to one side to present less of a target. "Where's Acheron?"

"I'm Quinton, second sorcerer to the Night Division of the OSA," he gave me a small bow. "At your service."

"Night Division?" I asked. "Shit."

The Night Division of the OSA was the equivalent of sorcery black ops. It handled all the off-record, unsanctioned and disavowed assignments the OSA swore never happened. They were the OSA grim reapers, and were feared through the sorcerous community—with good reason. They were scary as hell and powerful enough to back up their reputation as cleaners.

The rumor was, if you met the Night Division, it wasn't a matter of *if* you would die, but *how* horribly they would escort you to your last breath. If they were involved with Acheron's kidnapping, this had just gone from bad to horrendous.

"So you've heard of us? Good," he said. "Your demon is in the lowest level of this structure. If you survive long enough, you may make it in time to witness the rending of a Demon Lord."

"I don't want to fight you." I said, keeping my eyes on his hands for any renegade orbs coming my way. "Let him go."

"Gladly," he said. "Swear yourself to me, by word and blood, and I will let him walk free."

That was not what I was expecting.

"Come again?" I asked, confused. "You want what?"

"The Seven are exploiting you—"

"Oh and you want to offer me a job with benefits and a pension? Fuck off."

"I want to offer you the chance to fulfill your potential," Quinton said. "You can do some real good with the Order. We'll even let you keep your demon pet."

"Acheron is my friend, not my pet."

I was liking him less by the second. Images of burying my claws in his face danced in my vision. I quickly pushed them to the side. Maybe there was a chance I could negotiate Acheron free. I was going to channel my inner Swayze and be nice until it was time to not be nice.

"Of course, whatever you need to tell yourself so you can sleep at night," he said. "You have limited options. If you accept, you'll swear yourself to me completely, and I'll release your demon to you. I will make sure any repercussions from the Seven are mitigated and dealt with."

"If I refuse?"

"I will make sure your demon suffers before I rend him to nothingness. Then I will burn your entire world to the ground while you watch, helpless to stop me, then destroy you."

"I don't like threats," I said, my voice low. "They make for poor bargaining chips."

"This isn't a threat, Otherkin," Quinton said. "And I'm not bargaining with you. I'm informing you of your new reality. I *will* destroy your world and your demon, right before I obliterate you, if you refuse my offer. Do you accept?"

"I accept...I accept the fact that I'm going to enjoy burying my claws in your chest and ripping your heart out while it's still beating," I snarled. "I'm ending you tonight."

"That...was the wrong answer," he said and traced a sigil in the air. "I suppose it's to be expected, your kind aren't known for their intelligence. I'll make sure your demon knows you died defiantly and pointlessly. You won't be missed. Goodbye, Otherkin."

He stepped off the edge of the roof and vanished. The four corners of the roof were suddenly aglow with red summoning circles. The next moment, each of the circles held an angry-looking *Minoras* focused on me.

"Well, shit."

A series of low growls filled the night.

NINE

I stood equidistant from the four *Minoras* as they focused on me.

The sound of claws on the roof's surface brought my attention to the one that appeared to be the largest. It was to my right and closing in slowly, sniffing the air. I probably smelled as bad as Carter did. The other three hung back as the large *Minoras* closed in on me.

I turned slowly to give the large *Minoras* my full attention. If it attacked, I was outnumbered and out-clawed. This wouldn't even be a fight—closer to a bloody scuffle as they mercilessly eviscerated me.

I wasn't dying here tonight.

The *Minoras* were lower demons. They were intelligent and capable of language if you knew how to speak to them. Being an Otherkin meant demontongue came naturally to me. What didn't come naturally, was being surrounded by four of these demons.

Four hungry demons.

Even when I could cast, I would've never attempted to

summon one of these. They were irritable, nearly impossible to control, and acutely homicidal when dragged to this plane and trapped in a circle. It made for a short life expectancy.

I did, however, study up on them once I started encountering them out on the streets with Acheron. They were pack creatures and obeyed the laws of pack dynamics. That explained why the other three demons didn't pounce on me and attack outright. The largest one was being perceived as the dominant demon.

Whatever it said or did would be followed by the rest of them.

I was currently standing in the midst of what would be considered a free-cast. A free-cast meant both demon and caster were free to act as they wished. The only thing that restrained a demon from attacking a free-caster was power. The summoner had to be off-the-charts powerful to prevent the demon from ripping them to shreds.

I wasn't that powerful, but I could bluff.

The large *Minoras* stepped closer and growled. It shook its large body, rippling the red-orange scales that covered its skin. They always reminded me of a strange hybrid between a dragon and a large dog. The similarity ended at the six legs, enormous fangs and weaponized tail sporting a mace at its end. If I gave it any real thought, they were probably closer to manticores than dragons.

"Oh greatest of demons, I stand humbled before you," I said in demontongue. "How may I serve?"

Demontongue was similar to some of the original languages on earth—full of clicks, grunts and sounds not natural to what was considered 'civilized' culture.

Every demon I had encountered so far had demonstrated an ego the size of a mountain. When outnumbered four-to-one, the best strategy was humility sprinkled with a large dash of self-preservation.

The *Minoras* stood still and stared at me.

He unleashed a low growl that triggered my limbic system into immediate flight mode. The sound rumbled through my lower abdomen like a renegade bass beat intent on bouncing me off the roof.

I managed to remain still in front of the demon, because running and dying tired is never fun. It sniffed the air and scanned the roof, growling at the other three demons before focusing on where I stood. Its orange eyes fixed me with its unnatural gaze.

"I have been summoned freely to feast on you," It said with a growl, as it gave me the once-over. "You are not much of a meal. Who would seek your destruction so?"

"I have formidable enemies, but none as powerful as you," I answered, keeping my head down. "I do not know what I have done to cause such ire, I am a weak Otherkin."

"You are not Brood, not entirely," it said. "You are of my kind, but different."

"I know you must feast," I said, still keeping my head down, but ready to leap off the roof if necessary. "I can promise you a feast to last you all night."

The other thing I had learned about demons, was that they were total gluttons when it came to feeding. They could never get enough blood. In many cases, it was one of the easiest ways to defeat them. Provide them with enough blood to get distracted, then end them while they were busy feeding.

Okay, not easy, but definitely doable. Tonight I needed to change the menu from a main course of Otherkin to an all-you-can-eat buffet of sorcerer.

"Where is this feast?" it asked, padding one step closer, its claws clicking on the roof as it inclined its massive head in my direction. "Tell me."

"Search your senses," I said, cautiously, careful not to

sound like a smart ass. "Below us"—I extended an arm downward—"this structure is filled with sorcerers who entrap your kind and command you against your will."

"Sorcerers?" it said, swiveling its enormous head around. "Below us?"

I may as well have mentioned the best meat sausage to a starving dog. If there were a favorite food for demons, sorcerers would be at the top of that list. Demons despised sorcerers with a hatred that defied explanation.

Must've had something to do with all that summoning and enslaving demons to obey sorcerers against their will. It was not the sort of thing that was easily forgotten...or forgiven.

"Yes, great demon," I said, still not looking directly at it. "Please send one of these other great demons to confirm that my words are true."

"If you lie," the *Minoras* said, stepping even closer and buffeting me with its rancid dragondog breath, "you will die where you stand."

"I speak truth," I said, finally looking up into its eyes. "They are all here to trap and rend you."

"Go," the *Minoras* said to the other three. "Search this structure and see if this half-Brood speaks truth."

The other three *Minoras* silently stepped over the edges of the roof. The trio of horrors noiselessly crept down the side of the building. A few minutes later, the night became a light show of orbs and sorcery as the group of *Minoras* started attacking.

One of the three returned to the roof and knelt before the large *Minoras*.

"She speaks truth," it said. "Our enemies lie beneath us. A feast waiting to be devoured."

The large *Minoras* turned to face me and growled. The

smaller *Minoras* lowered its head, before leaving the roof again as it descended into the massacre below.

"Why should I let you live, half-Brood?" the large *Minoras* asked as it paced around, making me nervous. "I was summoned to kill you."

"Excuse me? I just provided you with a feast," I said, pointing to the ground. "That deserves *some* recognition."

"Some, yes," it said. "This is a free-cast. We would have feasted without your information. The presence of my enemies was known to me once I entered this plane. Try again."

Mental note: never, ever trust a hungry demon in a free-cast.

"I'm here to rescue a Demon Lord, my friend."

"You *befriended* a Demon Lord? Impossible."

"Definitely possible," I answered, defiantly. "Acheron is my friend."

The Minoras stopped pacing and focused on me with its creepy, large, orange eyes.

"He told you his...*name?*"

"I told you, he's my friend," I answered. "I know his *full* name."

Names were power. A demon's name was its one true vulnerability. With a name, a sorcerer could undo a demon, destroying it completely, provided they had enough time and power. This meant Demon Lords never revealed their true names, for good reason.

"The Brood have no friends, only enemies and adversaries. We do not understand friendship, only death and violence. How did you get his name?"—it peered closer and sniffed the air around me—"you are not strong enough to make it comply."

"We have an arrangement," I said. "He revealed his name to me, and I promised not to destroy him."

The *Minoras* rumbled with a low growl and shook its head.

"Either this demon is a fool, or you are more than you appear," it said. "Yet your words ring true."

"I have no reason to lie," I said. "Besides, I enjoy breathing."

"Your friendship, demon or not, means nothing to my purpose this night—your death."

"Maybe I wasn't clear, I have a demon *friend* on the lower levels," I answered, keeping my frustration in check. Demons could be single-minded about things like blood, killing, feeding, more killing. "I can't help him if you try and kill me. They are going to rend him at sunrise."

"Your situation, while pressing, is irrelevant," it answered. "I was summoned to destroy you—now."

"You get to make a choice tonight, then," I said, unleashing the power of the Darkin within and forming my chakram. It shone with golden light in the darkness. "You can go downstairs and have an easy meal, or you can stay here and try to kill me. I promise, I'm not an easy kill and I will do my best to take you with me. Your call."

"The meek half-Brood has claws and a bite. Good," it said, while cocking its head to one side. "You do well to hide your strength, but do not think you can stand against me and live. You think me lesser, and you are mistaken. You are not the only one that is more than it appears."

It growled and shook its body again, easily doubling in size in the process. The scales along its body transformed to a deep metallic red, and the orange eyes were now covered in bright red demonflame. I was staring at a *Majoras*. The larger, scarier, more lethal version of a *Minoras*.

"You...are definitely not *Minoras*," I said, looking up into its face with the realization that I had just challenged this demon to the death. "That explains why the others hesitated before attacking me."

"*Minoras* serve or die," It said, looking down at me. "Now, the terms of my summons. I was called to destroy an Otherkin."

"It's a free-cast," I said, thinking quickly about loopholes. "That means as a *Majoras*, you can pretty much do what you want. Technically, I'm not even your target."

It narrowed its flaming eyes at me. Demons were highly intelligent when it came to the following of a summons. If it wasn't spelled out, it meant they had latitude. A sorcerer never wanted to provide a demon with wiggle room. That was the whole point of the summoning circles and the binding. They forced demons to obey.

A demon with latitude usually meant a dead sorcerer.

This demon had been brought up in a free-cast and sent after an Otherkin. I was no longer strictly Otherkin, but more. That meant it had a choice, and I had a slim chance of not being dissected on this roof tonight.

"I am *Majoras*, yes, and you are not Brood. You are Darkin, dangerous in your own right, but no match for me."

Egos the size of mountains. In this case, it was probably right, and I had no intention of finding out.

"I'm beginning to see that," I said, and let out a deep breath. "Still, that doesn't mean I'm just going to stand here and let you shred me. Do we have an understanding, or do we get to the dying?"

The *Majoras* let out a long growl combined with a rumble. It took me a few seconds to realize that it was laughing at me. Not like I was offended; if it was laughing, it wasn't attacking.

I called that a win in my book.

"Your kind are known to the Brood," it said, once it stopped laughing. "Though I have not seen one of the Darkin in many cycles. You have strong enemies, young Darkin. To set me upon you requires power. Deep, dark power, not possessed by the human who opened the gate for me."

"Shit," I said mostly to myself. "Quinton was a tool? I mean, he's a tool, but I didn't realize he was being used."

"Indeed."

"Does that mean you aren't going to try and make me dinner?" I asked. It was best to be clear about these things, especially with demons. "Are we good?"

The *Majoras* narrowed its huge orange eyes at me.

"Good?" It asked. "Tonight, there will be a truce between us, for I will feast on the blood of my enemies below."

There was still the issue of four demons running free.

"This is a free-cast," I said. "Are you planning on attacking this city...*my* city, after dinner?"

"And if I do?"

"You and I are going to find out if I can stand against you and live."

"Excellent," it said. "Tonight, I will feast only on those in this structure, but I will accept your challenge. When we meet again, only one of us will remain standing."

I really needed to learn to keep my mouth shut.

"That's not exactly what I meant," I said, raising a hand. "I really don't want to do the whole *fight to the death* thing if you're going to leave my city alone."

"The word has been given and accepted," it said. "Tell me, half-Brood, how many Darkin have you met?"

"None," I said. "At least not to my knowledge."

"Have you ever wondered why this is so?"

Probably because we keep making stupid death threats to super demons that can shred us?

"Not until this exact moment when you mentioned it, no."

"Perhaps you should," it said as it crouched down. "There are greater threats than my kind to the Darkin. You would do well to discover them, before you too, become a meal."

It leaped over me and over the edge of the building. I

didn't even hear it land. I moved to the edge of the building and looked down. The large *Majoras* was walking along the side of the building. It paused for a moment, and smashed into a large window.

The screams followed a few seconds later.

TEN

I reabsorbed my chakram, headed for the stairwell, and took the stairs down.

To say the floors were covered in carnage would be a gross understatement. The floors, stairs and walls looked like someone had taken buckets of blood and decided to redecorate the space in a Jackson Pollock style of sanguine nouveau.

Splatters were everywhere, indicating where a sorcerer had taken their last breath, before meeting some horrific end from the claws or fangs of the *Minoras*. I stepped over limbs and remaining body parts so numerous it was difficult to determine how many OSA Agents were in the building.

"I thought they'd be neater than this," I mumbled to myself as I continued down the stairs. "This place is a bloody mess."

Six gore-filled levels later, I reached the ground floor and came face-to-face with one of the smaller *Minoras*. Its face was covered in blood and viscera. It shook its head as I approached, sending pieces of gore flying everywhere. I jumped back to avoid being showered with bits and blood.

"We have feasted tonight," it said. "The Demon Lord you

seek is below, behind that door"—it motioned with its head—"there are more sorcerers there."

"Not like your kind to leave a meal half-done," I said, looking around at the horrific scene of death surrounding us. "Did you get them all?"

"We have not feasted like this in some time," it said. "Thank you, Darkin. You will be remembered."

"No need, really," I said. "In fact I'd prefer it if you forgot you ever met me."

"We do not forget," it said. "You *will* be remembered, Darkin."

I didn't know if that was a threat or a promise, so I decided to let it go and focus on the immediate issue. If they were done, why was it still here?

"Are you saying you guys are full?" I asked. "Is that even possible?"

"Full?" it asked, then growled with another shake of its head, splattering more blood on the walls. "I am tasked with keeping guard to the lower levels."

"Won't they just get out some other way?"

"There are no other exits below us. The tunnels under this structure point to one location...this door."

I mentally reviewed the plans Gryn had provided. The *Minoras* was right. This was the only way down that didn't involve massive amounts of destructive power.

I turned to look at the massive steel door that led downstairs to the tunnels. Having only one way in or out was either poor planning or a deliberate choice.

It made for easy control.

The door was a chokepoint. If anyone or anything below was trying to get out, it would only take a small force to hold down this door. One exit was easy to watch, guard, or destroy if needed, containing everything downstairs in the tunnels.

"One way in and one way out?" I asked. "That doesn't sound too smart."

"The area below was meant to trap my kind. Yours too," it said. "Tonight, it will be the sorcerers' end—more of my kind are coming to the feast you provided."

I wasn't enjoying getting the credit for demon night at the all-you-can-eat OSA Sorcerer Buffet. Things like that had a way of getting around, and I had enough enemies to deal with.

"Don't mention it, really," I said. "My friend is down there somewhere. I need to get him, before you and the crew go on your ballistic demon shredfest."

"I was to instruct you to act with haste Death comes to this place tonight; all within this structure will feel our fangs and claws. None will be spared before the rising of the sun."

"None?"

It raked the floor with its claws, throwing up sparks along the concrete surface as it bared its fangs in what could only be the creepiest smile a demon could manage.

"None," it said. "Tonight, everything within these walls dies."

"Shit," I said, reaching for the door. "Thanks for the heads up. How soon before your demon pack returns?"

"Soon," it said. "Do not waste time."

"Thanks for the accurate timeframe there," I said, mostly to myself. No sense in picking a fight with a *Minoras,* even if it was just a guard dragondog. "Hope to never see you again."

I took the stairs fast. Demons weren't exactly known for their accuracy when it came to time. They were beings of millennia—what was an hour or two to them? I walked down a few corridors, when I realized the tunnels beneath the building were set up like a maze.

They had mimicked the labyrinth at the Seven HQ, using the confusing configuration of corridors to make it nearly impossible for anyone or anything to escape. I pulled up my mental map of the plans I had studied and looked for the corridor that led to the largest space.

Rending a Demon Lord was not a subtle affair. The sorcerer in question—I guessed Quinton in this case—would need room, a wide space to draw an enormous circle large enough to harness massive amounts of power—enough power to rend a demon like Acheron. I mentally pinpointed the room that made the most sense and started heading that way.

A few times I saw doors that led to small rooms. Inside these rooms, I could see operating tables, complete with straps and chains attached. Some of the rooms still had fresh blood on the floor or a half-dissected demon corpse strapped to a table.

Every so often I could sense OSA Agents in some of the rooms and corridors, but most of them were in hiding or heading away from me. If any of them had fled downstairs from the upstairs massacre, they had a rough night ahead of them.

These tunnels were a dead end...literally.

If I recalled the plans correctly, the *Minoras* was right: there really was no exit down here. These tunnels were devised as a containment and experimentation areas. That was Order code for torture and death. It dawned on me that this property was probably an OSA black site. A place where people and creatures—creatures like me— disappeared after being subjected to horrific treatment.

A quiet part of me wanted to warn the OSA Agents, to let them know hell was going to make a house call. The louder, stronger part of me said...fuck them. They persecuted and killed countless creatures with no provocation or justification, aside from their victims being different...being other.

They deserved what was coming to them tonight...with interest.

After a few more turns, I found the room I figured would serve best as the rending space. It was spacious enough to draw a large circle, but removed from the main network of tunnels. If I were going to destroy a Demon Lord, I would do it in this room.

I stood still at the entrance, adjusted my vision to the lower light and peered in. The darkened room was a large square with an upper level balcony overlooking the main area. It reminded me of an operating theater. Before stepping in, I checked the threshold to make sure it was sigil-free.

The last thing I needed was to get blasted by defensive sigils that rendered me unconscious or paralyzed. Quinton seemed like the type to use them, but the door was clear. Whatever nasty surprise he had left for me, I hadn't found it yet. There was a good chance the demons crashing his rending party had upset his plans.

As I stepped in farther, I saw the large Saint Andrews cross in the center of an enormous circle of sigils. Someone had been busy. I barely recognized any of the sigils in the circle, but I was familiar with the energy I sensed in the center of the circle.

X marked the spot, as I saw my friend bound to the wooden cross, with glowing bands of sigil-inscribed metal around his wrists and ankles.

"You shouldn't have come," Acheron said from the cross. "You do realize this is a trap?"

"Obviously," I said, looking around at the empty room. "It doesn't get more blatant than putting you on a cross in the center of what I can only guess is a rending circle?"

"Correct, complete with sigils to enhance my agony during the process," Acheron added. "It's good to see people take pride in their work. Even if the work is designed to destroy me."

"Can it?"

"Quite," Acheron nodded. "This is an ancient circle, not used in several centuries. Frankly, I thought it had been lost to time. Its construction is beyond any of the sorcerers I have encountered during my brief, but painful stay. This is an impressive display of skill."

"This whole setup is cliché, if you ask me," I said. "It's obvious and amateurish."

"Yet, here you are, springing the trap," Acheron answered. "Why are you here? It's not me they want, it's you."

"Me?" I asked, confused. "What would a bunch of third-rate wannabe sorcerers with an acute death wish want with me?"

"Must be for that wonderful demeanor of yours," Acheron said and coughed. "Apologies, this circle has had some deleterious effects on my recuperative abilities."

I stepped closer, but stayed outside of the circle. Acheron looked like he had been used as a punching bag by an angry troll.

"Those fuckers," I said, seething, and made to enter the circle. "Who did this to you?"

"Do *not* step into the circle, Nyx," Acheron said. "It's a trap."

"I'm not a demon."

"That's what they're counting on—your thinking you're immune. Kindly stay outside the circle."

"Who did this?" I said, looking around. "Where are they?"

"There were quite a few of them here earlier," Acheron said. "Then there was some commotion. Many of them fled. I'm sure they'll return...you should leave now while you can."

"Not without you," I said. "I came here to rescue you, and that's what I'm going to do."

"Forget me," Acheron said. "I'm a lost cause. Even if you could get past the circle, which you can't, I'm bound to this cross"—he tugged at the metal bands across his wrists—"with sigils even I can't break. Believe me, I tried."

I turned away from Acheron when I felt the energy signature on the upper level.

"I know you're there," I said. "Why not come down so we can talk about this?"

"I underestimated you twice," Quinton said. "I won't do so again. How did you turn the *Minoras*?"

"Turn them?" I asked, then laughed. "I didn't have to turn them. They were all too happy to feast on your stupid sorcerer asses."

"Impossible," Quinton answered. "I summoned them with the explicit purpose of destroying you."

"You used a *free-cast*," I said. "That was your first mistake."

"A free-cast?" Acheron said. "With a *Minoras*? That sounds foolhardy."

"Not *a Minoras*—*three* of them," I said, holding up three fingers. "That was your second mistake."

"I summoned *four* Minoras," Quinton sneered. "Are you blind as well as stupid?"

"Did you now?" I asked as I kept scanning the upper level. "Maybe you didn't read the summoning instructions? Seems like you may have miscalculated."

"Miscalculated?" Quinton said, his voice rising in pitch. He was getting angry, and judging from the scent I was picking up, fear had started taking hold. Good. "What do you take me for? A rank amateur?"

"Are you saying one of them wasn't a *Minoras*?" Acheron asked quietly. "Did he...did he open a gate?"

I nodded.

"Well, *I'm* not the one that summoned a *Majoras* by accident," I said, looking at Acheron. "That sounds like something only a rank amateur would do. I mean opening a gate and letting a *Majoras* in...well, *that* sorcerer would have to be a real fuck-up. Don't you think?"

"A free-cast with a *Majoras* would be downright suicidal," Acheron replied. "I truly hope you're mistaken, for all our sakes. They are nearly impossible to stop, much less kill."

"A *Majoras*?" Quinton said with a low growl as he slowly lost control. "You pathetic liar. You wouldn't know a *Majoras* if it sank its fangs into you. I summoned four *Minoras*."

"The sorcerer doth protest too much, methinks," Acheron said. "Tell me, this creature you saw, about twice the size of a normal *Minoras*, deep red scales, with flaming eyes?"

"I'd say that's an accurate description," I said, looking up into the balcony. "Said he was coming back—and bringing friends to sorcerer buffet night."

"Coming back?" Acheron asked. "Here? With more? Perhaps we should consider making an exit before that happens? No one on the premises is strong enough to deal with three free-cast demons, much less a horde of them."

"Quinton the Tool thinks he's powerful enough," I answered, pointing up to the balcony. "He thinks he can handle three *Minoras*, one *Majoras,* and whatever else they bring. Sounds like a very hungry group of demons."

"Lies of desperation," Quinton answered, but I could hear the undercurrent of fear in his voice now. "OSA Agents will be swarming the premises within the hour."

"About that,"—I said, holding up a finger—"did you miss the part where I said they're inviting more demons to the all-you-can-eat sorcerer buffet? If I were you, I wouldn't want to stick around to be dessert. Just a suggestion."

"You think you've won?" Quinton answered, his voice coming from a different location. He was moving. "By sunrise, that circle will rend your demon and there is nothing you can do about it."

"I can make sure you're not alive to see it," I answered,

still trying to pinpoint his location. "Why not come down and make me another offer? One I can't refuse?"

I glanced over at Acheron, who shook his head *no*...telling me not to negotiate.

If I survived tonight, I was going to start carrying a large gun. Something that held both demonkiller and asshole-sorcerer eradicator rounds.

"The window on that opportunity has passed," Quinton answered. "I'm here to make certain your demon dies by sunrise."

He had just overshared. I looked down at the circle around Acheron. I felt the energy thrumming around and in it. The circle was dormant but charged. It was waiting for a catalyst, something that had to do with sunlight or energy.

How would Quinton get sunlight down here into the tunnels? It didn't make sense—we were several levels under the building. There was no way sunlight could reach us.

The circle needed activation, and it needed activation by someone strong enough to manipulate the energy required to rend a Demon Lord. Which meant that anyone else that could have done it was probably in pieces upstairs, leaving only Quinton, or else he would have ghosted by now.

The *Majoras'* words came back to me: *Deep, dark power, not possessed by the human who opened the gate for me.*

Quinton wasn't strong enough to summon a *Majoras*. Hell, he didn't even have a clue one had piggy-backed into his summons. No, he couldn't rend Acheron, but maybe he didn't need to?

What if the circle was primed and on a timer? Then, it wouldn't require sunlight, or a massive amount of power, just some kind of activation. Any sorcerer could do it, not necessarily a powerful one, just one willing to take the risk and jumpstart the process.

That sounded more like Quinton the Tool.

OSA Agents weren't known for their bravery, especially not the Night Division. They preferred to fight from the shadows. Attacking left when you expected right. They hated direct confrontations and preferred to outmaneuver their targets, blindsiding them.

Except now, Quinton and his crew had become dinner. If he was tasked with this rending, he would have to stick around and do it himself.

I needed to remind him how alone he was.

"Did you get a chance to see all six floors of the building upstairs?" I asked matter-of-factly. "Or did you just see the level you and your minions were hiding on? Those *Minoras* shredded all of your people, I mean *all* of them."

"Their deaths are on your head, bitch. *You* did this."

"My head?" I asked, looking around. "I don't recall summoning, not one, but four hungry demons. I seem to recall that being you. Those sorcerer deaths are on *you*."

"There's no way for you to reach my location," Quinton answered, his voice echoing from the balcony. "You can stall all you want, but it changes nothing. At sunrise your demon pet dies."

At sunrise not sunlight. I was missing the obvious. The circle was on some sort of timer.

"Demon pet?" Acheron asked indignantly. "I am no one's pet."

I needed to communicate with Acheron, but I didn't know if it was possible now with the power of the Darkin I had within. I focused on him and searched for the bond we shared. It took some effort, but I managed it.

Is there any way I can break you out of there?

None. I'm trapped here due to the bond I share with you. They managed a deviously clever snare. It uses the energy of our bond to keep me affixed to the cross.

What happens if I break the bond?

You die. Do not even consider it.

I'm not the same Otherkin you knew. I've changed.

Turned over a new leaf? Well, good for you. Be that as it may, do not even think of breaking the bond. It will kill both the new and old you.

I pulled out the small slip of paper Gryn gave me.

For Emergency Circle Destruction Use Only.

If this wasn't an emergency, I didn't know what was. I examined the indecipherable sigils one last time, and tossed the paper into the circle holding Acheron.

ELEVEN

Normal sigils contain an immense amount of power.

Sigils created by an insanely accomplished sorcerer and imbued with his power, are staggering in the magnitude of energy they can unleash. When those sigils are designed to destroy a circle...the effects are impressive.

The paper floated over to the center of the circle near Acheron. For a few seconds, nothing happened.

"Littering, now?" Acheron asked. "What has this world come to?"

Quinton laughed above me.

"Did you think you would be able to disrupt *that* circle with a *piece of paper*?" he mocked. "You truly are clueless. To think I offered you a position with the Order. What was I thinking? I'm going to enjoy watching you die."

That circle, not *my* circle. Sorcerers had egos only slightly smaller than demons. If Quinton had drawn the circle he would've been boasting about his ability the moment I had entered the room.

A flicker of light caught my attention. It came from the

circle and steadily began increasing in brightness. The paper began glowing red and Acheron raised an eyebrow.

"Those sigils look vaguely like a—" Acheron started.

The sigils on the paper exploded with red energy. The force of the explosion knocked me across the room. I managed to twist my body and land in a crouch, as a beam of red and black energy shot up from the floor and slowly expanded, destroying the circle.

"No, no, no," Quinton yelled. "What have you done?"

"Destroyed your circle," I answered. "Shouldn't be a problem for an expert sorcerer like you to draw another one, right? You should have enough time before sunrise."

I was counting on the chance that he wasn't the one who drew the circle in the first place. He was just here to set it off. With the circle destroyed, Quinton would have to get hands-on. He would have to come down from the shadows and get his hands dirty.

My preferred style of fighting.

"You filthy, Otherkin bitch," he spat. "I'll kill you myself."

"He seems upset," Acheron noted as the circle of energy expanded further, obliterating the sigils of the circle. "Retreat is the better part of valor here. Get out now, Nyx...while you can."

"I told you," I said, as I formed my chakram, unleashing the power of the Darkin within. "I'm not leaving here without you."

"That's new," Acheron said, looking at my weapon. "Is that an upgrade? Nice to see you listening for once and taking my advice."

"We leave here together, or we don't leave at all," I said.

"I'm firmly in the *leave here together* camp, but the only way you can manage that is by—no, Nyx," Acheron said, as he finally understood what I was going to do. "I told you, it will kill you. You can't."

I flexed the muscles of my jaw and focused on tracking Quinton's energy as it moved from the upper level. He was coming.

"Let me know when the circle is completely gone," I said. "I'll get you off that cross."

"Touching, but futile," Quinton said, as he glided across the room, dropping to the floor from the upper level soundlessly and forming a swarm of black orbs around him. "You have no comprehension of the damage you've caused."

"Enlighten me," I said, drawing my claws. "If you can."

"With pleasure." Quinton unleashed the swarm of angry, black orbs in my direction. "This will take but a moment. Stand still, and accept your death."

"I've never been good at following orders," I said, separating the chakram in my hand. "How about...no?"

"You have a toy?" Quinton scoffed. "You think your little weapon is going to save you? I'm a Night Division sorcerer, and you are merely a stupid demon who has outlived her usefulness."

My conversation with Gryn came back to me:

"A blood sigil? I thought those were banned?"

"So is summoning a Demon Lord. It will require both of your blood to break the bond."

"Shit, how much blood?"

"Enough to make it dangerous."

"The circle is gone," Acheron said behind me. "I strongly suggest against this course of action. It's suicide."

I turned and ran toward Acheron. While I ran, I used the chakram to slice my forearm, causing a deep wound. I could feel the orbs behind me, and silently thanked Gryn for three weeks of obliterator dodging.

I rolled to the side, avoiding Quinton's orbs, coming to a stop next to the cross. I used my finger to trace half of the blood sigil on Acheron's face.

"This is going to hurt," I apologized. "Sorry."

"Don't do this. Not like this."

I sliced into his arm with the chakram and pressed my fingers into his wound. His dark blood covered my fingers as I traced the second half of the blood sigil on the other side of his face. I had just finished the sigil when several of Quinton's orbs punched into my side. I reflexively reabsorbed my weapon, as the orbs launched me away from Acheron and across the room.

"Now, you stupid demon, you die while your pet watches," Quinton said, then turned, looking at Acheron. "Don't worry, I will make sure she suffers long and hard before I put her out of her misery. Then, you're next."

A black cloud of energy began bubbling around the base of the cross. Quinton stopped in his approach and faced Acheron.

The sigils on Acheron's face smoldered with demonflame, burning his skin. His eyes slowly transformed into something dark and deadly, forcing me to look away. I willed myself to look again. As I watched, Acheron's skin turned scaly and metallic. Black energy crackled around his body as he laughed.

For the first time tonight, I realized I might have made a mistake.

Acheron's laugh made standing in front of the *Majoras* a pleasant memory. He had become something I had never seen. Not even when I summoned him did he look like this. He was revealing his true nature, and all I wanted to do was find somewhere to hide.

"Why wait?" Acheron asked, as he stared at Quinton. "Don't delay the inevitable...kill me now."

"Wait, what are you doing?" Quinton asked, holding up a hand as he backpedaled. "Stay back."

"I don't think so, sorcerer," Acheron said, as his body

burst into orange demonflame, incinerating the cross to ash, before returning to normal. "That was refreshing. Now, where was I?"

I was more surprised by the fact that Acheron's clothes were untouched, than the fact that he had just switched on and off bodyflames.

"Die, you demon spawn!" Quinton screamed, as he unleashed a barrage of black energy orbs at Acheron. "I'm sending you back to hell, where filth like you belong."

Acheron batted the orbs away with one hand, as he looked at the now dormant metal bands on his wrists. The sigils had stopped glowing. Our bond was broken.

Acheron was truly free.

"I was feared in hell," Acheron said with a smile, as he ran a finger under the metal bands around his wrists and popped them off with ease. "Something about even evil having limits and my surpassing them."

Quinton formed more orbs as Acheron approached.

"Keep back, demon," Quinton said. "I'll burn you where you stand."

"Burn me?" Acheron asked, his voice dark and lethal. "What do you know of burning? I'm a denizen of hell, human. Burning is an art form where I'm from."

"We trapped you once, we can do it again," Quinton said. "The OSA is sending reinforcements."

I almost felt sorry for Quinton in that moment. He was dead...his brain just hadn't gotten the memo yet. I chalked up the brief moment of pity to the loss of blood from my self-inflicted wound.

"It took them centuries," Acheron continued. "They imprisoned me in a circle not unlike the one used here. Now, tell me, you didn't draw this circle, did you?"

"What does it matter?" Quinton answered, surrounding himself in black energy. "We *will* trap you again."

"I'll take that as a no," Acheron replied. "Who drew the circle?"

"Fuck you," Quinton hissed as he backed away. "You're weak, nothing but a pathetic demon. You think I'm going to tell you anything?"

"I was tortured and broken, but in the end, they failed and died screaming," Acheron said as he formed a large, orange orb of demonflame and closed in on Quinton. "I killed them, but I was still trapped. Just when I thought I would rot in captivity"—he glanced in my direction—"a clueless sorcerer summoned me, liberating me from my prison."

"They should have destroyed you," Quinton spat as he created more orbs of energy. "I would have destroyed you."

"They tried," Acheron answered with another smile that froze my blood. "They failed."

"They may have failed," Quinton said. "But tonight, I won't. Tonight, you die."

"It's possible, considering my state and the horde of demons you foolishly unleashed," Acheron said with a nod. "I may die, but not before you."

Acheron released the orb of demonflame.

TWELVE

To give Quinton some credit, he didn't immediately shit his pants.

I'd say it was close, but his sense of self-preservation must have kicked in and overwritten the sheer terror that was filling the room as the orb of demonflame raced at him.

He tried to deflect it with an orb of his own. It was like trying to divert a wrecking ball with an egg. Acheron's orb swallowed Quinton's weak attempt at defense and crashed into Quinton, setting his arm aflame.

My senses rebelled at the acrid stench of demonflame in the air. The odor of rotten eggs was soon joined by the smell of burning flesh.

Quinton's burning flesh.

He started screaming as he reflexively tried to put out the flames by smothering them with his other hand. All he managed to do was set his hand on fire. He was in full-on panic mode and dropped to the floor. It was actually smart, but it didn't help. Apparently, Acheron had access to some insane variant of demonflame.

Nothing seemed to put it out.

Normal demonflame was similar to napalm on steroids. It burned through everything, taking real effort to put out if the blaze was large enough. Whatever Acheron was wielding was worse...so much worse.

"Stop it, Acheron," I said from across the room. "He deserves to die, but not like this."

Acheron made a fist and the flames went out. Quinton was moaning and writhing in pain as Acheron stepped close. He crouched down and slowly pushed the glasses up on the bridge of his nose.

"It burns...doesn't it?" Acheron asked. "Tell me who drew the circle, and I'll give you the death you deserve."

I slowly got to my feet and nearly toppled over. I had lost too much blood. I looked down at the still-open wound on my arm, in awe. Why hadn't it closed? I didn't have super-healing like a demon did, but none of my wounds remained open this long. I pressed my free hand over the wound and wobbled my way over to Acheron.

"Who drew the circle, Quinton?" I managed when I stood over his freshly-barbecued body. "Tell me. We know it wasn't you."

"Fuh...fuh—" Quinton stammered.

"Save it," I said, feeling slightly woozy. "I'm not going to let Acheron kill you. Do you know why?"

"You're not?" Acheron asked. "I think it's only proper, based on principle alone—not to mention my treatment under his supervision."

"I think Quinton here wants to do the right thing," I said, keeping my tone even. "He knows he fucked up. No one is going to rend a demon at sunrise. That means someone else is going to be pissed. Someone powerful, someone Quinton reports to in the Night Division."

Quinton's eyes opened wide.

"Kill...kill me," Quinton rasped through the pain. "Make it quick, please."

"Who drew the circle?" I asked, my voice harder this time. "Tell me and I'll consider it."

"Sigil...sigilsmith."

"Sigilsmith? Rodrigo?" I asked, not believing the words. "Are you shitting me?"

"It tracks," Acheron said. "He dislikes you, and is certainly no fan of demons. Two birds, one stone...one recovered artifact. It's neat and efficient."

I whirled on Acheron, and instantly regretted it as the room kept spinning. Acheron grabbed me by the arm to keep me from losing my balance.

"He's part of the Seven," I answered, keeping my voice low. "How did he know we were in the labyrinth?"

"The...the sigils," Quinton volunteered from the floor. "The ones in the labyrinth. He designed them."

"This presents more questions than answers," Acheron said, forming another orb of demonflame. He looked at me before glancing at Quinton below us. "Answers I doubt he has."

"Shit, Rodrigo? This means Vic must know something."

"Or Rodrigo is acting on his own," Acheron said. "In either case, this sorcerer has divulged what he knows. Shall I end him?"

"You promised to make it quick," Quinton said with a gasp. Fear danced in his eyes at the sight of the demonflame. "That's not quick. That's torture."

"No, I said I'll *consider* it," I said, looking down at Quinton. "You summoned four demons to destroy me. You were going to rend my friend, one of the only ones I have. You deserve to die in agony, but that's not who I am. I'm—"

"A sad, pathetic Otherkin bitch," Quinton answered. "You

have no idea what's happening, no idea what's coming for you."

I was about to answer when I felt a surge of energy behind me.

"Darkin," a voice said behind me, "you were warned."

It was the *Majoras*.

THIRTEEN

I turned slowly.

The *Majoras* had entered the room. Behind it, one on each side, were two more *Majoras*. Behind them, assembled in ranks of ten, were thirty *Minoras*.

All of them looked eager to get their shred on.

"This is not good," I said under my breath. "Seems like it's time to get to the dying."

"Wait," Acheron said, placing a hand on my shoulder. "Allow me."

Acheron gave me a glance and subtly waved me back.

I stepped back and let Acheron move in between me and the *Majoras*.

"Balorous," Acheron said, looking at the *Majoras*. "What are you doing here?"

"Acheron?" Balorous said, surprised. "Since when do you roam this plane?"

"It's been some time. What business do you have with the Darkin?"

"The word has been given and received," Balorous answered, with a growl. "When we next met only one could remain standing. This was agreed upon earlier, before I searched out my brethren. I left one of my own to warn her of my return. She has chosen to remain, therefore we must see who lives and who dies this night."

"One moment," Acheron said, raising a finger and pulling me aside. "Did you say you would fight him to the death?"

"It's a little more complicated than that," I explained. "I thought he was a *Minoras* at the time, then he shook his body and poofed, expanded into that thing."—I pointed at Balorous—"how was I supposed to know he was a *Majoras*?"

Acheron pinched the bridge of his nose and closed his eyes for a second. He took a deep breath and let it out slowly.

"Let me handle this," he said under his breath. "Can I count on you to remain silent for thirty seconds?"

"Thirty whole seconds?"

Acheron glared at me.

"Sure, thirty seconds, I can definitely do that."

"No matter what I say, do not under any circumstances respond to him. Is that clear?"

I nodded.

"Good," Acheron said, and turned back to Balorous and his crew of imminent demon death. "This is a waste of your time, Balorous."

"The word has been given and received, Acheron. You know our ways."

"But she does not," Acheron glanced back at me. "You would lower yourself to battle such a weakling? This is beneath you. Have you sunk so low?"

The demons around Balorous growled in response.

"What do you propose?" Balorous answered, raking a claw across the floor. "Will you stand in her stead?"

"As I see it, you could tarnish your standing here among your glorious brethren by"—he glanced at me again—"engaging this pathetic being."

"That was our word," Balorous said, but he sounded uncertain. "As agreed upon."

Acheron paused and transformed back into scary Demon Lord form, complete with bodyflames and a voice that would make James Earl Jones sound like a squeaky teenager in the middle of puberty.

"Allow me to counter with...facing your end at my hands," Acheron's voice boomed across the room. "I promise you it will be glorious, but it will be final. However, there is *one* more alternative."

All of the demons took several steps back. I didn't blame them. The demonflames around Acheron crackled orange and black. The only demon that held his ground was Balorous.

"State your alternative," Balorous said.

"Give her time to become a worthy opponent for a demon of your stature," Acheron replied. "When she is ready, I will convene an assembly, and we will see who remains standing. What say you?"

Balorous glared at me and then looked back at Acheron. He shook his body, making the scales covering it give off a metallic chime, before unleashing an ear-splitting roar. All of the demons behind Balorous bowed on their forelegs. The other two *Majoras* raked the ground throwing up sparks, and joined in on the roar.

I don't know how I managed to remain standing in the face of that contained fury, but I did. Acheron glanced at me and nodded.

"The word has been given and received," Balorous said, once the roar died down. "When she is worthy, the Darkin will face me in combat"—it padded over to where I stood —"then we will see who lives and who dies."

"More of his kind are arriving," Acheron said, pointing to Quinton, who probably had hoped we had forgotten him by this point. "He is the one who was used to open the gate."

Balorous looked over to Quinton and gave a low rumble. Quinton answered with a moan, and tried to crawl away. One of the other *Majoras* padded over quietly and blocked his way with a growl.

"Leave this place," Balorous said. "We will deal with him and his kind. Tonight, this will be a place of death and blood. You have no seat at this table."

"Understood," Acheron said with a nod, as he grabbed my arm. "May you feast long and deep."

"May your flame ever burn," Balorous answered, returning the nod. "We will remember, Darkin."

We stepped out of the room to Quinton's screams as one of the demons ended his pathetic life. Acheron transformed back into his normal form and picked up the pace until we were doing a slow jog.

"Are we late for something?" I asked as he picked up the pace. "You have somewhere to be I don't know about?"

"Anywhere but here," Acheron answered, taking the turns quickly. "Thirty-three demons, Nyx. We would have been dead in seconds."

"I thought you offered him a glorious death at your hands?" I said, barely keeping up as we spilled out into the street. It was still several hours before sunrise. I saw the headlights of several vehicles approaching. "This way."

We ran back to Eight, undetected. I unlocked her and we jumped in, catching our breath.

"That was close," Acheron said. "We almost didn't make it."

"Are you telling me you were bluffing?"

"Of course," Acheron answered. "I may be a Demon Lord and could, with difficulty—great difficulty mind you—dispatch one of the *Majoras*, but three of them? Impossible.

Not to mention the thirty *Minoras* who would lose their collective minds and tear us apart. No, a direct confrontation would have been suicide."

"You are one insane demon," I said after my heart calmed down. "The bond—I'm sorry I had to break it. You're free now. I'll understand if you want to go."

He showed me the wound on his arm. It had healed completely. I looked down at my arm and realized my wound was gone as well.

"Where did you learn the blood sigil?"

"Gryn, an old sorcerer, gave them to me," I said. "He studied under—"

"Circe, yes, I know Gryn," Acheron said. "You didn't break the bond, you transformed it. It's hard to explain. That blood sigil made us kin. The easiest way for you to understand it is...we're family now."

"What?" I nearly yelled. "What are you talking about? That sigil was meant to break our bond, not turn you into my creepy uncle."

"I prefer wiser and venerated older brother," Acheron said, pushing up his glasses. "I am older than you by a significant number of centuries."

"When I find Gryn, I'm going to hurt that old man."

"It was a smart—if dangerous—ploy," Acheron said, strapping in. "The *Majoras* could sense you were my kin. It was the only thing that allowed me to bluff our way out of there. Besides, I couldn't abandon my little sister, now could I?"

"Little sister? First and last time," I menaced as he put his hands up in surrender. "How did you know I was Darkin?"

"Your energy signature is different now, elevated. The only logical conclusion was a transformation to Darkin."

"What if Balorous had called your bluff?"

"We wouldn't be having this conversation," Acheron said,

his voice grim as he looked out of the window. "We'd be fighting for our lives this very moment, and losing."

"Shit," I said, slowly shaking my head. "I can't believe Rodrigo is involved in this."

"You have deeper concerns," Acheron said as I started Eight with a loud rumble that quickly became a growling purr. "By becoming my kin, you are officially a demon now."

"I'm not a demon."

"Semantics," Acheron said, shaking his head. "It doesn't matter that you are Otherkin or Darkin. To the Seven, the OSA, and the Black Cleavers, you are now enemy number one."

"Me against all of them?" I asked, keeping my voice low. "That's...I don't know—"

"Us," Acheron said. "It's *us* against all of them. I almost pity them...almost. Now, take us to Fongs. I'm absolutely famished."

"Fongs sounds perfect."

"Yes...yes it does."

I strapped in and crushed the accelerator.

THE END

THEY KILL
BOOK THREE

ABOUT THE STORY

When monsters come hunting...she will be their nightmare.

When Nyxia White transforms, she realizes she possesses a fearsome weapon and the power of the Darkin.

A power that threatens her enemies and makes her a target.

After rescuing Acheron, she understands her problems have only just begun. Someone wants them both dead and will tear their world apart to do it.

She must learn to control her new power in time, before the forces rising against her attack. Together, they must face overwhelming odds and confront a sorcerous enemy that believes the only good Darkin is a dead Darkin.

"What hurts you, blesses you. Darkness is your candle."
—Rumi

ONE

"They all die," I said. "Starting with Rodrigo."

"Ambitious, but suicidal," Acheron answered without looking up from his bowl. "This is absolutely delicious; you should try some. It's not really *that* hot."

He gently pushed a small bowl in my direction. It was full of Fong's famous Death Noodles, at least that's what I called them. They were officially known as something innocent, like Fong's Family Sweet and Spicy Noodles. The sweet part was absent, and the spicy was dialed up to over nine thousand. They were so spicy that they came with a warning.

"I'm not in the mood to incinerate my mouth, thanks."

"I'd like to test a theory," Acheron said. "Indulge me."

I grabbed one of the available forks; I wasn't going to use the chopsticks. The last time I had tried that, I had nearly skewered Acheron in the eye. I twirled the fork into the noodles. I marveled at how it retained its fork shape and resisted melting into some formless metal slag.

Yes, the noodles were *that* hot.

I placed the forkful warily in my mouth and, planning the

route to the bar for the special Extinguisher drink Fong's provided to those who chose to take their lives into their own mouths by trying the Death Noodles, braced for oral destruction.

Nothing happened.

"What the hell?" I asked, confused. "Why isn't my tongue melting?"

"You've been fundamentally changed," Acheron said, dabbing the side of his mouth with his napkin. "Your physiology has been altered."

"More than before?"

"Yes," Acheron said, and took another forkful from his own bowl while pushing the other bowl closer to me. "You transitioned into a Darkin, and then later, with the blood sigil Gryn gave you, into something more. I'd hazard you are more demon now than human. I'd say full demon, but I'd hate to insult demon kind."

"You have got to be kidding, right?" I asked, suddenly aware of the new guests arriving in pairs. They smelled like Black Cleavers. "Is there any way to reverse the blood sigil?"

"Of course," Acheron said, still focused on his bowl. "Death is usually the preferred method. It's direct, effective, and quite final."

"I meant other than death."

"Ah, no," Acheron said, with a slight nod as he glanced to the side. "I'm afraid I'm stuck with you being related to me. I may never live down the ignominy. I'm a Demon Lord, you know. Certain standards must be upheld."

"That's what you're concerned about? Your demon rep?"

"I'm not just *any* demon, I'll have you know," Acheron said, finishing his bowl of noodles. "I possess a certain standing in the demon community. This blemish will not be easily erased."

"Did you just call me a blemish?" I asked, glaring at him.

"Only in the best way possible," Acheron answered, dabbing the side of his mouth again. "Think of it as a term of endearment. Would you prefer stain? I do think stain is more appropriate. Our recently formed kinship is a stain I won't easily live down or wash away."

"A stain?" I said under my breath. "You're lucky I didn't let them rend your demon ass."

"This is precisely my point," Acheron answered. "I will have to educate you on the proper Demon Lord standards of conduct. This language of yours is completely inappropriate, considering the context of our present situation. Respectful deference to your elder demon kin"—he pointed to himself—"would be the better, and expected, course of action."

"I'm going to uphold your demon standards in a second, with a fist to your face," I said, noticing more suspicious guests arrive. "You seem to be attracting attention."

"You wouldn't hit a demon with glasses, would you?" Acheron asked, pushing his glasses up on the bridge of his nose. "These aren't inexpensive, you know."

"Why do you even wear those things? You have perfect vision, day or night."

"It allows me to hide in plain sight. It's my Clark Kent effect."

"Your what?"

"My Clark Kent effect," Acheron said. "Are you unfamiliar with the character?"

"Of course I know who he is," I said. "What does this have to do with you?"

"The Kent Effect, as I like to call it, is the ability to blend into your surroundings by playing on the expected and preconceived notions of what society deems to be reality."

"In English, please," I said. "So far, all I got is that you want to blend in."

"Exactly," Acheron said, raising a finger. "Kent blends in

by donning a pair of glasses, changing his posture, and adopting a meek demeanor, thus completely obfuscating his true identity."

"So, what you're saying is that secretly you're a super demon?"

"What I'm saying is that by wearing glasses and dressing in the manner of a college professor, my identity as a Demon Lord is safely kept from the populace," Acheron said. "What respectable Demon Lord would ever wear glasses? Even though,"—he tapped the side of his glasses—"I must admit, this pair makes me look dashing."

"I don't know *any* respectable Demon Lords, present company included," I said. "All that being said, it doesn't seem like your disguise is working on our new guests."

"What makes you think they are here for me?" Acheron asked. "They seem to be paying you an inordinate amount of indirect attention, and failing spectacularly at their attempts at subtlety."

He was right. The Cleavers kept glancing at our table, their looks lingering a little too long on me to be a coincidence.

"It would seem a surprise inspection is in order," Acheron mused.

"You better let Dan know," I said, trying my best not to stare back—yet. No point in scaring them off. "It doesn't matter who they're here for. I don't think these new patrons are here to enjoy the Death Noodles."

"Indeed," Acheron said, raising a finger to get the attention of one of the waiters. "Perhaps these fans of yours just want to talk? Maybe a profound conversation on your new demon status?"

"Fans of mine?" I shot back under my breath. "I'm not the demon here—"

"Pardon?" Acheron interrupted. "That almost sounded like present tense."

The waiter came over to the table. He gave us a smile, along with a slight bow, then pulled out a small notebook.

"Anything else, sir?" the waiter asked. "Are the noodles to your satisfaction?"

"Delectable, as always, Charles," Acheron said. "Could I request a word with Dan?"

Charles' face dropped, no doubt afraid that he had committed the cardinal sin of providing poor service. Acheron knew all of the staff by name. He was considered their most important guest, with a reserved corner table in full view of the entrance and what appeared to be an unlimited tab.

We would often get our food served by Fong personally, which spoke to the esteem Acheron was held in. Fong's was bustling at every hour of the day. To have the owner serve us personally meant he had to step away from all of his other business to take care of us.

The rumor was that Acheron had saved Fong's life years ago, then provided the seed capital to help him start the restaurant, but remained a silent partner, never taking an interest in the business, just the food.

It was possible. I knew Acheron was well off, although I didn't where his money came from, or why he would invest in a restaurant. What I did know is that he loved Fong's Noodles.

"Sir? Are you sure?" Charles asked nervously. "Was there something else you needed? Mr. Fong is very busy at the moment. Is it possible I could assist you?"

"Certainly, Charles," Acheron said, with a small smile; his voice gentle, like a dagger pushed into your side. "You can assist me by informing Dan I need to see him—now."

"Yes, sir," Charles said, nodding quickly. "I will let him know."

He walked away quickly.

"You could have let him know he provided great service," I said. "Now he thinks he failed in some way. Dan will have to talk him out of quitting."

"Charles can't quit," Acheron answered, folding his napkin and placing it on the table just so. "He's part of the family. In fact, all of the staff here are related to Fong in some way. I will make sure his exemplary service is noted."

A few minutes later, after more pairs of Cleavers filled the restaurant, Fong arrived at the table with Charles in tow.

"Ah, Acheron," Fong said with a deep bow. "Is something wrong?"—he glanced sidelong at Charles—"I am sure that whatever it is, we can fix it."

"Nothing is wrong, my friend," Acheron said, looking at Charles. "Charles was the consummate professional. Thank you for your outstanding service, Charles."

Charles bowed deeply, and let out a short sigh of what I imagined was relief.

"It seems you have a vermin problem," I said, keeping my voice down and looking across the floor at the Cleavers. "Large, disgusting vermin."

"I'll have you know, we are impeccable in how we conduct business," Fong said, insulted. "Especially the cleanliness of our establishment. We have no vermin on the premises."

"Even so," Acheron said, motioning with his chin to the Cleavers, "I do fear, my friend that you may need to conduct a surprise inspection."

Fong turned slowly, and casually looked around the restaurant, waving and smiling to some of the guests. When he turned back, his expression was dark.

"I understand," Fong said stepping close to Charles and

whispering something in his ear, too quiet for me to make out, before focusing on Acheron again. "How long?"

"I'd say we have ten to twenty minutes before they feel brave enough to approach," Acheron said. "In the meantime, one more bowl, for each of us, before pain starts. Please make mine extra spicy."

"For both of you?" Fong said, looking at me. "Are you certain, Miss? Last time..."

"I know," I said, raising a hand. "I'll pass. I don't want to push my luck."

Fong nodded to Charles, who hurried off to spread the word to the staff and to bring Acheron another bowl.

"Do you need assistance?" Fong asked. "I can stay and—"

"No," Acheron said, his voice a guillotine, cutting off any further suggestion of Fong's assistance. "Your skills are needed in the kitchen. Remember our agreement."

"I will never forget it," Fong said. "We will conduct the inspection now. Please be careful."

"I shall," Acheron said. "Besides, they aren't here for me"—he motioned to me with his fork—"they're here for her. It seems she's making friends in all the low places."

"These are bad men," Fong said, looking at me and keeping his voice low as Charles brought another bowl of Death Noodles to the table. "They are dangerous."

"I know," I said. "I promise not to break too much of the place."

"That is no problem," Fong said, glancing at Acheron. "We have all kinds of insurance. Make sure they don't break you."

"I'll make sure," I said. "Thank you."

Fong bowed again to both of us and hurried off with Charles. I could see the other waiters speaking to the patrons and packing food. They avoided the Black Cleavers as they weaved through the tables, clearing out the restaurant.

"Extra spicy?" I asked incredulously, as I examined his bowl of noodlebliteration. I marveled at how the bowl remained intact. The noodles were just this side of lava red and looked lethal to touch, much less eat. "How spicy is extra spicy?"

"Fong has a special batch of Carolina Reapers in the warehouse," Acheron said, gesturing to the bowl of death. "These approach an average of two million Scoville Heat Units."

"Is that even legal?" I asked. "That sounds a last meal type of spicy. As in eating them means it's your last meal—ever."

"They are painfully intense," Acheron said, with a smile. "You should try some."

"No, thanks," I answered. "I make it a policy to stay away from any food actively trying to reap me."

"Your loss," Acheron said, nodding as the restaurant emptied. "In a moment, your fans will know we are aware of their presence."

"How did you ever manage to have this arrangement?" I asked, looking around with a mild sense of shock at the efficiency of the 'surprise inspection'. "This has to be one of the busiest restaurants in the city, if not the busiest. Yet Fong manages to clear it out in minutes."

Acheron glanced around and nodded, his mouth full. He took a few moments to chew and savor before answering.

"The last time I was attacked in here, it ended badly," Acheron said, enjoying his second bowl of culinary death. "Lives were lost, and I had to forcibly remove the threat. I promised Fong that would be the last time, thus the surprise inspection was created."

"That explains the staff, it doesn't explain the patrons."

"The clientele that frequents this fine establishment does so with the awareness of the danger," Acheron said. "I dare say, it adds to the cachet. They dine here with the understanding that they may be required to exit the premises at a moment's notice. Quite exciting, I think."

"It's only exciting if they avoid becoming collateral damage," I said. "These Cleavers are looking twitchy."

"I do hope they have the decency to wait until I'm done. These noodles are simply awe-inspiring. You really should have gone for the second bowl."

"Pass," I said, eyeing the Cleavers in the room. I counted ten low-level sorcerers and one mid-level potential threat. That must have been the leader. "How did they even know we were here?"

"Perhaps you're getting predictable in your old age," Acheron said. "I hear complacency is the first step toward extinction."

"This is *your* favorite place, not mine," I said with a low growl. "If anyone is getting old and slow, it's a certain Demon Lord I had to rescue recently."

"As your newly appointed elder demon kin, I object to the insinuation and your tone," Acheron replied. "Haven't you been taught to respect your elders? For the record, you didn't *rescue* me, you facilitated an extraction, one I was in the midst of executing when you arrived."

"The only thing about to be executed was you," I hissed, picking up the movement in my peripheral vision. "Oh, look, we have a contender."

One of the Cleavers approached our table. I suppose it was better than encountering the OSA. The Order of Supernatural Affairs would have just started flinging orbs of energy in our direction, obliterating the restaurant. Many of the patrons would have been caught in the attack, becoming needless collateral damage.

Things would've gotten bloody, and the body count would've been unacceptable. The Cleavers may have been bright as bricks, but they preferred to be in the shadows, not attracting attention. The OSA counted on the strength of the Order to act with impunity. They didn't care if they attracted attention.

In other words, they were gigantic assholes.

"Nyxia White," the lead Cleaver said. "We're here to take you in."

TWO

"Take me in where, exactly?" I asked, leaning back and giving Mr. Brave Cleaver the once-over. "I don't seem to recall hearing an invitation. What if I don't want to go wherever it is you want to take me?"

Judging from his expression, Brave Cleaver must have been unaccustomed to resistance. He looked from me to Acheron, who was still enjoying his noodles, and then back to me. His expression ran the gamut from surprised to shocked to angry in the space of a few seconds.

"Then we will take you by force," the Cleaver replied. "We're not scared of you or your second-rate demon. You come with us or you both die here."

Like I said, bright as bricks.

"It's been my experience," Acheron said in between forkfuls of noodles, "those that feel the need to inform others of their fearlessness are usually either filled with fear or about as intelligent as a slug. Which one is it for you?"

"You must be a special kind of stupid," I said before the Cleaver could answer. "I'm going to give you a chance to walk away with all your body parts attached while you still can. Take it."

"They told us you would be too scared to act," the Cleaver said with a smug look. "Surrender or die."

I pushed back from the table and eyed Acheron, who was still eating. He waved me on as he went about getting another forkful of noodles.

"There's only eleven of them," Acheron said. "I still have most of this bowl to finish. Fong's Noodles cannot be rushed, nor can they be left to grow cold. I'll join you as soon as I'm done—if any of them are left to pose a threat."

The Cleaver turned to face me.

"You think you can take on all of us—alone?" Brave Cleaver said with a sneer. "You must have inhaled too much demonflame." He glanced at Acheron. "Serves you right, hanging around demon filth."

"Right," I said, looking at the Cleaver. "What's your name, and how did you know we were here?"

"I don't give my name to demon scum, and we found you because you were sloppy," the Cleaver said. "They know where you are. They always know."

"It's so refreshing to see that the recruiting practices of the Cleavers have maintained such a low bar to clear," I said, stepping away from the table and extending my arms forward. "I'm going to call you Doe. You don't mind, do you?"

Doe produced a pair of large black restraints covered in sigils—demonic suppressors—that looked like the evil version of police handcuffs.

"I don't give a shit what you call me, trash," Doe said, approaching with the cuffs. "I'm here to take you in or put you down if you resist. Please resist."

I looked at Acheron.

"He did say *please*," Acheron said, glancing at Doe and

then refocusing on his bowl. "Don't kill him. We need to know who sent him and how they knew you were here."

The other ten Cleavers stood scattered around Fong's in pairs. As far as strategies went, it was laughably stupid. They should have approached us in a staggered formation with weapons and orbs drawn, using overwhelming force as a deterrent.

It wouldn't have worked, but it was better than standing around waiting to get picked off. I got the impression that whoever briefed this crew hadn't done their homework, or truly felt I wasn't much of a threat.

Either way, I felt insulted.

"Last chance to walk away," I said, stepping closer. "If you stay, you're going to die hard after you tell me everything you know."

"The way I see it"—Doe turned and nodded to the other Cleavers—"we have you out-numbered, and out-gunned. You don't get to negotiate. You get to die."

Doe went to place the suppressors on my wrists. I pulled my arms back, extended my claws and buried them in his abdomen, retracting them before he could take his next breath. I moved faster than his brain could process.

A look of shock crossed his face as he collapsed to his knees, dropping the suppressors and grabbing his midsection with a grunt.

"Kill…" Doe managed between gasps, tracing a sigil to stop the bleeding as he fell forward, "kill them."

I jumped to the side, as a barrage of red orbs headed my way.

THREE

I upended a nearby table into a makeshift shield.

I saw Acheron gesture, creating a shimmering barrier in front of him.

"Really?" I asked, as I ducked behind the table. "You're just going to sit there?"

"No, I'm also going to enjoy this delicious bowl of noodles *while* I sit here."

"You realize they're going to attack any second now?"

"No imminent danger," Acheron answered. "If you can't handle this group of cannon fodder, I may be forced to disavow you as my kin. Besides, I'm still eating. Do you expect me to interrupt my meal?"

"Yes, I do actually," I said. "If I go nuclear, they all die."

"You say that like it's a bad thing," Acheron said. "What do you think 'taking you in' means? They aren't planning a spa day for you."

Several of the red orbs missed me, sailing into the wall behind me. A few of them punched into the table, which didn't immediately shatter into pieces. I was amazed that the table had withstood the onslaught, then I noticed the softly glowing sigils inscribed on its surface.

"You had the tables inscribed? All of them?"

"Yes. Along with most of the items in the interior," Acheron said. "Fong didn't want to have to replace the furniture. I went to the added expense of making sure the defenses were sufficiently robust to prevent excessive destruction."

"Nice touch," I said. "Do you want to do your 'Demon Lord' thing and just scare them shitless? Would save me the trouble of shredding them."

"Not particularly," he said, pointing to his bowl of noodles. "I think they deserve a good shredding. If you can, do it without killing any of them. Think of how the word would spread. You would become notorious...and feared. Nyx—the Darkin Menace. Has a certain ring to it. An air of impending doom."

I answered with a scowl, and rolled away from the table. I knew he was right; I just didn't want to admit it. There was also the nagging question of how the Cleavers had found us. Either someone in Fong's informed them or we were somehow being tracked.

There was no way I could believe anyone in Fong's would betray our location. That left me with only one option: we were being tracked.

I ran to the closest pair of Cleavers who, surprisingly, were not overjoyed to see me closing in on their location. Black Cleavers were bold when they had the numbers, but cowered in direct confrontations.

Seeing the leader of their little group writhing on the floor in pain, unnerved most of them. The orbs they were launching my way were more a fear reflex than a concerted attack.

They were bullies. Worse, they were bullies with power,

who used that power to intimidate and hurt others. Acheron was right, they all deserved a good shredding, and I was in a shredding mood.

I extended my claws, and heard one of the Cleavers behind me let out a yell as he bolted for the door. I saw Acheron flick his wrist, sending an orb of demonflame to intercept the only smart Cleaver in the group.

The demonflame orb smacked the escaping Cleaver in the back of the head, lifting him off his feet and sending him face first into the still closed door. He was unconscious before he crumpled, noisily, to the ground in a heap.

I sliced through the closest Cleaver's leg, careful to leave it attached. These were foot soldiers of stupidity. They deserved to get beaten, repeatedly, but not death. He screamed and grabbed his thigh as he fell back. His partner, completely spooked, turned and ran.

I glanced at Acheron, raising my eyebrow and pointing with my chin to indicate the remaining Cleavers.

"Some assistance?"

"Fine," Acheron said with a small sigh. "Only because if I don't, they'll end up killing each other as they trip over themselves."

Acheron waved a hand and unleashed a small swarm of demonflame orbs. They sped across the floor faster than I could track, which, considering my heightened senses, was impressive.

Each of the orbs slammed into a Cleaver with force, bouncing them off the walls, counters and other assorted furniture. The furniture remained intact, the Cleavers; not so much.

With the exception of the leader I gutted, and the minion I sliced through, the rest of the Cleavers were in various states of unconsciousness—victims of Acheron's demonflame attack.

I walked over to where the groaning Doe writhed in pain and crouched down next to him. He scooted back, trying to get away from me.

"Who did you piss off?" I asked as Doe ran out of real estate and found himself up against a wall. "Who hates you to the point of sending you on a suicide mission?"

"What are you talking about?" Doe answered, trying to slide sideways along the wall away from me, and failing. "We have the authorization to apprehend you."

"Authorization?" I asked, somewhat surprised. "Who gave you this authorization?"

"I don't know," Doe admitted. "We were contacted and given instructions."

"Stop squirming, or you're going to bleed out. That sigil you cast isn't going to save you. Now sit still."

Doe sat still.

"You stay away from me," he said with a tremble in his voice. "Stay away."

"Trust me, there is nothing more I would prefer than to stay away from you Cleavers," I said. "Who briefed you on this op? Who gave you the information we were here?"

"OSA. They said that you were a dangerous threat and needed to be apprehended."

"Well, they were right on that," Acheron said. "You are a dangerous threat."

I glared at Acheron, who shrugged in response.

"The OSA would never stoop so low as to use Cleavers for their dirty work," I said. "Not when they enjoy it so much. Someone lied to you."

"They said they were OSA and had the credentials," Doe said, still trying to slide away. "They had the sigils—I saw them."

"I seriously doubt Flint sanctioned this."

Doe's eyes grew wide at the mention of the Black Cleaver leader's name.

"How...how do you know about Flint?"

"Focus," I said, turning to glance sidelong at Acheron. "Can you seal this wound? Before he kills himself?"

"You mean the wound you inflicted by burying your claws in his abdomen? That wound?"

"Yes, *that* wound," I said. "Preferably before he spills his guts all over the floor."

"I thought that was the point of the impaling followed by questions?"

"The goal is information, not viscera," I snapped. "Can you close him up?"

"I can, but the question is, do I want to?" Acheron said. "It would be simpler to remove his head and call it a night."

Doe visibly paled at Acheron's words.

"We need information," I said. "He may have something we can use."

"I highly doubt it," Acheron said. "This is a ploy. Someone expected you to tear through these expendables. Death by proxy."

"Someone wanted you dead, and they wanted me to do the killing...why?"

"I don't know what you're talking about," Doe said. "We got a tip that you would be here. They instructed us to bring you in, and said we would be compensated for your successful apprehension...dead or alive."

"And you thought, what?" I asked, amazed at the level of sheer ignorance. "I would just cooperate?"

"Well, yes," Doe said after a brief pause. "There's eleven of us and only one"—he glanced over at Acheron—"two of you. We have the greater numbers and firepower."

I glanced around Fong's at the unconscious Cleavers tossed around the floor.

"Not so much," I said. "Now listen closely. You're going to let my partner seal that wound—"

"He's a demon," Doe spat. "I'd rather eat a bullet."

"That can be arranged," Acheron said, stepping over to where I stood. "It would certainly be more efficient."

"You will *not* eat a bullet," I said. "You *will* let my partner heal you, and then you will take your sorry asses and get out of this restaurant before I decide you're better off as fertilizer"—I extended one claw and placed the tip of it under Doe's chin—"am I being clear?"

Doe's pupils increased in size and I heard his heart rate double.

"Yes, I understand," Doe said, as the rest of the Cleavers slowly regained consciousness around us. "This means nothing, though. You're still filth. We will hunt you down and take you out."

I retracted my claw and slowly shook my head, stepping back to give Acheron some room to operate.

"You're only breathing because he was having dinner"—I glanced at Acheron—"and I don't feel like cleaning up a bloody mess of Cleaver bits. But keep talking, you're changing my mind."

Acheron moved close to Doe.

"It would be wiser to refrain from threats and insults until after the 'filth' that's going to heal you, does so," Acheron said, tracing a sigil over Doe's wound. "Once you're well, feel free to come after us. I promise you"—Acheron lowered his voice—"the next time we meet, I won't be so cordial."

Acheron placed a hand on Doe. It began to give off a deep orange glow, mingling with the violet light that came from the sigil he had traced. Moments later, I could see the wound was gone.

Doe looked down in amazement.

"How did you?" he started. "That's impossible."

"Go. Now," I said. "The next time I see you, or any Black Cleaver, blood will be spilled."

"Count on it," Doe said, getting unsteadily to his feet. The rest of the Cleavers were making their way to the exit. "I do recall one thing, and I'll tell you because you can't do anything to prevent what's coming for you."

"Illuminate us," Acheron said. "I wait with bated breath."

"That OSA call we got, They didn't tell us how to find you specifically, they mentioned your vehicle," Doe said, removing a small, flat, rectangular stone from his pocket and tossing it on the floor. "They gave us that; it's how we found you."

Acheron picked up the stone and held it between his thumb and index finger. A blue sigil glowed on both sides of the stone.

"What the hell is that?" I asked. "What is that sigil?"

"This is not from hell," Acheron said, "trust me."Acheron looked at Doe. "How did you obtain this?"

"Courier package along with a burner phone," Doe said. "I wouldn't be worrying about Black Cleavers if I was you. We may have been played, but someone with influence is running this game, and you're on the losing side."

Doe and the rest of the Cleavers stumbled out of Fong's.

FOUR

"What is it?" I asked, looking at the stone. "I've never seen that sigil before."

"Your knowledge of sigils is underwhelming, at best," Acheron said, his expression concerned. "This is known as a tracker stone. The sigil inscribed on it acts as a tether—it's attuned to a specific energy signature."

"A tracker?"

"It's tethered to a specific energy signature and with the right cast you can follow the tether," Acheron said. "This appears to be a short-range tracker."

Acheron traced the sigil from the stone in the air. A thin beam of blue energy shot out from the stone and led outside.

"He said they mentioned Eight, not me," I said. "Do you think...?"

"I do, indeed," Acheron said, "but there's only one way to make sure."

Fong and some of the staff came in as I straightened out the table. He surveyed the interior and started directing the clean up.

"Thank you for not destroying the restaurant," Fong said

with a short bow. "We should be able to meet the dinner rush. Would you like some noodles to go?"

"No, thank you, my friend," Acheron said. "Two bowls of extra spicy deliciousness is enough for the evening. You may, however, reconsider conducting business tonight."

"Are we in danger?" Fong asked. "Will they be coming back?"

"Unlikely, but you can never be sure," Acheron said. "Discretion is the better part of valor."

"Yes," Fong said with a nod. "But when you are accustomed to grabbing a tiger by the tail, you learn to expect the fangs. We will be careful. We are not entirely defenseless. You have seen to that."

Acheron nodded.

"True, the defenses withstood most of the damage," Acheron said. "We have other business elsewhere tonight. Be vigilant."

Fong nodded as we headed for the door. Once we were outside, I saw the thin beam of blue energy connect to the underside of Eight.

"Shit, seriously?" I asked, scanning the area outside of Fong's. "This tether is visible?"

"Apparently so," Acheron said. "It would seem that whoever inscribed the sigils on Eight placed a special symbol to allow your vehicle to be tracked."

"Rodrigo," I said, seething. "He was the one who inscribed Eight."

"It would seem this symbol was some kind of insurance," Acheron said. "Something placed to know where you were at all times, or at least your vehicle."

"He knows I don't go anywhere without using Eight," I said as the anger simmered over into a slow, churning rage. "I need to know if Rodrigo did this by himself, or if Vic gave the order."

"Does it make a difference?"

"Yes, it does," I said. "It helps me decide if I'm adding Vic to the victim list."

"Even with your Darkin abilities, I strongly advise against confronting Victoria," Acheron warned. "Her position as leader of the Seven is not an accident, nor the result of some equitable hiring practice. She killed her way into that position. I'm certain she would kill to remain in it."

"If she sanctioned your kidnapping, she's looking at early retirement," I said, my voice low. "I need to talk to her."

"I'm going to reluctantly decline another visit to the Seven HQ," Acheron said. "The last visit resulted in an unpleasant detour."

"This time she comes to us," I said, keeping my rage in check. "We'll use the neutral hub."

"Grand Central?" Acheron asked. "Large enough to be fairly safe. Not even the Seven would launch an attack on neutral ground. It would create too many ripples in all the wrong ponds."

"Grand Central works," I said. "Let's go see if Liv can do something about the sigil on Eight. I don't like the idea of being tracked."

"Ahh, a visit to Liv," Acheron said, his voice suddenly husky. "First Fong's, now Liv. My favorite hungers will be satiated. This evening gets better by the second."

"First, ew, and second, TMI. The evening will get better when we get rid of this tether thing," I said. "Liv is strictly business, she is not there to sate any of your hungers."

"Fong's and a femme fatale," Acheron said. "You just described my near perfect evening."

"Do I really want to know what would make it perfect?"

"Fong's, femme, and fear," Acheron said with a wicked smile. "The trifecta of perfection. I'm sure Liv would be willing to oblige, if I gave her the right incentives."

"You are a sick puppy, and she's celibate," I said, shaking my head. "Is there any way to mask this tether thing? I don't feel like being followed."

"I can mask it temporarily, but we can't go to the Grimoire at this hour," Acheron said, crouching and looking under Eight. "Liv will not accept visitors this late."

"Even you?" I asked. "She won't make an exception for her favorite Demon Lord?"

"Astounding as it may sound, no, she won't," Acheron motioned for me to back up. "It's a security measure. Too many valuable artifacts in the Grimoire and too many creatures of the night who would find it irresistible. Much like Liv herself. Now, back up."

"Why, you're just casting a mask?" I asked, confused. "You *are* just casting a mask, right?"

"It's too complex to explain," Acheron said, interlacing his fingers and extending his arms as he cracked his knuckles. " Explaining it to you would most likely do more harm than good."

"Do I look like I want a brain aneurysm? Just don't blow up Eight, I'm serious."

"As am I," he said. "You will need to move back a bit farther. I haven't cast a transportational mask in decades. They are quite volatile."

"Not exactly filled with confidence in your abilities here."

"Well, fortunately for me, my execution of casts doesn't rely on your assessment of my abilities," he said, crouching once again to look at where the tether ended. "Don't worry, I won't blow up your—"

"What's that sound?" I asked, looking into the sky and pointing north. "Over there."

"What sound?" Acheron said, looking where I pointed. "Perhaps you suffered a head injury during my extraction? I don't hear anything."

"I'm serious. That sounds like a—"

"Wait, I hear it now," he said, his expression darkening. "Curious, it sounds like a—move back!"

Acheron whirled on me and pushed.

His shove sent me sailing back, just as the blast the explosion engulfed him and Eight.

FIVE

I slammed into the nearby wall, leaving a Darkin-sized crater in the brick.

My claws were extended and scales covered my body. The scales probably saved me from major damage. I had never taken a rocket to the face—not the kind of thing I ever wanted to practice. I looked around for Acheron and saw him lying on the sidewalk next to Eight, that had somehow survived a direct rocket impact.

I made a mental note to thank Rodrigo for the sigils that kept Eight intact right before I eviscerated him. I ran over to Acheron as he got to his feet. I skidded to a stop a few feet away.

He was beyond pissed.

His vest was shredded, along with most of his clothing. The lenses of his glasses were shattered and his dress shirt was a tattered mess. One of the sleeves barely held on, the other had decided to leave his shirt entirely.

He ripped off the remaining sleeve as his body burst into demonflame.

"Acheron," I said, keeping my voice even. "Calm down."

"Calm down?" he said. "Do you see the state of my clothing? This is, was my favorite Burberry suit"—he looked down at his destroyed clothing—"ruined, absolutely ruined."

"We'll get you another suit," I said, looking around at the destroyed sidewalk. "But we can't do this here, too much collateral damage. That wasn't an orb. It was a rocket."

"I am well aware of what it was," he said, each word laced with anger. "I managed to receive the brunt of it, thank you very much."

He removed his glasses slowly and folded them, placing them inside the pocket of his vest.

"I know, and thanks for the shove, but you're not listening."

"I hear you perfectly," he said, turning north. "I'm going to make sure that whoever fired that rocket regrets it for the rest of their very short life."

"No," I said, my voice hard. "That's what they want. All that rocket did was ruin your clothing, Eight is still in one piece. So are we. What if the next rocket gets past us?"

I turned and looked at Fong's.

"That would be costly," Acheron said with a short nod. "What do you propose?"

"We ID the shooter, then deal with them later," I said. "Can you see them from here? My vision is good, but not that good."

"Your hearing has vastly improved," Acheron said, peering into the night. "You heard that rocket before I did. I'm sure your vision will improve as well. I have them. Bloody hell."

"What is it? Can you tell who it is?"

"Judging from the vehicle make and model, we're dealing with undercover OSA Agents and the Seven."

"Are you sure?"

"The vehicles are OSA issue for clandestine work. The

energy signatures are a mix of low-level Agents and Seven operatives. They are quite distinct."

"Rodrigo? Is he there?"

"No, but I know who fired the rocket. His energy signature is clear to me."

"Damn," I said, unlocking Eight, and jumping in, hitting the wheel with my palm. "If Rodrigo were there we could have—"

"Rushed into a gauntlet of armored vehicles and Agents possessing enough firepower to mow us down several times over," Acheron said without looking away. "You're right, a direct confrontation would be foolish."

"I don't understand," I said, "The Order and the Seven never work together."

The engine started with a roar.

"Naïveté will get you killed," Acheron said, strapping into his seat. "It would appear that they are aligned in bringing about your destruction."

"Shit, this is bad," I said. "Dealing with the OSA is a pain in the ass, but dealing with the Order *and* the Seven is going to be nearly impossible."

"Everyone dies, remember?" Acheron said. "They're just facilitating your mission."

"When I said everyone dies, I wasn't including us," I said, swerving around traffic. "This changes everything."

"I thought we were included, considering your driving skills," Acheron said. "Speaking of change, there is no way I'm going to see Liv dressed like this. I need a change of clothing."

"You want to stop and change? Now?"

"Yes, make a stop at the Tailors," Acheron said, grabbing the vehicle phone. "They never close. I'll ring him to let him know we are on our way."

SIX

The Tailor was an enigma.

No one really knew who, or more importantly, what he was. He kept a shop downtown near the South Street Seaport, away from the busier section of the tourist attraction.

It was an old warehouse located at 44 Fletcher Street that appeared to be abandoned, and for all intents and purposes was, unless you happened to belong to a select group of clientele.

Clientele like Acheron.

We arrived at the Tailor's ten minutes later, traffic being non-existent at this hour of the night. Fong's was located off Hudson Street, near Duane Street which usually made getting downtown a nightmare due to the traffic, except in the early hours when traffic wasn't an issue.

"Has anyone ever asked who the Tailor is?" I asked. "Or what, for that matter?"

"Of course," Acheron said, getting out of Eight. "They usually only ask once. Are you curious?"

"I was, but not anymore."

"Wise choice," Acheron said, walking up to a nondescript door. "Tailor doesn't like questions unless they have to deal with style, measurements, and material. Anything else is off-limits."

"Is Tailor his name or what he does?"

"Both," Acheron said. "Make sure you keep any questions focused on clothing and things of that sort."

"Why?" I asked. "I mean, I get that everyone has a past, but he provides a service."

"It's because of the service he provides," Acheron said. "He has a very diverse and discreet client list."

"The abandoned warehouse kind of gave it away." I looked up at the building. "Not exactly Madison Avenue."

"It's not supposed to be," Acheron said. "The clients who visit him could never go somewhere like Madison Avenue."

"At least not without causing a mass panic," I said. "Doesn't explain why he's so tight-lipped."

"Hypothetically, let's say the Order was looking for a particular person of interest—a rogue Darkin, for example, no one we know personally. Just some random Darkin, out causing havoc on the streets."

"Right, some random Darkin," I said. "Because Darkin are just roaming the streets these days."

Acheron nodded with a slight smile.

"The Order knows of Tailor's existence and they come knocking on his door," Acheron said, knocking on the door in a particular sequence. "They proceed to ask him if he has seen the Darkin in question. What do you suppose he will say?"

"He wouldn't," I said. "The Tailor only discusses style, measurements, and materials."

"Precisely," Acheron said, as the door opened inward. "Which is why everyone leaves him alone. His discretion is legendary; as is his wrath. Don't anger him."

"Anger him? How am I going to anger him?"

"With you, it usually starts when you open your mouth," Acheron said. "Have you ever considered a vow of silence? The city would be a more peaceful place. At the very least it would be quieter."

I glared at him, but remained silent as we crossed the threshold. We stepped into a dim waiting room furnished with a large, leather chaise on one side, and smaller chairs and tables on the other. Each of the small wooden tables held a small tray with cups. A large espresso machine sat on a long table, and the smell of rich, strong coffee filled the room, reminding me that I hadn't eaten much in the last few days.

A tall, thin, older man, impeccably dressed in a dark suit greeted us. He could have easily doubled as someone's idea of the typical butler, complete with the air of disdain for us lesser beings who were privileged to be in his presence. He raised an eyebrow as he gave Acheron the once over.

"Conventional or mystical?" Tailor asked, still examining Acheron. "This destruction looks conventional."

"Correct," Acheron said. "Blast force of a rocket at close range."

Tailor stepped closer to Acheron and pinched the material of Acheron's shirt, what was left of it, between two fingers.

"This material is not rated for heavy warfare," Tailor said after a moment. "Will sir be needing an upgrade in material?"

"That would be most helpful," Acheron said, glancing my way. "It would appear we've made some unpleasant enemies."

"When are enemies ever pleasant?" I asked.

"When they try to kill you like civilized beings," Acheron said. "Not like cowards with long range rockets."

"Burberry?" Tailor said with a slight accent. "Without the additional ventilation, I presume?"

"Yes," Acheron said. "I'm meeting with Liv Rei at the Grimoire. Something appropriate for the occasion."

"I see," Tailor said, tapping his chin with a finger. "Business or pleasure?"

"Business," I said. "There will be no pleasure tonight."

"Or ever, if you have anything to say about it," Acheron said, with a scowl. "Business, please."

"And for the miss?" Tailor asked, examining my combat armor. "Is this business storming a fortified encampment, or would you prefer something more respectable?"

I looked down at my combat armor. It was my turn to raise an eyebrow.

"This *is* my business attire. Do you want to know what business I'm in?"

"Not particularly," Tailor said with a sniff, unimpressed. "If the gentleman will follow me. The lady may join us if she feels so inclined, or she can wait here."

"I'm joining," I said. "You don't happen to carry large handguns, by any chance? You know, the type that can take down a *Majoras* or demons of similar size?"

Acheron gave me a look and shook his head as Tailor walked ahead of us.

"You could have waited out here," he said. "This is terribly boring."

"This is exciting; he's going to dress a Demon Lord," I said. "Can you ask him if he has Burberry in kevlar for you?"

"I will ask no such thing," Acheron said under his breath, indignant. "Tailor only provides the best materials. Burberry kevlar would be an insult."

"You'd think with an operation like this"—I looked around the space as we walked—"he could provide reinforced materials, considering his clientele isn't exactly the gentle type."

We crossed a few more rooms until we arrived at a large fitting area. I sat down in one of the large wingback chairs while Tailor escorted Acheron to a set of three mirrors resting on a raised platform.

He pulled out a measuring tape that gave off a subtle green glow as he took measurements. When he was done, he motioned for Acheron to enter a small closed off area to undress while he left the room.

A few minutes later, he returned with a large case and a dark suit. He handed the suit to Acheron, before walking over to where I sat.

He extended the case to me.

"I believe this is what you requested," Tailor said, pointing to the box in his best Vanna White impression. "If you would be so kind, I may have to adjust the fit."

"I told you, *this* is my business attire," I said, taking the case. "I don't need some fancy dress that's going to get destroyed."

"If I may be so bold," Tailor said. "Your *business* attire is lacking the necessary accessories. Please open the case."

I opened the case.

An enormous handcannon made of black metal gleamed in the dim light. Next to it, I saw a custom-made thigh holster designed to hold the gun, with a waist belt outfitted to carry extra magazines.

"Whoa," I said, surprised, removing the gun from the case. "She's beautiful."

"Her name is—?" Tailor said, waiting for me to respond.

I held the gun for a moment until the name came to me.

"Dark Justice," I said. "It's the only justice I know how to give."

"A fitting name," Tailor said with a curt nod. "Please stand."

I stood, and he fitted the thigh holster and waist belt around me in one smooth motion. He stepped back and motioned to me. I holstered Dark Justice.

The balance was perfect, with the weight of the weapon evenly distributed around my body. The gun itself was almost as long as my forearm, but rested easily on my thigh.

"It feels perfect," I said. "How did you...?"

"A shipment of additional ammunition will be sent to your address of record every week," Tailor said. "Please store this ammunition carefully. It is designed to deal with most threats."

"Most threats?"

"If you face a threat this weapon cannot deal with," Tailor said, "My suggestion would be to employ a swift retreat in order to preserve your life."

"Thanks for the advice," I said. "I'll keep that in mind."

I saw Acheron step out of the dressing area and onto the raised mirror platform.

"Please do so," Tailor said, turning toward Acheron. "You're done. Let me see the fit, if you please."

Acheron was wearing a black vest and pants ensemble with subtle silver accents. The vest material was covered in a black flame motif, that could only be seen when Acheron moved and the light hit it at the right angle.

The shirt was off-white, with a dark tie that complemented the vest perfectly. Tailor may have been a creepy butler, but he knew his clothes.

"You've outdone yourself, Tailor," Acheron said, reaching into his old vest and removing the glasses. "I'm afraid the lenses on these—"

Tailor reached into his suit and pulled out a small case, handing it to Acheron.

"The finishing touches," Tailor said. "Please try these on."

Acheron opened the case. Inside was a another pair of glasses, identical to the ones that were destroyed, and a silver pocket watch complete with chain.

"A pocket watch? Really?" I asked. "You do realize we have advanced a bit in timepieces."

"That is no ordinary pocket watch, any more than what you are holding in your hand is an ordinary gun," Tailor said, glancing at me then turning back to Acheron. "The usual method of payment?"

"Of course," Acheron said, placing the watch in the vest pocket and running the chain through the slot designed for that purpose. "Thank you again, Tailor. We'll be on our way now."

"Very well. It is always a pleasure," Tailor answered. "These garments, unlike your previous set, have been heavily inscribed. It may not be as effective as our Burberry Kevlar Collection"—Tailor glanced at me—"but it should protect you from conventional and unconventional attack."

"Once again, thank you," Acheron said, glaring at me. "*We* are appreciative of your splendid service."

I caught the glare and the hint.

"Yes, of course," I said. "Thank you. I don't know what to say."

"You've said plenty," Acheron said under his breath. "We will see ourselves out."

"I look forward to your next visit," Tailor said, leaving the room. "Please secure the door upon your exit."

Acheron remained silent until we were inside Eight.

"I think he likes me," I said, patting Dark Justice. "Did you see my gun?"

Acheron leaned back in his seat and sighed while pinching the bridge of his nose. He pushed up his glasses and stared at me.

"I don't know how he didn't blast you for that kevlar remark," Acheron said. "I've seen him unleash his fury for far smaller infractions. You, he gives a gun. Maybe he's lost his mind?"

"I'm special," I said. "He even let me name her."

"What, pray tell, did you name your gun?" Acheron asked. "Something atrocious, like Bloody Vengeance?"

"Her, the gun's a her."

"Of course it is, what did you name *her*?"

"Dark Justice."

"Apt," Acheron said with a nod. "Let's go see Liv. The mask on the vehicle will wear off in an hour or so, and then we will have unwanted stragglers following us."

"If they do," I said, patting Dark Justice again, "I'll introduce them to DJ, here."

"Does that thing even come with a silencer, or are you planning on notifying the entire city every time you discharge that handcannon?"

"Trust me," I said, starting Eight. "If I'm using Dark Justice, being quiet is going to be the least of our worries."

"I'll call Liv," Acheron said. "It's close enough to sunrise that she may agree to meet at the Grimoire."

"She's going to be blown away by your new look," I said, glancing at him with a grin. "She may even reconsider her vow."

Acheron glanced down at his new clothes.

"I have been known to break a heart or two, you know."

I laughed and then grew semi-serious.

"Liv is going to be more of a challenge, I think," I said, stepping on the gas and roaring away from Fletcher Street. "The clothes are sharp, but her wit is sharper. Besides, this is business, remember?"

"Business, yes," Acheron said. "Everyone dies, starting with Rodrigo."

"Exactly. Once I get things straight with Vic, it's time to unleash some justice...Dark Justice."

Acheron groaned and closed his eyes.

"This is going to be never-ending, isn't it?"

"I don't know what you're talking about," I said, accelerating Eight. "Today, the dawn is going to be bright, and the justice, well the justice is going to be dark."

He groaned again as I swerved around traffic and headed to the Grimoire.

SEVEN

"She agreed to open the Grimoire early for us," Acheron said. "We're to use the private entrance."

"That was nice of Liv," I said. "Maybe we could avoid Becca, for once."

"Unlikely," Acheron said, pulling down on his vest. "Becca is a guardian. They guard Liv constantly."

"I thought their focus was primarily the Grimoire," I said. "Not Liv."

"There is no Grimoire without Liv," Acheron said. "Frankly, I think Liv is perfectly capable of defending herself, but having a handful of guardians on the premises must make life relatively easier."

"I disagree," I said, parking in front of the Grimoire. "If you need to have five guardians around you at all times, either you've attracted the wrong kind of attention, or you're surrounded by dangerous artifacts."

"I'll take your word for it," Acheron said, getting out of Eight. "After all, you started the day dodging rockets, which clearly denotes your adept attention getting, and currently you are in possession of an ancient demonic artifact. I'd say that makes you an expert in these matters."

"Does that make you my Demon Lord guardian?"

"My presence around you makes me question my sanity," Acheron replied, as we made our way through the small park that led to the Grimoire's private entrance. "The intelligent course of action would be to put as much distance between us as possible."

I stopped walking.

"Why didn't you?" I asked. "It's not like we're bound any longer. You could just walk away and roam the earth."

"I could," Acheron said, turning to face me. "I don't for several reasons."

"Which are? My charming personality?"

"If you are now cataloguing homicidal tendencies with a dash of sociopathy as charming, then yes," Acheron said. "The thought of you alone in this city, makes me fear for its continued existence. Besides, thanks to Gryn and his blood sigil, we are now kin. One does not abandon kin—ever."

"Like I said, my charming personality," I said, as we continued walking. "Oh, look it's Becca."

Standing in front of the private entrance was a six foot tall threat of controlled destruction. Becca's black hair was pulled back in a long, tight braid, contrasting starkly against her pale skin. Today she was dressed in black combat armor similar to mine. Her violet eyes shone with latent power, her gaze focusing on Dark Justice as we approached.

"Nice hardware," Becca said, staring into my eyes. "It stays holstered while on the premises. Understood?"

"Completely," Acheron said, before I could add something about how my Dark Justice will only come out when it's needed most. "*All* weapons will remain holstered."

I nodded, because I didn't trust myself and I needed to see Liv and get the tether removed. I made a mental note to work on my Dark Justicisms, especially for moments like these.

We stepped into the Grimoire, and Liv greeted us with a smile. She was dangerous most of the time, but as a retired succubus, her smile had enough wattage to power a small city.

She wore a short black dress that showed off all her curves without revealing any of them, her auburn hair hung loose, framing her pale face. Her eyes, similar to Becca's, radiated a soft violet light, with the only difference being that Liv's irises were actually violet—a rare trait.

Acheron wasn't joking when he referred to Liv as a femme fatale. Aside from her obvious and over-the-top beauty, Liv radiated real power.

The kind of real power that killed you.

Liv was beyond beautiful. She was nearly perfect, which was the first red flag if you were paying attention. That whole saying about something looking too good to be true applied here.

The truth was that by the time your brain got the memo, it was too late. Liv was lethal, and I was doubly glad for her vow of celibacy and neutrality.

She was, literally, deathly beautiful.

I heard Acheron gasp and glared at him.

"Not my fault," he muttered. "Do you see her?"

"Of course I see her, can you keep it under control?" I asked. "Did you forget why we're here? Rocket to the face? Ring any bells?"

Acheron composed himself.

"I am in complete control," he said, without looking at me. "We are here to conduct business, starting with the black dress...tether. I meant tether."

"You're hopeless," I said, moving past him. "Good morning, Liv."

"Good morning, Nyx," Liv said, and then dropped her

voice several levels into Ultra Husky. "Good morning, Acheron."

Another ten-thousand watt smile blinded Acheron, and I knew by this time he had lost all capacity to form thoughts, much less coherent sentences. By this point, I was getting the impression Liv was being cruel, intentional or not. I took it upon myself to save Acheron from himself.

"I was just thinking," I said. "That vow of celibacy, is it still in effect?"

All the sexiness left the room in a hurry.

"Yes," Liv said, dryly. "It's still in effect. Why do you ask?"

"No reason," I glanced over at the slowly recovering Acheron. "Just wondering if your vow allows wiggle room for Demon Lord seduction."

Liv narrowed her eyes at me and nodded.

I returned the stare and let her know, *do not toy with my kin*. I wasn't in the habit of shutting down Acheron's love life. He was a Demon Lord and I...well, I was some kind of demon mix. He could be with whomever or whatever he wanted, but not like this.

It felt wrong.

I didn't know if he had love interests in hell, and I didn't care, but I wasn't going to let him get seduced into stupidity by a succubus—a demon whose sole purpose is seduction.

Acheron snapped out of it and cleared his throat.

"Pardon, it would seem I was taken aback by your beauty this morning, Liv," Acheron said. "You look stunning, as usual."

"Thank you," she answered with a low powered smile this time. "You're too kind. You called about something urgent?"

The private entrance led to a smaller room in the Grimoire. It was as secure as the rest of the space, with subtly glowing sigils inscribed in the walls. This room, however, was reserved for private meetings between Liv and select clients.

There were no books or artifacts in this room. It had a large oak desk and several comfortable chairs for guests. The furniture was minimal, but sturdy.

"We need to break a tether," I said. "A powerful one."

"Do you know who created this tether?"

"Not for sure, but I think it was Rodrigo."

"Rodrigo, the sigilsmith from the Seven?" Liv asked. "That Rodrigo?"

"Yes," I said. "That bastard."

"Impossible," Liv said, shaking her head. "The reason he's a sigilsmith, and not a sigil apprentice, is because he possesses enormous skill."

It was Acheron's turn to narrow his eyes.

"You are a *sigilmaster*, are you not?" he asked. "Surely that denotes considerable skill. Even comparable to a sigilsmith?"

Surprise flitted across Liv's face, but she regained her composure almost instantly.

"How do you know that?"

"I hear things," Acheron said, waving a hand. "Rumors here and there."

"Those rumors are unfounded," Liv said, giving nothing away. "Undoing a sigilsmith's work is deadly."

"Which is why we are here," I said. "You were the first one we thought of."

I left out that she was the *only* one we thought of. We didn't have many options. Any of the sorcerers we could've approached would refuse for several reasons.

No one wanted to get on the wrong side of the Seven. I was so far over on the wrong side, I was practically right. Liv also made a good point; no sorcerer in their right mind would tangle with a tether created by a sigilsmith. It required a high level of skill and competency with an ample dose of insanity.

Liv fit all of the criteria.

In addition, she ran and owned the Grimoire. In essence,

she was untouchable. No one dared attack Liv. Not even the Seven wanted that fight, and if they tried, it would go badly for them.

Acheron handed Liv the stone. The glowing blue sigils on its surface were currently dormant. I figured it meant the mask was still intact.

"What is this tethered to?" Liv asked, holding the stone in her palm. "One of you?"

"No, to my vehicle, Eight."

"The solution is simple, then," Liv said, placing the stone on her desk. "Get rid of the vehicle. Drive it into the river and abandon it."

"Not an option," I said. "They took everything else from me, they aren't taking Eight."

Liv looked over at Acheron, who shook his head.

"Not negotiable," he said. "The tether must be undone."

"Undoing this tether will alert its creator," Liv said after a moment, picking up the stone again. "Whoever made it will know the moment its undone."

"I'm counting on it, that's why I want you to undo the tether two nights from now."

Both Liv and Acheron looked at me.

"Two nights from now?" Liv asked. "Why?"

"At this location," I said, writing down an address on a pad. "Can you do it?"

"Yes, yes I can do it, at great personal risk," Liv said, looking down at the address. "What I don't see is any incentive to anger the Seven."

"I was recently abducted and nearly subjected to a rending," Acheron said, his voice cold. "Many of those responsible have been dealt with, however, this happened on my most recent visit to the Seven HQ. This tether was instrumental in providing them with information as to our whereabouts."

Liv's face darkened and the energy of the room shifted. I

made a mental note to never, ever piss her off. Whatever reluctance she felt evaporated. I don't know if it was a demon solidarity thing, or she really cared for Acheron. What I did know was that she was now determined.

"What time?" Liv asked.

"Midnight, two nights from now," I said. "I have one more meeting to get things straight, then Rodrigo and I will settle this."

"Can you enhance my mask?" Acheron asked. "I don't think it will last another two days."

Liv took the stone between her thumb and forefinger. She whispered something under her breath and traced a sigil on the stone itself.

"I've modified your mask," Liv said. "The tether will seem to be active, but if another tracker stone is activated it will point to various locations throughout the city, misleading whomever is searching for you."

"That works," I said. "Like hiding in plain sight."

"It won't hide your vehicle," Liv said. "If they see you—"

"Another rocket surprise, got it," I said. "Stay out of sight."

"Do I even want to know what a rocket surprise is?" Liv looked at Acheron. "They're using conventional weaponry. Do you remember the danger?"

"I do," Acheron said, his expression dark. "Two days. We will resolve this matter in two days."

"Or throw us into a war with the Seven," Liv said. "I am prepared for either outcome."

"If we do go to war, I plan to make it a short one."

"Your self-confidence is astounding," Liv said. "Will it be just the two of you against all of the Seven?"

"We can deal with them," I said. "They may have numbers—"

"And overwhelming firepower," Liv added. "Don't forget

the top-notch sorcerers as well. What exactly is it that you bring to this battle? Spunk?"

"Death," I said, serious. "I bring death."

"Well, I'm certainly convinced," Liv said. "I hope the death you're referring to isn't your own. Now take me to your vehicle."

"We're parked out front. Why do you need to see Eight?"

"I need to see the originating sigil," Liv said, walking away. "Give me a few minutes to change into something more practical for a vehicle inspection. Bring your vehicle around back, to the garage."

EIGHT

"I had no idea the Grimoire had a garage this large," I said, pulling up to the large space in the rear of the building. "What did she mean about the danger?"

"Some time back, before the Order was formed, groups of sorcerers began using conventional weapons to attack demons and supernatural beings."

"That seems counter-productive," I said. "That sort of weaponry has little to no effect on demons."

"They knew," Acheron said. "It was the optics. Demons were being blamed for the damage and, worse, for the loss of life."

"That's what they tried to do at Fong's," I said. "If we had stayed—"

"It was very likely the next rocket would have headed right into Fong's," Acheron said. "The defenses at Fong's are considerable, but the outcome would have been disastrous."

"We would have been held responsible," I said, pensively. "That's what they wanted with the Cleavers. If I had gone on a rampage and killed them—"

"The OSA, the Seven, and any other authorities that

govern supernatural activity would have appeared shortly thereafter to apprehend you or, at the very least, paint you as a menace to society."

"To be hunted down—"

"And destroyed," Acheron finished. "Do you understand now? You no longer work with the Seven."

"I need to call Vic."

"That will resolve nothing," Acheron said. "Let's pretend she doesn't know about any of this, and that would require an impressive suspension of disbelief. Do you think she's going to come to your aid? To our aid?"

He was right.

The last conversation I had with Victoria rushed into my memory:

"The Seven is not a charitable organization. You either have a use, or you don't. You're either an asset or a liability."

"What are you trying to say? Are you saying I'm a liability?"

"Partnering with a demon can be viewed as such. They are our enemies."

"Keep your friends close and your enemies closer?"

"Precisely. Every contingency is planned for, Nyx. This is The Seven. We don't like, or entertain surprises. You do good work, in spite of a demon partner, which we, which I, tolerate—within reason. I'd suggest you don't become a liability."

"Liabilities are removed, right?"

"Like the cancer that they are."

Liv appeared at the garage door in jeans and a black t-shirt. The new outfit did nothing to lessen the distraction she posed. She looked amazing in everything she wore.

I stepped out of Eight and approached her.

"Could you turn down the succubus a bit?" I said under my breath. "We both know he likes you, no need to pour salt on the wound."

She smiled.

It was one of those smiles that made you reassess how dangerous a person could be. She leaned in and whispered in my ear.

"Trust me," she said, keeping her voice low. "I'm not using any abilities. If I were, he would be mine right now."

"Shit, really?" I asked, surprised. "No abilities?"

She shook her head.

"None," Liv said, turning to Acheron. "Now, Acheron, can you show me where the originating sigil is. I need to see what I'm up against."

"Over here," Acheron said, crouching down near the rear of Eight. Liv got in close and I rolled my eyes so hard I nearly saw my brain. "Right here."

Liv moved to one side of the garage and grabbed a small dolly. She placed it on the floor and rolled under Eight. I stayed back, letting Acheron have his moment.

"Someone wants you dead," Liv said as she rolled out from under Eight and stood. "That's an ancient sigil of destruction, and it's primed."

"Primed?" I asked, taking a few steps back. "What do you mean, primed?"

"You're driving around in a bomb waiting for activation."

"Do you know what the catalyst would be?" Acheron asked. "What could prime it?"

"It could be anything with this kind of sigil, it's old and broad in application," Liv said. "They are primarily used to set traps on property. I've never seen it used on a vehicle this way."

"Can it be primed with a large dose of kinetic energy?"

"I suppose so, but that would require an incredible amount of force," Liv said. "You would need—"

"Something like a rocket?" I asked, knowing the answer. "Would that work?"

"Yes, actually," Liv said, turning to look at Eight again.

"Whoever attacked you this morning knew what they were doing. Neither of you were the targets"—she pointed at Eight—"your vehicle was."

"If it's primed, they plan to set it off."

"It's a devious, but effective setup," Liv said with a nod. "They wait until you are within a target of their choosing, set off the sigil, destroy you and their intended target. Two birds, one bomb."

"If this is Rodrigo, who does he think you will see?" Acheron asked, turning to me. "He thinks he knows you."

"He knows I take Eight everywhere."

"Granted, but given the current events, where does he *know* you're going to go?" Acheron asked. "You would go to this place without fail. Where and who?"

"I'd go see Vic," I said. "Shit, he wants to take out Vic?"

"It would seem like the ideal situation," Acheron said. "You arrange a meet. He knows you won't go to the Seven HQ, not after last time. Vic agrees to meet you. Once he knows she's near your vehicle, he finds a way to set it off."

"So, Rodrigo erases us and Vic and then what? He takes over the Seven?"

"I don't know," Acheron said. "I'm not that familiar with the inner workings of an organization that has gone through great pains to not exist, but it makes sense. If he removes Victoria, perhaps he can maneuver in the power vacuum her absence creates?"

"Plausible," Liv said. "All of the blame would fall upon Nyx and her demon partner, absolving Rodrigo of any guilt. He could even blame the sigils failing on Nyx's particular biochemistry if anyone were to investigate further."

"Fuck me," I said under my breath. "I knew he was an asshole, I just didn't think he was this much of one."

"It's elegant and simple, really," Liv said. "Even the attack this morning was designed to throw you off. You would drive away thinking you were lucky that the sigils held. How did you find out about the tracker stone?"

"Cleaver who should've been dead told us," I said. "If I had killed him—"

"Then you would have never discovered the tether," Liv said. "Whoever set this in motion would have eliminated you both."

"Can you remove the destructive aspect of the tether?" I asked. "Can you make it go off, but not explode?"

Liv looked at me as if I had asked her to burn her books.

"You don't know what you're asking," Liv said. "This isn't a conventional explosive device. I manipulate one part, it affects the whole. It's all connected."

"Can it be done?" I asked. "Or are you saying *you* can't do it, but someone else can?"

"This thing is set to detonate if it's undone," Liv said, glaring at me. "I can undo part of it, but we are going to need countermeasures."

"What kind of countermeasures?" I asked.

"The kind that require your vehicle to be sitting in the middle of a circle while I work," Liv said. "Something that can contain a detonation."

"How bad if it goes off?"

"Bad? Try horrific. The sigils on the chassis will act as force multipliers for the initial blast," Liv said. "Most of the chassis is inscribed, but the undercarriage isn't. Once detonated, all of the energy will travel upwards and outwards."

"Like a mushroom cloud?"

"Precisely like that," Liv said. "Anything and anyone within a square block of your vehicle will be disintegrated. Think mini-nuke, without the radiation."

"It's good to know your knowledge of sigils is so limited," Acheron said with a small smile. "Thank you for this."

"Don't thank me yet," Liv said. "Besides, my knowledge of

sigils is mostly hearsay and information I gather from the odd book here and there."

"Of course."

"Son of a bitch," I muttered. "He planned this."

"It would seem leaving an area of the vehicle uninscribed was some kind of contingency plan," Acheron said. "A method of neutralization of sorts. It would appear Rodrigo doesn't like you."

"Thanks for the tip, Captain Obvious," I growled. "What gave it away? Turning Eight into some kind of massive bomb, the rocket to my face this morning, or his general hatred of me?"

"I'd say all of the above," Acheron said. "But he seems particularly fixated on your elimination. Perhaps we can ask him why?"

"I'll make it a point to do that," I said. "Right after I bury my claws in his chest and remove his heart."

"May I suggest questioning before you remove his internal organs?" Acheron said. "I find conversation is easier while the victim is still alive."

"Well, if I don't contain this vehicle within a circle when I undo the sigil, I'm the one being neutralized," Liv said. "I suggest you leave your vehicle here. Take one of the Grimoire vehicles in exchange."

Liv pointed to the other vehicles in the garage.

"Are they inscribed?" I asked. "I seem to have a negative reaction on most vehicles and their internal working mechanisms."

"Hmm," Liv said, giving it thought. "Take that one"—she pointed to the far corner—"the cat should be sufficiently destruction proof."

I looked over to where she indicated and saw a blood red Dodge Challenger SRT Hellcat.

"Are you sure?" I asked. "It looks—"

"It will stop bullets and most small arms fire," Liv said. "It will not, however, stop rockets or any ordnance of that sort, so try to avoid exploding while driving it. Keys are on the wall."

Liv pointed to a large board holding sets of keys.

"Thank you," I said, taking the keys and heading over to the Hellcat. "I'll bring her back in one piece."

"Make sure you do," Liv said. "That's Becca's ride."

I stopped mid-stride.

"Maybe there's another vehicle?"

"There isn't," Liv said, shaking her head. "The sigils on your Eight are too complicated to duplicate in such a short time. Take the Hellcat and don't break it. All the vehicles technically belong to the Grimoire."

"Becca will not be pleased," Acheron said once we were in the Hellcat. "I know I wouldn't be."

"It's not like we have much of a choice," I said, starting the engine. "I need to contact Vic and set up a meet, ASAP. She needs to know what Rodrigo is up to."

"Indeed," Acheron said. "Preferably before she hunts us down."

I backed out of the garage and merged into traffic east, leaving the Grimoire and Eight behind.

NINE

"You need to come in before I bring you in," Victoria said. "You can even bring your demon."

"The last time I went to visit you, Acheron got kidnapped and I caught an orb to the face. Pass."

"Where are you? You're not calling from Eight."

"No I'm not," I said. "We need to meet."

"I just said that," Victoria snapped. "Where are—?"

"The Terminal, at sunset," I said. "If you don't show, that will be answer enough."

"You have no idea what you're doing, do you?"

"Staying alive," I said. "If you want to do the same, meet me tonight."

"Is that a threat?"

"Take it anyway you want," I said. "Meet me at the Terminal. I'll be there for one hour once the sun sets. One second after, I'm gone."

I hung up the call.

"That sounded like a threat to me," Acheron said. "*Do* you know what you're doing?"

"The Terminal is ideal, and I haven't had a decent meal in

days; Fong's Death Noodles don't count. Why am I not starving to death?"

"You won't need much food as your body changes," Acheron said, glancing at me. "I enjoy food for the taste, but I don't need it for sustenance. The Terminal is an excellent choice. Their latin-seafood fusion cuisine is simply singular. I hope Hector is still there. He makes a phenomenal paella."

"I could eat a salted brick right now and it would be delicious."

He scrunched his face at my mention of culinary masonry.

"We do not eat salted bricks, or bricks of any kind," Acheron said, and paused pensively. "Victoria is way above your power level, and is not known to take threats lightly."

"Neither am I," I said. "Rodrigo is planning on blowing me up. You too."

"I think he really just wants to blow *you* up," Acheron said. "He most likely just wants to banish me."

"Oh, like that's any better? He hates demons. Last time I checked, that included you."

"He may hate demons," Acheron said, "but he feels threatened by you somehow. How was he involved in your obtaining the Darkin weapon?"

"He was the one who had it," I said. "Rodrigo runs the Vault where all the Seven artifacts are kept. Gryn convinced him to hand it over."

"Convinced him? How?"

"Gryn vouched for me," I said. "Rodrigo thought giving me the weapon was a mistake. He thought I posed a threat to the general populace."

"Did it become violent?" Acheron asked. "Gryn is known for his particular brand of power diplomacy, and Rodrigo has a violent temper. Did they fight?"

"Almost. Gryn gave him the opportunity, but Rodrigo

backed down," I said, swerving around traffic. The Hellcat handled like an unleashed beast wanting to tear up the road. "I don't think Rodrigo can take Gryn."

"Very few have confronted Gryn in lethal combat and survived to tell the tale," Acheron said. "I'm actually surprised you survived his training. Did you know he was an apprentice to Circe?"

"He mentioned it, yes."

"Do you know what happened to the other apprentices who trained alongside him?"

"I heard the training was too brutal—it killed most of them."

"Close," Acheron said. "In the last phase of the training, Circe pits all of the apprentices against each other in a Battle Royale of sorcery—a no-rules fight to the death. Whoever is breathing at the end, graduates."

"Damn, that must have been rough," I said. "Did they know beforehand?"

"They discover the terms on the final day," Acheron said. "Those who refuse to participate are eliminated instantly by Circe."

"That's brutal."

"Like I said, I'm surprised you survived Gryn's training," Acheron said. "What was Rodrigo's response when you attuned to the weapon?"

"He lost his shit, to put it mildly," I said, recalling Rodrigo's response. "He was angry, furious, but something else as well. I think he was scared of me."

"Rightfully so," Acheron said, gripping the dashboard. "If I may inquire, where exactly are we racing off to?"

"Black Cleaver territory."

"Why? Do you need target practice?"

"I need insurance," I said. "Flint and I need to come to terms."

"When you say 'come to terms' is that similar to 'meet your maker'?"

"We need a truce," I said. "I can't fight on three fronts. If I can take the Cleavers off the board, even temporarily, I can focus on the Order and the Seven."

"It makes for a sound strategy, provided we reach Flint without a bodycount," Acheron said. "The Black Cleavers are not known for their expert negotiating skills."

"If I need to make an omelet," I said, patting Dark Justice, "I'm going to have to break a few eggs."

"Then you wonder why everyone wants to kill you," Acheron said with a sigh. "Why don't you let me do the talking? I can at least get us to speak to Flint without bloodshed."

"Really?" I asked. "Cleavers aren't big fans of demons, you know."

"Who is?" Acheron said. "Besides, in this guise, I'm a concerned third party who wants to avoid violence."

"Right," I said, driving down the FDR Drive and getting off at the Houston Street exit. "I see this lasting about thirty seconds before one of them wants to blast you."

The Lower East side belonged to the Black Cleavers. You stepped into their neighborhood at your own risk. Occasionally they ventured out, but they kept mostly to themselves, unless they were on the hunt, like what happened at Fong's.

Black Cleavers were self-appointed sorcerers that hunted demons. Most of them were dangerous. All of them were egocentric idiots. Only a small handful were actual threats.

Flint had managed to consolidate his power base by keeping the Cleavers contained. The Order mostly left them alone and the Seven turned a blind eye to their operations, as long as they were conducted below Houston Street.

It was an uneasy detente. The OSA only used Cleavers for field work, but would just as easily wipe them out if given the chance. The only wrench in that plan was the Seven, who operated in the shadows and who could and would retaliate against the Order.

Victoria had sent them the message a few years back: Cross that line and we will burn you to the ground, even if we incinerate ourselves in the process.

This truce gave Flint and the Black Cleavers plenty of latitude. Over time, they expanded their numbers and operated as freelance sorcerer muscle. Flint would hire out squads to the Order when the OSA wanted plausible deniability.

In other words, the Cleavers were the grunts that got shit duty and were usually the first ones killed when an OSA op went sideways. Flint didn't care. He had numbers on his side and led an army of low-level sorcerers.

He was paid well by the OSA and the Seven, if he kept to his designated corner of the city. The moment that changed and the Cleavers became ambitious, the OSA would stomp them down hard and fast, or the Seven would arrange for Flint to quietly disappear while installing a leader who understood the game.

This situation gave Flint leverage, but it also made him vulnerable. It was a vulnerability I could exploit.

If I could avoid getting killed in the process.

TEN

The nexus of the Black Cleaver territory was on Water Street.

The location was unofficially known as the Zipper, because the housing complex buildings were designed in a zig zag fashion resembling the teeth of a zipper. Officially the location was known as the Vladeck Houses. It was a series of twenty six-story buildings forming thirteen acres of self-contained no man's land if you weren't a Cleaver.

In the over 1500 apartments, all inhabited by Cleavers or their relatives, lived over three-thousand people. When I said Flint had an army, it was with the understanding that the Vladeck Houses only formed one corner of the Lower East Side.

Driving into their neighborhood was a necessary risk.

I had several advantages working for me. Flint knew who I was, and that I was loosely associated with the Seven. This would get me past the entrance of the territory. The fact that I could possibly shred any one Cleaver gave me some street cred, and would make sure I didn't get attacked, unless it was by a mob of Cleavers.

Having a Demon Lord partner would get me to the inner area—Vladeck Park, where I could actually speak to Flint. None of this would guarantee I could leave Vladeck Houses alive.

If Flint considered you a Cleaver enemy, the area would lock down around you, converting it into the ultimate Hotel California. You could check out any time you like, but you could never leave.

I parked the Hellcat on the corner of Water and Gouverneur Streets, making sure it was throughly locked. The sigils on the vehicle were defensive, and I doubted any of the Cleavers would try to tamper with it, but they weren't exactly the brightest bulbs in the store.

We walked down Gouverneur Street to the central building that served as the main entry point and gatehouse. Several Cleavers stood by the massive gate as Acheron and I approached.

"Are you sure you want to do this?" I asked under my breath. "I could shoot these few and—"

"Alert the entire complex?" Acheron finished. "Let's try my method first, before you mete out your Dark Justice."

"Hey, I like that," I said. "I'll meet the Cleavers to mete out some justice...some Dark Justice."

"No," Acheron said. "No justice will be meted out here, dark or otherwise. Let me do the talking."

"After you," I said. "Thirty seconds, tops. Before one of them gets trigger happy and starts the dying."

We stepped up to the main gate and faced a barricade of heavily armed Black Cleavers. Most of them held rifles, while a few carried guns in holsters. One of the Cleavers, larger than most stepped forward. I guessed he was the main Cleaver on guard duty.

"I think you two are lost," the Cleaver said, blocking our path. "Why don't you run off, while you still can?"

He wore the basic black on black ensemble of all Cleavers. Black shirt, black jeans and finished off with black combat boots. All of this was covered by a long black trench coat filled with hidden weapons. A nasty surprise for the unsuspecting victim.

Some of the Cleavers around the gate snickered.

"Tell them, Boris," one of the gate guards added. "They're no Cleavers. They smell like Order scum."

"The tall one smells like a demon to me," one of the others called out. "Shoot him, Boris, and see what color his blood is."

"We're here to see Flint," Acheron said, in his best professor voice. "We have an appointment."

"Oh, well, now," Boris said, turning to his Cleaver clique. "They have an *appointment*. William, why don't you check the guest book and see if their names are on the list? Your names?"

"It would seem you were correct," Acheron said turning to me. "Would you be so kind as to introduce us?"

More snickers from the group around the gate.

I extended my claws as I stepped close to Boris. The snickers stopped immediately, replaced by the sounds of weapons being raised in my direction.

Men in general seem to be very protective of their nether regions. I raised one hand to Boris's face, but the other I kept low, hovering near his jewels. His expression went from one of mockery to complete focus.

"It's her," I heard a few of the minions mutter under their breaths. "The freak."

"That's right," I said to a completely focused Boris. "It's me. Your boys may be able to drop me, but not before I make you a eunuch. Tell Flint, Nyx wants to have a word, without spilling blood or removing body parts."

"We'd burn you before you could make a move," Boris

said, but he was sweating. "We have you outnumbered and outgunned."

It was always the big frogs in the small ponds that needed convincing. Granted, the Zipper was a fairly large pond, and the Cleavers were a force to be reckoned with, but they were a speck of dust compared to the city they operated in and the combined forces of the OSA and the Seven.

I focused and let my scales emerge, covering my skin, in the same instant, I slid to the closest Cleaver and slashed through the strap holding his rifle: I snagged the rifle before it hit the ground and slid back to Boris in one smooth move. I placed the muzzle of the rifle gently under his chin and smiled.

"Your guns are meaningless, and your numbers just mean more targets for me," I said, keeping my voice low. "Call Flint or you get to die first as I shred my way to him. I'm sure he'd like that."

"Call him," Boris said, his expression dark. "Now."

I managed to make my point without embarrassing Boris too much, which was the point. If I had stripped his weapon, he would have lost face and been forced to uphold his standing. That would've become bloody, fast. By stripping one of the minion Cleavers, I allowed him to retain his status as top dog in his small pack.

Some days it's the small wins that matter.

One of the Cleavers pulled out a radio and contacted the main house, explaining the situation. A long string of curses, followed by some moments of silence came across the radio. Then another voice.

Flint.

"Nyxia, I'm assuming you can hear me," Flint said. "I would appreciate it if you left my men intact. Boris will escort you to the park. Boris?"

"Yes, sir?" Boris asked, wincing. "I'm here."

"Please bring Miss Nyxia and her associate to me," Flint said. "If she is attacked in transit, I will hold you personally responsible."

"Yes sir," Boris said, as I lowered the rifle. "Understood."

"That wasn't so difficult now, was it?" I said as I tossed the rifle I held back to its owner, keeping my gaze focused on Boris. "After you."

Boris turned and motioned for the large steel doors to be opened. I had no illusions of storming the Zipper. The place was an enormous fortress. I could diminish their numbers considerably, but the entire complex was full of Cleavers and their families.

If I tried to shred my way to Flint, it was the textbook definition of a suicide attack. I'd have to deal with thousands of Cleavers, while looking out for small arms fire, snipers, and a wide assortment of deadly orbs, all focused on Acheron and me.

No thanks.

Not to mention that Flint's inner circle were actually dangerous sorcerers. If I somehow managed to get past all of the Cleavers in one piece and made it to Flint, I'd still have to deal with two fairly accomplished sorcerer lieutenants.

As far as plans went being escorted to Flint was the best outcome I could hope for. Now, getting out was an entirely different story. There was still a chance I would have to cut my way out of the Zipper.

"This way," Boris said, as he moved forward past the gate. "We don't keep him waiting."

We followed Boris in the glare of the gate group. Some of them muttered curses in our direction. I heard a few threats, but nothing I hadn't heard before.

Like I said, most of the Cleavers were bullies in a group and cowards when faced alone. It didn't mean they weren't dangerous, it just meant I needed to keep my distance from them.

We headed down a wide path that led to the center of the complex. Boris remained silent for the whole trip. I made a mental note of potential exits and angles of attack.

"One way in and one way out," Acheron said, taking note of what I was doing. "Difficult to attack and easy to defend."

"I noticed," I said, glancing at Boris walking ahead of us. "We may still have to leave this place violently. Don't let your guard down."

"My guard is never down," Acheron said. "I must, however, commend you on your tactful handling of our entry."

"Thanks," I said, "But we're not out of here yet."

"True. Do you have a proposal in mind for Flint?" Acheron said, still looking around. "I don't think he will react positively to you threatening his manhood with your claws."

"We're just going to talk," I said. "I'm going to make him an offer he can't refuse."

"I see," Acheron said after a brief pause, before looking down at his new set of clothing. "I was just enjoying my new look."

"Trust me, I got this."

"That's what I'm afraid of."

ELEVEN

We arrived at Vladeck Park a few minutes later.

Boris remained on the main path and pointed ahead of us. In the distance I could see a large gazebo. In the center of the structure, I saw several tables and chairs situated around one large round table with three chairs.

I guessed this is where Flint held court.

The three chairs were occupied, but the rest of the small park was empty. At least, it appeared to be empty. I doubted Flint would face me or Acheron without a sizable contingent of Cleavers ready to throw at us. He was ambitious and mildly unstable, but he wasn't stupid.

The most likely scenario was that he had several groups of masked Cleavers waiting in the area around the park, along with snipers placed in firing positions, ready to put holes in us at a moment's notice.

Once we stepped close to the gazebo I noticed the sigils. The gazebo floor was inscribed with a series of defensive symbols. Some I recognized, but most I didn't. The ones I didn't understand were still familiar, the way a skull and crossbones didn't need an explanation to convey a message—danger.

Gryn's words came back to me:

"What are sigils?"

"A way to express power?"

"Close. Sigils are symbols used in chaos magic. It is an intention given form and condensed into a symbol. Always remember, the intention is as important as the symbol itself."

The sigils on the gazebo floor spoke to keeping the area safe from any attack. They spoke of protection and defense. It was possible I was standing in the most protected area in the entire Zipper.

Flint stood when we walked up the small flight of steps into the gazebo proper. He was a large, imposing presence condensed into an average sized man. His slight frame held considerable power and the promise of spectacular violence. A raw intelligence danced in his eyes as he took in our arrival. He ran a hand through his short, salt-and-pepper hair, and gestured for us to sit in the chairs at the main table.

He wore a variation of the basic black on black Cleaver uniform, with the exception of the trench. He wore a dark grey wool peacoat that covered the black dress shirt and slacks. The two beside him, one male and one female, were dressed similarly and felt just as dangerous.

These two were actually more well known than Flint. This was by design; Flint preferred to operate behind the scenes. They were loosely known as the Duo of Death.

The male was enormous, making Boris look tiny by comparison. I knew he went by Bear. Ogre would've been more fitting. He focused on Acheron with a cool expression as we sat. The woman was slight and svelte, with a dancer's body. I only knew her as Espada. Her reputation was impressive. According to the rumors, she took on a horde of *Minoras* on her own while wounded, with only her wits and a blade, and survived.

She gave me a short nod as I sat. It was one of those 'like knows like' nods.

Both Bear and Espada were accomplished demonhunters with considerable skill. I didn't know their real names, I doubted if anyone did. What I did know is that Flint never went anywhere without the two of them.

This was our first official meeting and so far no one was bleeding or in the process of trying to kill anyone.

It was going well.

"Welcome, Nyxia and Acheron," Flint said, as Acheron raised an eyebrow in mild surprise. "Yes, I do know your name, though I doubt it's your true name."

Flint was informed. It made sense. If you were going to lead a small sorcerer army in this city, information was your most important resource and currency.

Acheron gave Flint a small nod.

"This is Bear and Espada," Flint said, motioning to the two beside him. "My sword and shield. To what do I owe the pleasure of your visit, Miss Nyxia?"

"I prefer Nyx," I said. "I have a situation that I think would benefit both of us."

"Really?" Flint said, sitting across from us. "Word is, you are blacklisted. OSA and even the Seven want you retired. What could you offer me that would be of any benefit? As I see it, it's you two against them. I would do you a favor by killing you now."

I let his words hang in the air for a few seconds.

"Then you would be cutting your own life short," I said and watched both Bear and Espada subtly tense up. They were good. Their energy shifted slightly, but I knew, one move from me and they would be all over me in an instant. "Something I'm sure you'd prefer to avoid."

"Are you offering me death?" Flint asked with a slight smile as he leaned back. "You do realize where you are sitting?"

"I'm only here to offer a truce," I said, "and stability."

"Stability?" Flint asked, now interested. "How so?"

I explained what we suspected about Rodrigo's plot to take out Victoria, and how that would negatively impact Flint in both his business, but his standing in the sorcerer community. If Rodrigo managed to take out Vic, it would create a power struggle among the three most powerful groups.

No matter how I felt about Vic, she and the Seven were the check and balance between the OSA and the Black Cleavers. If she were gone, the presence of the Seven would be diminished. This would send the city into a mini-civil war, one I thought the Cleavers would lose, even with their superior numbers.

I waited while Flint came to the same conclusion. He may have been somewhat uncaring about putting his Cleavers in dangerous situations, but he didn't send them to their deaths needlessly. An all out, knockdown war with the OSA would change all of that.

Black Cleavers would die by the thousands, and we were sitting in ground zero. If I wanted to deal a devastating blow to the Cleavers, I would obliterate the Zipper first, wiping it from existence and leaving a crater in its place.

The OSA had the power to do that. The only thing holding them back was a reprisal from the Seven. If the Seven were weakened by internal fighting, the OSA would jump at the chance for a power grab. The first order of business would be erasing the Cleavers.

"You think you can face the sigilsmith?" Flint asked after a few seconds. "Just you two? A demon and an otherkin?"

"Yes," I said, not sharing about being a Darkin. "What do you have to lose? If I succeed, you can say you helped keep the peace. Your standing with both the Seven and the OSA goes up, even though the OSA hates your very existence."

"There is no love lost between us."

"If I die—"

"When you die," Flint interjected. "Not if."

"Right," I said, continuing, "*if* I die, you can wash your hands of me. Who's going to question you? At the very least, you have advance notice to prepare against the OSA, and you know they will be coming for you. Either way it's a win-win situation for you."

"What do you want?" Flint asked. "I know what you offer, but what do you want?"

"I want you to stand down."

"You want me to stand down," Flint said with a small laugh. "Stand down for how long?"

"Until I resolve this situation with Rodrigo—a few days at most."

"A few days?"

"We both know you supply the OSA with redshirts. Everybody knows actually. If I'm going to face them, I don't want their numbers reinforced by Cleavers."

"You want them to get their hands dirty," Flint said, a smile forming on his face. "You want this to be personal."

"I want them to get their hands bloody," I said. "I'm going to make this as personal as it gets. The OSA will curse me and no place will be safe. I'm going to live in their thoughts. Every sound, every shadow will bring the promise of death. I will hunt them until my very name brings them to their knees in fear."

Flint leaned in, staring at me and steepling his fingers as his elbows rested on the table.

"There is risk to me if I do this," Flint said. "They will suspect my motivations."

"Tell them there's been an uptick in demon sightings and

you need to divert your men to that. Doesn't have to be true, just plausible."

"And if I refuse?" Flint asked. "You are, after all, not only partnered with a demon, but part demon yourself. We are demon hunters—killers of your kind."

"If you refuse, I will grant no immunity to anyone that comes after me," I said. "I will treat them like any other enemy, and terminate with extreme prejudice. Unlike what happened to your people last night."

"I heard," Flint said. "Aside from a near evisceration and a serious leg wound, you and your demon allowed my men to leave. Why?"

"He was having dinner," I said, glancing at Acheron, "and I really didn't feel like cleaning up the mess. Besides they were being played, someone sent them there to die. I prefer to deal with the ones giving the orders, the ones who are hiding behind the foot soldiers."

"The sigilsmith," Flint said, leaning back again. "I will do this, because you allowed my men to walk away from facing you. You have two days."

"Two days is perfect. Thank you."

"On the third night, this armistice is lifted. You will revert to just another target to be eliminated for a price. Understood?"

"Completely," I said, getting to my feet. "In two days we can get back to the dying between us. Understood."

"Bear will escort you to the entrance," Flint said, standing and giving us a slight bow. "Perhaps, one day, I can give you both the warrior's death you deserve. Until then, may our paths never cross."

"On that day, only one of us will be walking away," I said returning the slight bow. "I will do everything possible to make sure it's me."

"I would expect no less," Flint said, turning to walk away while holding up two fingers. "Two days."

TWELVE

Bear escorted us all the way back to the Hellcat.

Under normal circumstances I would've said that was overkill, but walking in, and more importantly, out of the Zipper intact was rarely done. If having Bear lead us out meant we could do it without having to fight to within an inch of our lives, I'd take it.

I started the Hellcat and roared away from the Zipper.

"Frankly," Acheron said, pulling down on his vest, "I'm surprised we're not facing a gauntlet of death."

"The day is still young," I said, jumping on the FDR heading north. "How soon to sunset?"

"You have about two hours," Acheron said. "Do you think Victoria will agree to the meet?"

"Would you?"

"Hmm. You have been known to be dangerous," Acheron said. "However, Victoria is in no imminent danger from your abilities."

"She's that strong?"

"Yes," Acheron said, with a short nod. "I would refrain

from confronting a sorceress at that level for a few centuries, if I were you."

"Right, mental note not to commit suicide by attacking Vic, got it."

"I think your selection of the Grand Central Terminal will be a deciding factor," Acheron said. "She knows not to expect an attack on neutral ground."

"Not unless I want to get incinerated," I said. "Are the sigils in there strong enough to stop her?"

"She's strong, but she's not *that* strong," Acheron said. "The nullifying effects of the sigils in the terminal are connected directly to the ley line that runs underneath the space. The terminal was intentionally constructed on its location, like most of the old churches, to harness and amplify the currents of power they possessed."

"So she won't be able to cast?"

"Neither will you be able to tap into the power of the Darkin," Acheron said. "The terminal is an energetic dead zone. It is the ideal neutral ground."

"Maybe you should wait outside," I said. "This place sounds too much like the labyrinth in the Seven HQ."

"Quite the opposite," Acheron said. "The terminal should have no adverse effects on me."

"Why not? Is it because you're a demon?"

"Because I am a being of energy," Acheron said, as I turned off the FDR at 42nd Street. "As are humans, but they have forgotten and are now forced to 'tap' into energy that is always readily accessible to them."

"Does that mean that people like Vic are remembering?" I asked. "If she's that powerful, does that mean she can tap into more of the energy?"

"Not really," Acheron said. "The energy that exists permeates everything, because everything has a vibrational frequency—everything. What humans have forgotten is how to attune to those frequencies. Sorcerers, and the like, are only just beginning to attune to the energy all around us."

"That's what I had to do with the Darkin," I said, nodding. "Gryn called it attuning."

Acheron nodded.

"Since you are becoming more like me, you will discover, over time, how much easier it is to manipulate energy and power."

"Yet Vic is too strong for me?"

"She's had more practice, and you have to approach this sort of thing from a different angle, since you can't cast anymore," Acheron said. "For you, it now must be through the expression of the Darkin. It's like you learning how to walk when Victoria has been running marathons. She has had time and experience on her side, but eventually you will close the gap."

"Do you think she will believe me?"

"I don't know," Acheron said. "She saved you and facilitated your becoming a Darkin. That works in your favor, but—"

"But?"

"She's also the leader of a worldwide clandestine sorcerous organization that prides itself and excels in subterfuge, misdirection, and misinformation," Acheron said. "I'm sure on some level her curiosity is driving her to find out why you want to meet, but that is different from accepting what you present as fact."

"I'll just tell her what I discovered."

"There's also the possibility that she knew all along."

"That would suck," I said. "It would mean she's working with Rodrigo."

"Victoria is difficult, if not impossible to read or predict," Acheron said. "She's formidable, unpredictable, and saved your life."

"I remember," I said, turning onto Vanderbilt Avenue and parking the Hellcat across from the terminal building. "That's the only reason I'm approaching this situation like this."

"Well that, and the fact that taking on the Seven head-on would get you killed instantly," Acheron said. "No one even knows who all of the members of the Seven are. Is it seven, seven hundred, seven thousand, or seven million? No one knows."

"I'm sure Vic knows."

"You could always ask her," Acheron said, as we stepped out of the Hellcat. "She may even give you an honest answer, but I doubt it."

"Me too," I said, crossing the street. "Let's go."

THIRTEEN

The entrance to the terminal neutral ground was accessed from the ground floor.

In the center of the main floor in Grand Central Terminal sat the clock. It was situated above an information booth which dominated the center of the main concourse.

The clock itself was an integral part of the neutral ground, providing the doorway to the space every five minutes. The four convex faces of the clock were made of opaline, not opal, contrary to the myth, and inscribed to give off a warm glow. The compass that rested on top of the clock aligned to true north, and helped channel the energy of the ley line into the hidden spiral staircase below that led directly into the underground neutral area.

Descending several levels would allow access to another hidden area—the Terminal Restaurant and neutral ground proper.

Acheron and I stood near the entrance and waited.

Five minutes later, the clock faces glowed a little brighter and the seams around the door in the rear of the information booth gave off a quick pulse of white light like a flash.

Unsurprisingly, no one noticed. In this city, unless something was tearing buildings in half or causing massive delays in transportation, it barely got a second look. It was one of the major reasons supernaturals could live here in relative peace and anonymity. It was easy to hide in plain sight.

I opened the door and headed downstairs.

We descended four levels below the main concourse and tracks, down into the neutral area. The Terminal neutral space and restaurant was an architectural wonder, with vaulted ceilings covered in warm terracotta tiles and a spacious open floor plan designed by Rafael Guastavino, who later designed the Oyster Bar several levels above the Terminal which was open to the normal populace.

At first glance, both restaurants were identical; the subtle difference was only apparent in the staff and the design work. Each of the tiles of the Terminal were specially inscribed with sigils of nullification and obfuscation. Rumor was that Guastavino, who designed the place, was a sorcerer of the Seven. Although that was never proven or disproven, no one could deny his incredible talent.

The staff in the Terminal were known as Voids. Unofficially they were called 'MT's'. Voids were immune to sorcery of any kind, which made them ideal for a place like this. They also possessed one special ability—they had the ability to neutralize any sigil or cast at will.

If there was ever a natural counter to a sorcerer, it was a Void. Hector, the manager of the Terminal, made it a point to have only Voids on his staff. He had never had a problem in the Terminal because of this.

The entrance archway of the Terminal contained several sets of glass doors that allowed visitors an excellent view of anyone entering the neutral space.

We crossed the threshold and the frame of the doors gave

off a subtle golden glow, probably reacting to Acheron's demonic presence.

"Acheron, hola!" a voice with a slight accent said from behind us. "It's been too long."

We turned to face Hector, who apparently never aged and looked like the long lost twin Antonio Banderas never knew he had. His jet black hair was pulled back into a tight ponytail and he wore an impeccable black tuxedo ensemble, complete with sigil accents in the fabric. He was nearly as tall as Acheron. He came over and clasped Acheron by the shoulders, kissing him twice, once on each cheek.

"Hola, Hector," Acheron replied warmly. "Tell me we are in season for your wondrous paella."

"Of course, my friend," Hector replied, before turning to me. "The paella is always in season for our favorite customers."

He grabbed me gently by the shoulders and looked down at me with a small smile, before narrowing his eyes.

"*Señorita, un placer. Has cambiado, como?*"

"Long story," I said, answering his comment about my change. "The pleasure is mine, Hector. How have you been?"

"Good, but much better now that you are both here," Hector said. "Your guest is expecting you."

"She's here?" I asked, lowering my voice. "How long?"

"The *Directora* has been here for ten minutes," Hector said, without missing a beat. "I took the liberty of seating you in our executive lounge. That will provide you some privacy. This way, please."

We followed Hector into a small lounge. It was like walking into a restaurant within the larger restaurant. Seated in the back, I saw Victoria. She was facing the entrance and saw me immediately. She acknowledged me with a short nod as we approached her table.

Hector seated us and promised to return with our meals

shortly, leaving us alone with Victoria. She wore her usual slate gray suit with a white blouse. In the dim light of the Terminal, she looked more like the scarily powerful sorceress she was and less like the power broker CEO. Her hair, peppered with gray, was cut short, in a severe hairstyle with the sides shaved close and the top fairly long.

"Hello, Nyxia," Victoria said, before glancing over at Acheron. "Acheron."

She said his name with barely concealed disgust.

Acheron smiled and gave her a curt nod.

"Director, a pleasure as usual," Acheron said. "Thank you for meeting us."

Victoria turned to face me.

"The Terminal," Victoria said, glancing around. "Fitting, considering your trajectory."

"I like the food," I said. "Plus, it's a neutral ground. I've been a little popular lately."

"I heard," Victoria said. "Seems like the OSA and the Cleavers consider you a threat. One to be eliminated."

"But not the Seven?"

Victoria smiled unapologetically. It was the smile of an apex predator that is comfortable knowing its place at the top of the food chain, and that the only threat you present is indigestion.

It was a bone-chilling smile.

"You have *never* been a threat to the Seven," Victoria said. "Even now, after"—she waved a hand in my direction—"your transformation. At best, you and your demon partner are a necessary distraction."

"Well, now I'm feeling all warm and welcome."

"Do not mistake my presence here for some kind of acceptance," Victoria said, her tone serious. "I'm here because you are my responsibility. Need I remind you that there are some within the Seven that feel you"—she glanced at Acheron—"and your demon are better off as a memory?"

"No you don't," I said feeling the rage bubble within. "Those that feel that way can go fu—"

"What Nyxia is trying to say," Acheron said, cutting me off, "is that we feel there is a credible threat against your life."

"I'm the Director of the Seven, demon," Victoria said. "There are credible threats against my life every day I decide to get out of bed." She turned to me. "This merited an in-person meet?"

"This is different."

Victoria wasn't known for her sense of humor. The fact that she was actually here, meant the threat posed by Rodrigo *was* credible, even if she acted like nothing fazed her. Unless she was just here to erase Acheron and me.

Both were viable possibilities.

"You have exactly sixty seconds to explain why I'm here, before the Seven Agents in this room apprehend and rend you both."

"This is neutral ground," I countered. "They won't tolerate violence here."

"Even now you still don't understand," Victoria said. "Who do you think bestowed neutral status to the Terminal?"

"The Seven?"

"No, be more specific. Try again."

"You?" I said, shocked. "You gave them neutral status?"

"And I can take it away faster than it would take a bullet to perforate your dense skull," Victoria said. "Now, explain your pointed invitation."

FOURTEEN

"Before we get to the violence," I said. "Who authorized the inscribing of Eight?"

"I did, of course. You had gone through several company vehicles by that point," Victoria said. "The next step would have been to get you a tank. What does that have to do with anything?"

"You gave Rodrigo that assignment?"

"No, he requested it, insisted actually. Why?"

I explained what we had discovered with Eight, the sigils, the tether and the tracker stone. Victoria's expression darkened.

"Where is the vehicle now?"

I glanced over at Acheron who nodded slightly.

"The Grimoire," I said. "Liv is working on it."

"You placed a volatile sigil car bomb in proximity to a repository of ancient, highly powerful artifacts?" Vic asked. "In what reality does that sound like a good idea to you?"

"When you put it that way—"

"There's no other way to put it. What is Liv doing with it?"

"She's disarming the sigil nuke that Rodrigo placed on my ride."

"You've made a serious accusation, and your proof is a little thin," Victoria said. "Actually, it's more than a little thin, but I believe you."

"You have other evidence," Acheron said. "That's why you agreed to meet us here."

Victoria nodded.

"We've been monitoring the Vault and Rodrigo for some time," Vic said. "Artifacts have been 'destroyed' and are then showing up on black markets or in the hands of the OSA. Never here in the city, always overseas."

"He was funneling artifacts to the OSA?"

"For a price," Victoria said. "Everyone we tried to place in the Vault was either dismissed or met with an unfortunate end."

"No witnesses," Acheron said. "He was systematically removing them."

"Yes. So I needed to have someone who could go in and place the right sigils in the right places without his suspecting I was aware of his activity."

"Who?" I said. "Who did you send?"

"You," Victoria said. "You and Gryn."

"What?" I nearly yelled, attracting the attention of some of the nearby patrons, who quickly looked away when I glared at them. "What do you mean, me and Gryn?"

"The Darkin weapon," Acheron said. "He was planning to sell it?"

"You're quite quick for a demon." Victoria said.

"You have no idea," I said. "He's one of the only—"

"Demons to need a rescue from a rending orchestrated by a combined effort of the OSA and Rodrigo," Victoria finished. "I said quick, not intelligent. In any case, I'm impressed you managed to rescue the big, bad, Demon Lord."

"It was not a rescue, it was an extraction," Acheron said. "One I was in the middle of executing when Nyxia arrived."

"Of course," Victoria said. "Whatever you need to tell yourself to keep that massive ego intact. To answer your question, he has a transaction arranged to offload the Darkin weapon."

"You knew it was Rodrigo and you didn't tell me?"

"You were focused on your demon's rescue," Victoria said. "I didn't want you distracted."

"Gryn knew?"

"What do you think?"

"Of course he knew," Acheron said. "The actual mission was to stop the sale of the Darkin weapon and plant the sigils. What did he use? Sigils of surveillance?"

"He used a sigil of omnioculus."

"An omniocular sigil?" Acheron asked, impressed. "I knew Gryn was formidable. I didn't realize he wielded that much power."

"He is and he does," Victoria said. "We knew Rodrigo had a buyer set up to move the Darkin weapon. Fortunately, I had an Otherkin"—she looked at me—"one eager to increase her power. It was an ideal situation that provided us access."

"You *used* me?"

"Yes, like I said, a necessary distraction," Victoria said. "The fact that you attuned to the weapon was a bonus. Unexpected, but a contingency we planned for."

"You expected her to fail?" Acheron asked. "Failure to attune with the weapon would have resulted in her death. The weapon would have killed her."

"I'm aware," Victoria said, her voice just this side of arctic. "It was a calculated risk. That weapon in the wrong hands"—she glanced at me again—"and I'm still not entirely certain that's not the case, was an untenable position. With

Nyxia's attunement we managed to meet two of our three objectives."

"Two out of three?" I asked. "What was the final goal, erase me?"

"If that were an objective, it would have been met long ago," Victoria said. "The final objective is why you're here, is it not?"

"You're going to eliminate Rodrigo," I said. "That was the plan all along?"

"No, I'm not going to do anything, except attend your detention and subsequent rending at the Vault tomorrow."

"My what?"

"You broke the bond between you and this demon, yes?"

"I had no choice, they were going to rend him," I said. "I wasn't going to let that happen."

"Thank you," Acheron said, with a nod. "At least someone appreciates my presence."

"Be that as it may, you unleashed a Demon Lord," Victoria said. "He is a potential threat to this city and everyone who inhabits it."

"What are you talking about?" I asked, confused. "It's Acheron. You're talking about him like he's going on a rampage of death and destruction."

"He is," Victoria said matter-of-factly. "By this time tomorrow, your demon will be shackled and prepped for rending. The Vault also houses a very specific detention area. I will assume you attuned to the weapon in the Room?"

"Yes, not exactly my idea of fun," I said. "I hope I never have to—"

"That is where you will be tomorrow, and most likely where you will have to face Rodrigo."

"He's a sigilsmith," I said. "I don't cast. Is the plan still my termination? Because this seems like suicide."

"It will be your only opportunity," Victoria said. "The interior of the Vault is inscribed to diminish abilities."

"Diminish, not neutralize?"

"Neutralized sigils react poorly with some of the artifacts. We discovered that the hard way," Victoria replied. "By diminishing their power we were able to contain them in homeostasis without blowing up the city in the process."

"That's why he backed down when Gryn challenged him," I said. "Even in a diminished state, Gryn was stronger than Rodrigo."

"Gryn is stronger than Rodrigo inside and outside of the Vault," Victoria said. "It's why I chose him. Don't misunderstand. This is your only opportunity, but it won't be easy. Even in the Vault, Rodrigo is a sigilsmith and wields a formidable amount of power. Your only advantage is that the diminishing sigils do not seem to affect demonic entities."

"You're saying I need to use my Darkin abilities."

"I hope you've been practicing."

"How is this supposed to happen? I can't just stroll into the Vault, he'll try to blast me on sight."

"I, along with a security detail, will be escorting a rogue Otherkin and her Demon Lord partner for a scheduled rending," Victoria said. "Prior to your demise you will be stripped of all standing and be cast out of the Seven for releasing a Demon Lord into the world."

"Clever, by casting her out, you've given her the freedom to attack the sigilsmith," Acheron said. "I must admit, your thinking is practically demonic in its deviousness. She doesn't need to abide by the rules of the Seven.

"Not that she ever did," Victoria said, glancing at me. "This will make it official, and Rodrigo will be beside himself to partake in your rending."

"The premise is to return the artifact and destroy the two of us," Acheron said. "Will he believe it?"

"His hatred for your kind will help cloud his reason," Victoria said. "Nyxia will be relinquishing the Darkin—a weapon she shouldn't have attuned to in the first place—and any other equipment provided to her by the Seven."

"This could actually work," Acheron said. "It would put us all in proximity to the vehicle."

"How do we get him to try and detonate Eight around you?" I asked. "I'm not exactly going to drive to my own execution."

"It will be towed to the location, to arrive shortly after we do," Victoria said. "All decommissioned vehicles are stored in the Vault. It's SOP."

"Once he has us all in the same place, he will make his move," Acheron said. "Provided he can assure his own safety. A sigil of destruction is no small matter."

"Did Liv assure you she could defuse the sigil?" Victoria asked. "I'd rather not go out in a blaze of glory."

"She said she could do it," I said. "I told her to remove the explosive components and leave the light show."

"If she can manage to reverse engineer an ancient sigil of destruction, that would be impressive," Victoria said. "I'll have containment circles standing by just in case, although, with a sigil like you described, it may not do much."

"You don't think she can do it, do you?"

"I prefer not to place my life in the hands of a succubus, retired or not. She's still a demon," Victoria replied. "I don't trust demons, or anyone else *that* much."

"Rodrigo will try to kill you."

"He's not the first," Victoria said, holding my gaze, "nor will he be the last. It comes with the position."

"What happens if he manages to remove you?" Acheron asked. "Does it create a power vacuum?"

"Another Director will be chosen," Victoria said. "It's not as easy as it sounds."

"Can Rodrigo take your place?"

"As sigilsmith he can appeal for the position. If he manages to survive the interview, then theoretically he could become the next Director."

"That's why he needs to remove you," I said. "He needs you gone."

"You first," Victoria replied. "My sources tell me he still has the sale of the Darkin weapon set up—two days from now. What does that tell you?"

"He's confident he will have the weapon for the sale," Acheron said.

"The only way he can get the weapon back is—" I started

"To eliminate the Otherkin it's attuned to," Victoria finished. "That means *you* need to die first."

"That bastard, he's been after me ever since I attuned to it," I said. "Can I kill him twice?"

"If I may inquire," Acheron asked, "how much is he selling the Darkin weapon for? This seems like an inordinate amount of effort for monetary gain."

"It's not for money, he's trading it for another artifact—the Archimedes Magnifier."

"He wants to trade my weapon for a magnifying glass?"

"A magnifying gem," Acheron said. "It was my impression that the last gem of that nature had been destroyed."

"It seems your impression along with that of the Seven is wrong," Victoria said. "With a magnifying gem, Rodrigo could increase his power tenfold. Stopping him would be impossible."

"That would guarantee his attaining the directorship of the Seven," Acheron said, "and its vast worldwide resources."

"If he manages that, it would be a bad day for everyone. At least those still living."

"We need to stop him."

"Or die in the process," Victoria said. "Though I prefer to avoid the latter."

"Liv needs time to defuse the sigil," I said.

"She has one day," Victoria said. "We will apprehend you and your demon at the Grimoire tomorrow afternoon and set this plan into motion. Once Rodrigo is neutralized, one of my Agents will take his place at the trade. I'd like you to be there."

"Why?" I asked. "I don't need some magnifying gem."

"Proximity," Victoria answered with a small sigh. "You've attuned to the weapon, which means you need to stay close. It also means you can track it. You *can* track it?"

"Yes," I lied. "I can."

"Good," Victoria said. "We make the trade, you track your weapon and lead us to the buyer. We retrieve your weapon, the buyer and the gem, and call it a night."

"That sounds too simple."

"It isn't," Victoria said, getting to her feet. "No plan survives contact with the enemy. Be prepared for the unexpected. Enjoy the meal. It's on me."

Hector arrived with delicious smelling plates of food.

"Thank you."

Victoria looked at the food, glanced around the Terminal, and nodded.

"As last meals go, this is a good choice," Victoria said, and then looked at Hector. "This meal is covered."

"Understood, Directora, *buenas noches*."

"Have a good evening, Hector," Victoria said, then focused on me. "Get whatever rest you need. We'll pick you up at the Grimoire. Stay out of sight until then."

FIFTEEN

"Can you track your weapon?" Acheron asked when we were back in the Hellcat. "I was under the impression you barely had a handle on its use."

"I just need some practice, that's all."

"So it's a no, then. Can you at least sense its presence?"

"Yes," I said, sensing the Darkin within. "It's complicated. The Darkin isn't just a weapon, it's also an entity; it's more than the weapon."

"That would be a result of your attuning to the weapon," Acheron said with a nod. "What about the weapon itself? Can you sense it?"

"When it's close I can sense it easily. It gets harder when distance is involved, but I'm pretty sure I can track it."

"Pretty sure won't be enough," Acheron said as I roared the Hellcat into traffic. "We need to rectify that at the Grimoire. That is, if we ever make it there in one piece."

"Stop criticizing my driving. I'm an excellent driver."

"Is that what you're calling it? 'Driving'? I would describe it as something closer to continual accident avoidance."

"Shut it. I'm a great driver."

"We have distinctly different definitions of 'great', it seems," Acheron said, gripping the handle on the passenger side with one hand while the other grabbed the dashboard. "Perhaps I could meet you at the Grimoire. I'll take a cab, it's safer."

"In this city? Are you insane?"

"I ask myself that every time I step into a vehicle with you at the wheel."

"I don't trust Victoria," I said after a pause. "She's holding too much back."

"She probably views it as a survival mechanism, but I agree. There is a high likelihood she is using you—again."

"I can't do this on her terms," I said. "That will end up with me being shredded. I need to shift my leverage."

"Shift your leverage? What exactly do you mean? You can't possibly be thinking of attacking Victoria—that would be immediate and horrifically agonizing suicide."

"I'm insane, but I'm not that insane, no. I need to increase my standing with all of them. I need to become a threat they fear and respect."

"All of who?"

"The Seven, the OSA, and the Cleavers, along with anyone else that thinks I'm an insignificant target or pawn to be moved around the board. That's going to stop, I'm making sure of it."

"How?" Acheron asked. "They view you this way—please take this with no offense—because they outclass you in power and experience. You are not a threat to them. Perhaps in a few hundred years you will be; right now you are an afterthought."

"Read me," I said, as we approached the Grimoire. "How powerful do I appear?"

"With or without the Darkin ability coursing through you?"

"Both."

"Without it you would be considered angry and dangerous, but not much of a threat," Acheron said, gazing at me. "With it, you're angry and dangerous, and pose a minor threat. In your defense, the power hasn't had time to grow within you."

"How long before I would be viewed as a threat to someone like Victoria?"

"Victoria? Try never," Acheron said with a chuckle that died away when he saw my expression. "You're serious?"

"Yes. How long?"

"You understand that she's the Director of the Seven, a group of sorcerers powerful enough to hide their presence from most of the world, yes?"

"I know who she is."

"I don't think you do," Acheron said. "In order to become Director, they took a page from Circe's manual of graduation and intensified it. All candidates undergo a blood ritual and then they are forced to fight to the death."

"A blood ritual? What kind of blood ritual?"

"I'm not sure of the details, not being a sorcerer, or part of the Seven. From what I have learned it involves an assimilation of power. Whoever remains breathing at the end, absorbs the powers of the vanquished."

"How many candidates in a typical Director interview?"

"It varies, usually anywhere from three to five," Acheron said. "Victoria could have the power of three insanely powerful sorcerers, or five elite-level sorcerers combined. Either way, it's a losing proposition for one marginally enhanced Darkin."

"What if I could increase my power?"

"How and where?" Acheron asked, incredulous. "You plan on stopping by the power store and leveling up your ability?"

"Two days from now," I said. "Using the magnifying gem.

If I use it before Victoria gets it, I could—"

"Potentially explode in a bloom of mystic energy," Acheron said. "Are you serious? We don't even know if it's a real gem. What if it turns out to be fake and destroys you instead?"

"If it were fake, Victoria wouldn't be trying to intercept it."

"All of a sudden you're trusting Victoria?" Acheron asked. "You said it yourself, she can't be trusted."

"I know and I don't," I said, my voice firm, "but if she's going through all of this to get the gem, I'm getting it first. Do you think Liv has information on how to activate the gem?"

"Of course she does, the information is in the Grimoire somewhere," Acheron said. "That doesn't mean she's going to share it with you."

"You need to convince her," I said as I parked the Hellcat at the rear property of the Grimoire. "As your kin, I invoke the law of elder brother protection."

"There is no such law, and frankly I'm reconsidering your kinship to me," Acheron said as we exited the Hellcat. "We may be reckless, but what you propose to do is suicidal."

"What does she propose to do?" Liv said, stepping out of the darkness. "It sounds dangerous."

"Inside," Acheron said. "We can't discuss this out here."

"Let Becca know I brought her car back in one piece," I said, proudly.

"I never let her know you borrowed it," Liv said. "Do you think you would have gotten very far if she knew you were driving it? As far as she knows, it was getting detailed."

Liv opened the garage door with a gesture, causing the sigils it was inscribed with to flare. We followed Liv into the Grimoire through the private entrance.

"Were you able to defuse the sigil bomb?" I asked. "Was it

even possible?"

"Yes and no," Liv said, sitting behind her desk. "I managed to remove most of the explosive aspects of the sigil sequence. It will explode—"

"Will it destroy Eight?"

"It's comforting to know that your first concern is the welfare of your vehicle, not the others who will be standing next to you, should Rodrigo decide to detonate the bomb."

"Vic will be standing in a containment circle, I'm sure, and you're practically indestructible. Eight isn't."

"Incredible," Acheron said. "Your concern for my safety is simply staggering. Please try not to care so much."

"Hey,"—I pointed at Acheron's chest—"I ran into a building full of sorcerers and faced off against some pretty vicious demons to save your ass. I care, but this is Eight we're talking about. Liv?"

"Your vehicle should survive the blast, but I wouldn't stand too close when it goes off," Liv said. "If I tried to unravel anymore than I did, the Grimoire would be a crater right now. I think I've reduced the explosive potential to one tenth of the original energy output."

"You think?" I asked, walking over to where Eight sat parked in the center of a glowing red circle. "Can you be a bit more specific?"

"No," Liv said. "This is not an exact science. I'm manipulating forces of chaos, not cutting the red or green wire. One tenth is the best I can do, and, considering what it's supposed to do, one tenth will still be a considerable explosion."

"I understand," I said. "I'll do my best to be away from the blast zone. What do you know about Archimedean magnifiers?"

"Aside from the fact they're all gone, they were volatile and dangerous," Liv said, looking from me to Acheron and then back to me. "They were designed to magnify the power of the person who activated them. In most cases it was permanent."

"Most cases?" I asked. "What happened to the other cases?"

"The gem would explode, disintegrating the person trying to activate it."

"Oh," I said. "That does sound volatile and dangerous."

"It was, but they're all gone now. Why are you asking?"

I explained Victoria's plan to Liv, including the trade off of the Darkin weapon for the magnifying gem.

Liv shook her head.

"It's too dangerous," Liv said. "Let's pretend this is a real magnifying gem. You can't cast. You would need to be able to cast the activating sigil."

"She can't, but I can," Acheron said. "Once I have it."

"You're supporting her in this madness?" Liv asked, whirling on Acheron. "She's going to kill herself and you're going to help her do it?"

"She's my kin," Acheron said, as if that was enough. "I won't let her blow herself up."

"Bold words," Liv snapped. "Like you have a choice." She turned to face me. "There's also the small matter of your current power level. If you're not strong enough it will devour you. Why do you think they were destroyed?"

"To prevent misuse?"

"Misuse?" Liv scoffed. "To prevent power-mad idiots from detonating themselves and killing innocents in the process. If this is a real gem, and that is an enormous 'if', there's no way to reduce the explosive potential. When a gem of this kind goes off, the resulting explosion makes a nuclear blast look insignificant."

"Fuck," I said. "I don't have a choice. I have to take the chance. Is there a way I could do this someplace that won't take out half the city?"

"No," Liv said with finality, crossing her arms. "There isn't."

"Yes," Acheron said, staring hard at Liv. "You can let her use the portal."

Liv stared hard at Acheron.

"Both of you are insane," Liv said. "You're going to anchor her?"

"Yes," Acheron said. "I can anchor her."

"Oh really, genius? Who is going to cast the sigil if you're busy anchoring her in place?"

They both looked at me and I raised my hands in surrender.

"Don't look at me," I said, shaking my head. "You lost me at the portal."

"Liv," Acheron started. "I know it's presumptuous of me to ask, and if you refuse I will understand, but can you cast the activating sigil?"

"No, absolutely not," Liv said. "I will not be part of your destruction. I will allow you the use of the portal, but more than that I refuse to do."

"I understand, I truly do," Acheron said.

"Do you, really?" Liv asked, placing a hand on Acheron's cheek. "Do you know what it would take for me to cast that kind of sigil?"

"I will find a way to do both or locate a proxy," Acheron said, placing his hand over hers. "Thank you for the portal."

"You can use the guest quarters downstairs," Liv said, heading for the door. "Whatever you do, don't move your vehicle from the containment circle tonight."

"What happens if we do?"

"The partial defusing process will be complete shortly after midday tomorrow," Liv said, stopping at the door. "If you want to see the sunrise, don't move the vehicle."

SIXTEEN

"What is the portal?" I asked as we entered the guest quarters. "What does it do?"

"It's not just a what, but more of a when," Acheron said, settling into a large chair. "You should try to get some sleep. Tomorrow we have a rending to attend."

"Don't even joke like that," I said. "Tomorrow, we take care of Rodrigo."

"Or he takes care of us," Acheron said, closing his eyes. "Get some sleep."

I had never seen Acheron sleep.

It seemed to me that demons didn't need sleep. What he would do on occasion, is sit on the floor cross-legged in a meditative pose or on a large chair, closing his eyes while deepening his breathing.

These moments never lasted longer than ten to twenty minutes and he could step out of his power demonaps instantly. For the time being, I was still human enough that the bed looked comfortable.

I closed my eyes as soon as my head hit the pillow.

What felt like ten seconds later, Acheron was waking me.

"Are you kidding me? I just managed to close my eyes and you're waking me up?"

"You've been sleeping for hours," Acheron said. "It's after noon. Honestly, how do humans get anything done if they spend most of their lives sleeping? In any case, that is not why I woke you."

He pointed to the large television which was currently muted.

The news line on the bottom described the massive destruction perpetrated by a pair of terrorists. Several buildings had been destroyed, and authorities were looking for the male and female pair.

"Shit, that's bad," I said, "but I don't see how—"

"Wait for it," Acheron said, arms crossed. "Victoria is making sure she sells this."

He pointed to the screen again and I saw the two images of the suspects. They were pictures of Acheron and me.

"Holy fuck," I said. "They're saying *we* did that?"

"Officially it's a pair of highly trained and dangerous terrorists," Acheron said. "Unofficially—"

"The OSA is going to be all over this," I said. "Any casualties?"

"None, just massive property damage," Acheron replied. "This will not be an easy situation to extricate ourselves from, even after we deal with Rodrigo."

"It smells," I said. "Vic is declaring us redshirts—shit."

"Demon Lord on the loose, and the Otherkin who released him," Acheron said. "The OSA will hand out the A&D order before the broadcast is done. My guess is that the Seven will intervene and inform the OSA that it's an in-house issue, which they will resolve internally. At least until we get the gem."

"Suddenly, I'm really glad we worked out that truce with the Cleavers," I said. "Apprehend and Destroy orders are premium rate missions. Flint must be kicking himself right now."

There was a knock at the door.

It was Liv.

"Seems like you managed to destroy a fair part of our city," Liv said, nodding at the television. "How you managed that while being here is a considerable feat."

"It's all part of the ruse," Acheron said. "This is to convince Rodrigo of our guilt."

"You don't see it?" Liv asked. "This is no ruse. Once Victoria is done with you, she feeds you to the wolves. The story has been put in place. There's no coming back from this. She gets the gem, neutralizes Rodrigo, and gets rid of the both of you in one fell swoop."

"We've come to the same conclusion," Acheron said. "We are not in a position to alter the events, at least not presently. We will have to see this through. Better to spring the trap you can see."

"I wouldn't put it past her," I said. "That's why I'm going for the gem first."

"The two of you can't do it alone," Liv said, looking at Acheron. "I will anchor Nyx, and you cast the sigil. An anchor is safer for me, but you have to promise me, Acheron, if you see the process destabilizing, you stop and come back."

"I promise," Acheron said. "If the situation devolves we will return immediately."

She handed Acheron a small scroll. It was covered in intricate writing I couldn't decipher. I did manage to make out a large sigil in the center of the scroll.

"Is that it, the activating sigil?"

Liv nodded.

"It took me some time, but I knew we had a copy of it here," Liv said. "You may as well learn it, even if you can't cast it. It's a sigil of assimilation. If you really get a gem and manage to pull this off, the gem will magnify your current level of power at least tenfold."

"It can be more than tenfold?"

"Yes," Liv said, and stared at Acheron. "Some of the gems had no upper limit. The energy multiplied on a cycle. More energy equaled a greater magnification which would then repeat."

"Why does that sound like a bad idea?"

"Because it is," Acheron said, taking the scroll from me after I examined it. "The gem didn't have an upper limit, but the sorcerer in question inevitably did. Eventually they would reach critical mass and—"

"Disintegrate from a power overload," Liv finished, giving me a hard stare. "The portal will remove the danger you pose to others, but not the danger you pose to yourself or Acheron."

"If I don't do this," I said, "Vic is going to hand us over to the OSA. I'd rather not give her that opportunity."

"I just want you to go into this with your eyes open," Liv said, as Becca appeared in the doorway. "If you manage to succeed, come see me. If not, this is goodbye. I can assume the Seven will be here shortly to collect the two dangerous terrorists hiding out in a bookstore?"

"Apparently, we're nerdy terrorists," I said with a slight smile. "Thank you, Liv, for everything. If I don't see you again—"

"I know," Liv said, turning to Becca. "How long do they have?"

"There's a convoy of vehicles leaving the Seven HQ," Becca said. "I'd say about ten minutes, twenty on the outside."

"You have the Seven under surveillance?" I asked. "How did you manage that?"

"The Grimoire is a hub of power in this city," Liv said,

nodding to Becca who left us alone. "We've managed to become so by consolidating the most important currency in the city."

"Information," I said. "How connected *is* the Grimoire?"

"Enough to know you managed to broker a two-day armistice with the Cleavers—impressive actually—had dinner at the Terminal, and will be traveling to the Vault under the watchful eye of Victoria and her security team."

"That's good," I said. "You wouldn't happen to know who wants to trade the gem for the Darkin weapon, do you?"

Liv shook her head.

"We're good, but we're not that good," she said. "That information is only known to Rodrigo and I assume, the Director.

I nodded.

"And Vic is not big on sharing."

"If I had to guess, I would say it's another Otherkin," Liv said. "It's the only thing that makes sense. That weapon has little value to anyone else."

"Another Otherkin," I said, surprised. "I can't believe I didn't think of that."

"Once you stop Rodrigo, if you stop him—"

"I will stop him," I said. "Or die trying."

"Well, *if* you stop him, you need to get that information before the handoff," Liv said. "I will have the portal prepared, since I'm an optimist, but we can provide you some support if we know where the trade is going to take place."

"We'll do what we can," Acheron said. "The situation will be fluid and we don't want to alert Victoria to our intent. If she finds out we intend to abscond with the gem, she will blast us once it's in sight."

"Make sure she doesn't find out," Liv said. "And don't get yourselves dead."

SEVENTEEN

I was looking out of the large bay window that dominated one wall of the Grimoire and faced out to 6th Avenue when Victoria arrived. Five large, black SUVs rolled up in front of the Grimoire. I imagined there were several in the back as well to prevent our 'escape' in case we wanted to beat a hasty retreat.

Victoria stepped out of the lead vehicle as a small squadron of Seven agents poured out of the other vehicles, weapons drawn and moving in a tight formation toward the Grimoire.

I looked at Acheron, who nodded back at me.

"Showtime," I said as the Seven Agents headed inside. "Keep your eyes and ears open. I have a feeling this is just another misdirection move for Victoria."

"Agreed," Acheron said, raising his hands as the Seven agents entered the Grimoire. "Look, it seems we have guests."

The Seven agents all wore dark suits and angry expressions. The Lead Agent approached us and holstered his gun.

The rest of the agents around us kept their weapons trained on us.

They were all sorcerers, men and women highly trained to eliminate threats like Acheron and me. These weren't Cleaver level minions. The Seven was made up of the elite. Any one of these agents would be a handful. Dealing with an entire security detail was a fight I didn't want—not yet.

"Under the jurisdiction of the Seven, I'm here to detain you and this demon," Lead Agent said. "If you resist we are authorized to use deadly force. Do not resist."

"The Seven?" I said. "I thought the Seven didn't exist?"

The Lead Agent just stared impassively at me and motioned to the agents behind him.

Several of the agents approached Acheron and me, placing sigil covered cuffs on our wrists. Immediately, I felt a disconnection from the Darkin energy within.

"Are these demonic suppressors?" I asked, holding up my wrists and trying to feel for the Darkin energy without success. "Someone's been doing their homework."

"Take them downstairs," Lead Agent said, turning to another group. "Get your team and secure her vehicle. That's Seven property. It comes with us."

The agents led us outside to a waiting Victoria.

"You've been running around this city like a rabid dog," Victoria said, looking directly at me. "I allowed it because you were effective, but I warned you not to become a liability. Wanton destruction of property aside, you unleashed this... this demon into my city."

"I did what I had to do," I said, playing my part. Except it was feeling all too real. "They were going to rend him."

"All you did was delay the inevitable," Victoria answered. "You did what you had to do, now I must do the same. Now I must put you and this creature down to keep my city safe."

"You could exile us," I said, testing a theory. "You could banish us from the city."

"I could," Victoria said, her voice slicing through me, "but I won't. The only reason you're still breathing is because the destruction you two caused avoided fatalities. Had that not been the case, we'd be sweeping up your remains right now."

"So it's a no on the banishing?"

Victoria smiled at me then and I knew. She was going to use this situation to remove Rodrigo, Acheron, and me.

"I'm afraid I'm going to have to decline," she said. "I hear rendings are exquisitely agonizing, but quick. This will all be over soon enough." She turned to the Lead Agent. "Get her out of my sight and make sure her vehicle is retrieved."

"Being done as we speak, ma'am."

"Good," Victoria said, stepping into her vehicle. "Make sure the Vault knows we're on our way. If we don't handle this today, the OSA will do something foolish and force me to take measures."

"Yes, ma'am," Lead Agent answered, turning to his team. "Separate vehicles. Put her in two and the demon in three. Make sure those cuffs stay on at all times."

They secured us in the vehicles with five agents for each of us. Either Victoria was going full drama queen or we were in deep shit. I was leaning toward the deep shit side of the equation.

I glanced outside as a tow truck slowly drove past us. It held Eight on a large flatbed. I followed it with my gaze until the driver turned a corner and vanished from sight. Eight would get there before us. I never did get to tell Victoria about the fact that Liv only managed to cut down on the sigil bomb's explosiveness, not remove it entirely.

I almost felt bad for omitting that small detail but I had a feeling, a deep, uneasy gut feeling, that it was possible

Victoria didn't have Acheron and my best interests in mind with this little exercise.

I focused and tried to reach Acheron mentally. The demon-bond we shared allowed us to communicate silently, if we were close enough, but that bond had been broken. We were now kin and I didn't know if it would work with the demon cuffs on, but I had to try.

Distance would interfere with the process, but since he was only one SUV away from me we were close enough. I hoped.

"Acheron. Acheron can you hear me?"

"I had my suspicions," Acheron answered in my head. *"These suppressors only work on full demons. You may be my kin, but you are not entirely a demon."*

"How can you hear me?" I asked. *"I can't feel the Darkin."*

"It seems after you initiate contact I can respond, but I couldn't initiate contact with you. You can access the Darkin, but you have to use another method."

"Another method? What other method? I think Vic is seriously going to try to erase us."

"It is a distinct possibility. I'd suggest you extricate yourself before that happens. I'll see what I can do on my end. We have to stop, my cuffs are beginning to smolder."

"Shit," I said, breaking the connection. It was good to know I could reach out to him, but I didn't want to give this advantage, however slight, away.

I heard several of the SUV doors slam shut and we drove off to the Vault.

EIGHTEEN

We arrived at the Vault as the sun set.

There was a larger contingent of agents waiting for us outside the building. Located on 14th Street and Eighth Avenue, the Vault was situated inside the building that housed the Museum of Illusions.

The corner of Eighth Avenue and 14th Street was barricaded off, allowing our convoy to come to a stop directly in front of the building. To the general public, the building was an old bank converted into a museum. For the Seven, the museum was the perfect cover to house artifacts of power.

Victoria stepped out first and climbed the steps into the Vault. We followed shortly after. Her security detail came in after us, but the agents that were outside remained on the perimeter as the door was closed and sealed behind us.

The interior of the museum was a large, open plan with exhibits designed to fool and trick the mind into seeing or believing something other than what they presented. Somehow the exhibits felt sinister at night. It was either that or the whole 'walking into a trap' vibe I was getting.

More agents were situated inside.

They remained so still that for a brief moment I thought they were part of the exhibits. One of the interior guards stepped forward and intercepted Victoria. He walked ahead of her and led us to a smooth marble wall.

Victoria nodded and he stepped back. She placed a hand on the wall and a section opened inward. The guard went back to the main floor to resume mannequin duty.

This all seemed like overkill.

I counted ten agents as part of Victoria's security detail. I knew Acheron and I posed a threat, but I didn't think it was this much of a threat. Part of me was actually impressed that Victoria went through this charade, until the smarter, wiser part of my brain reminded me that there was a good chance this wasn't a charade.

The large section of the wall whispered closed behind us and we stood in a large, empty atrium. There were cameras mounted in every corner, covering the entire floor space. Under each of the cameras were nasty-looking mini-Gatling guns with oversized magazines.

I remembered that they were loaded with Gorgon rounds, nasty things that would dehydrate a target on impact. A fight in this space would be over quickly if those guns were activated.

We followed Victoria as she crossed the large tiles that made up the sigil floor of death. It was a different path from the one I took with Gryn, which made sense since the sigil sequence changed the path randomly every few seconds.

There was no way we were leaving the same way we came in.

We stepped forward into a large alcove, and a wall of blue energy descended behind us, enclosing us in the space. The floor shifted slightly and we began dropping down into the Vault proper.

When we reached the lower level, Rodrigo stood waiting

for us on the opposite end of the floor. This level was a wide-open space, similar to the one above, but minus the Gatling guns and tiles of death. Two large doors sat at opposite ends of the room. The rest of the room was filled with small cases holding various low-level artifacts.

Off to the side, hidden behind one of the large exhibits, I saw a ramp I hadn't noticed on my last visit here.

Rodrigo was dressed casually in a white dress shirt and dark jeans. His sleeves were rolled up, revealing some of the sigils inscribed on his arms. His brown hair was cut short, making him look younger than his years.

"I told you she was a security threat," Rodrigo said, approaching us. "Her vehicle is secured downstairs, it arrived about twenty minutes ago. It contains some irregularities I need you to see."

"Irregularities?" Victoria asked. "What irregularities? We have more important matters to attend to"—Victoria glanced at Acheron and me—" the vehicle can wait."

"No, it can't," Rodrigo said, walking toward the ramp. "It's been rigged to explode"—Rodrigo glanced my way—"probably by this bitch here. I need you to look at the sigils, I don't recognize them."

"How could *you* not recognize them?" Victoria asked, as we followed Rodrigo down the ramp. "This is your area of expertise."

"These sigils seem to be demonic in nature," Rodrigo admitted. "I may be a sigilsmith, but my area of focus was never demonic inscriptions."

"Demonic?" Victoria asked warily. "What are you saying?"

"I don't recognize the inscriptions on the vehicle," Rodrigo said. "Considering my areas of study, the sigils I don't recognize are limited to a finite amount. That's why I need your input. You've dealt with demonic castings more than I have."

"I don't see how my opinion on the matter will change anything," Victoria said. "You said it's rigged to explode. You don't need me, you need a sigil demo team."

"They're on their way," Rodrigo assured her. "But I think if you could decipher them, it could help with the containment."

"It's not contained?" Victoria asked, stopping on the ramp. "Are you insane? Why would I go near an exposed sigil bomb?"

"I would never expose you to that kind of danger," Rodrigo said. "I have it contained, just barely. If you can tell me what I'm facing, I can inform the demo team and strengthen the current circle I have around it."

Victoria gave a Rodrigo a hard look.

"This is sloppy," she said. "Are you saying we brought a volatile bomb into a repository of our most important artifacts?"

"I'm saying that either the Demon Lord or your pet project Otherkin placed sigils on the vehicle to cause us damage," Rodrigo said, glaring at me. "Thankfully, *I* caught it before it triggered and placed the entire vehicle in a containment circle."

"If you have it contained, even nominally, then why do you need me to examine it?" Victoria asked. "You dealt with it. The demo team will be here soon and they can take it from here."

"That's what I'm trying to explain to you," Rodrigo said. "The circle is unstable. You were always much better at these things than I ever was. I'd prefer you contain it, then we can proceed with the evening's events. Or we can wait until it explodes. My circle may or may not contain the blast. Your call."

"Fine," Victoria said, her expression dark while glancing at me. "You never did focus on containment when we were apprentices. Where is the vehicle?"

"On the far side of the garage, bottom of the ramp and to the right, this way," Rodrigo said. "I figured it was better to keep it isolated."

"It's still in the Vault," Victoria pointed out. "If it detonates, there are artifacts in here that will level not only the building, but the entire block."

Victoria turned to me.

"What the hell were you thinking?" she asked. "I'm going to enjoy taking you out of commission."

"If you ask me," Rodrigo said with a nod, "this was long overdue."

Victoria turned to her security team.

"We may be dealing with a volatile explosive device," Victoria said. "You and your team secure this level until the demo team gets here. Bring them to me when they arrive."

"Yes, ma'am," Lead Agent said, glancing at Acheron and me. "What about them?"

"They're with me," Victoria said. "The cuffs will stay on."

"Yes, ma'am, be careful with the hybrid," Lead Agent said. "She's not exactly a demon. We don't know if the cuffs are completely effective with her."

"Noted," Victoria said, continuing down the ramp. "If I notice anything, I will take the necessary precautions. Set up a perimeter at the top of the ramp. No one is to come into the garage level except the demo team."

Lead Agent nodded and stared instructing his team as we kept moving.

Rodrigo led us down a level and turned to the right. We faced a large, partially open blast door. Rodrigo pulled it aside and led us inside the garage. Eight sat inside a glowing red circle on the far end of the large parking area.

"Since when do garages need blast doors?" I asked under

my breath, marveling at the thick steel door. "Paranoid much?"

"Blast doors are a needed precaution when our vehicles are inscribed. It's a contingency in all of our facilities. Rodrigo, secure that door, just in case."

Rodrigo nodded and pushed the door closed easily.

"We didn't do whatever it is you're accusing us of," I said. "I can barely read most sigils, and I don't go around blowing up buildings."

"You fucking liar," Rodrigo said, burying a fist in my midsection and doubling me over, before turning to Victoria. "I should kill her right now. Why are we bothering with protocol? Let me end her now. We toss the demon into the Room, rend him and call it a night."

"No," Victoria said. "The property destruction has the OSA involved. We're going to follow protocol, so I don't have to deal with them later. We do this right, so we only have to do it once."

"I'm going to kill you so hard," I said between clenched teeth, as I straightened up. "I'm going to start by removing your non-existent balls and work my way up, you fuck."

"I'm going to enjoy seeing you beg for your life," Rodrigo said with a laugh. "Victoria should've never saved your life. I told her it was a waste of time and—"

"Enough," Victoria said, as we approached Eight. "Show me these demonic sigils you mentioned."

"I'm sure they would know," Rodrigo said, when we were close to Eight. "Have the demon take a look."

It was a perfect setup.

By having Acheron look at the supposed 'demonic sigils' Rodrigo managed to get us all in proximity to Eight. Once he triggered the sigils, it would detonate, blasting us to particles.

Victoria glanced back, and motioned for us to step closer to Eight as she examined it.

"Is this true?" she asked, pointing at the symbols inscribed on the chassis. "Do you recognize these sigils?"

"Some of them, yes," Acheron said, pushing his glasses up on the bridge of his nose, "but I can assure you these are not demonic sigils of any sort."

"Of course they aren't," Rodrigo said, tracing a sigil as he backed up. "I'm sorry, Victoria. At least you get to die with your pet scum."

"What are you doing?" Victoria asked, stepping toward him and stopping as bright orange symbols flared on the floor. "What is this?"

"This is your funeral," Rodrigo said, moving back even farther. "The sigils on that vehicle will detonate in a few moments, removing you and the demon filth. A two-for-one special, actually."

A larger orange circle surrounded us as the smaller, red containment circle slowly disappeared. The orange circle rose around us and formed a dome of energy enclosing us and Eight.

"Don't do this," Victoria said, and for the first time I thought I heard actual emotion—sadness. "It's not too late to stop this."

"It is too late," Rodrigo said, looking at me. "You have something I need, demon bitch. Once that thing destroys you, I'll be back for the weapon you stole from me."

"This will destroy the Vault," Victoria said. "Are you insane? The artifacts—"

"Have been relocated to secure locations," Rodrigo said, cutting her off. "You've been lax in your duties, *Director*. While you weren't looking, I offloaded most of the important artifacts, I just need one more."

"The Darkin weapon," Victoria said. "What use is it to you? You're not an Otherkin."

"That weapon is my key to power," Rodrigo said. "I'll be

back for it once you're all gone. Unfortunately"—he looked around before pulling the blast door open—"there may not be much left to search through once those sigils go off. Goodbye Victoria, I never did like you."

Rodrigo pulled the blast door from the other side and secured it, before I heard him run up the ramp. The sound of gunfire and orbs crashing into walls followed soon after, then quiet.

"I trusted that bastard," Victoria said under her breath. "Against my better instincts, I trusted him."

The sigils on Eight began glowing.

"I think this would be a good time to inform you that Liv only managed to reduce the potential intensity of the blast," I said, moving away from Eight. "It's still going to explode."

"By how much?" Victoria said, as she stepped close and removed the cuffs from Acheron and me. The flow of power into my body was instantaneous, crashing into me like a wave and making me slightly dizzy. "Nyxia, focus. By how much?"

"She said ten percent," I said, getting my bearings. "She reduced it to ten percent of the original blast."

"Ten percent?" Victoria said, looking at the glowing sigils. "That's still enough to level the Vault."

"What about this dome?" I asked. "Will it keep us safe?"

"It would," Victoria replied, as she crouched to look under Eight. "If the blast were occurring outside. Since the bomb is in here with us, the kinetic energy will just bounce around in here first until we're bloody paste. Eventually, it will overwhelm the dome, but by then it will have multiplied in force several times."

"The firecracker scenario," I said.

"The what?" Victoria asked, as she traced the sigils on Eight. "What does this have to do with firecrackers?"

"If you hold a firecracker in your open palm, and it explodes, it will hurt, but cause minimal damage. If you close your fist around the firecracker and it goes off, you lose fingers."

"This is something like that, but the firecracker in question would blow off your entire arm, palm open or closed."

"Oh, hell," I said. "Can you reroute the energy?"

"Perhaps an energy funnel to siphon the energy of the explosion downward and away from the Vault?" Acheron said. "Can we assist?"

"No, I don't need or want your assistance with this," Victoria said. "This was because of my error in judgement, and I will rectify it. I will not lose the Vault because of one arrogant, self-absorbed, prick. I do, however, need one thing from you."

"What do you need?" I asked. "Please say it's shredding Rodrigo."

"I need you to stop that bastard," Victoria said. "I'll deal with this."

""I'd love to, but we can't leave the circle," I said, stepping to the edge and feeling the dome of energy stopping me. It felt solid as I placed my hand forward. "We can't get through this."

"I can," Victoria said, and traced a sigil. The force of the energy she unleashed punched a hole in the energy dome, launching Acheron and me across the garage. "Go, now. We don't have much time."

NINETEEN

We reached the top of the ramp to a scene of carnage.

Victoria's entire security detail had been slaughtered. Judging from the guns in holsters and the lack of extensive orb energy, the attack had caught most of them by surprise.

"That fucker," I said, kneeling down next to the broken body of the Lead Agent. He was one of the few who had drawn a weapon "He didn't have to kill them."

"Yes, he did," Acheron said, looking around. "It needs to look like we tried to escape. This looks plausible. We killed the Director and her team, before he managed to heroically stop the vicious Otherkin and her deranged Demon Lord partner."

"Where is he?" I said, looking around. "He couldn't have gone far."

"There"—Acheron pointed across the floor—"I presume that fortified area is the one place he could weather a massive explosion with little to no personal damage."

The door to the Room was slightly ajar.

"Let's go."

"You do realize this is a trap," Acheron said, as we crossed the floor. "He's had time to prepare and set this up."

"Is it still a trap if you know it's a trap?" I asked, pulling on the Room door. "Doesn't it just become a difficult obstacle then?"

"Your logic is flawed," Acheron said. "Knowledge of the trap doesn't change its inherent state. Even if we spring this trap, as we will, we don't know the extent or parameters of the trap in question. It is still a trap."

"Fuck that," I said, drawing Dark Justice. "This is my trap equalizer. Let's find him before he thinks about—"

An explosion rocked the Vault, followed by a series of tremors that traveled throughout the building. The first explosion was followed by a series of smaller detonations.

"What the hell," I said, turning to the door, which had vanished. "Shit, Victoria."

"Is probably cursing your name right about now, if she's still alive, that is," Rodrigo said, stepping into the center of the Room. "Victoria saved you—again. That containment dome should have trapped you all. This is, unexpected...but perfect. I get to kill you with my own hands."

"You know, I didn't expect you to be such a monumental asshole. Oh wait, yes, yes I did," I said, raising Dark Justice. "Why don't you just get on your knees before I put several bullets in you in the most painful places imaginable?"

Rodrigo slowly raised his arms.

"Don't think so," Rodrigo said, sliding to the side. "You need to die."

He was fast, faster than me, tracing a sigil before I could fire. My gun flew from my hand and vanished through the wall behind me.

"Are you kidding me?" I said, pissed and surprised. "I just got that gun."

"You are in my Vault, hybrid scum," Rodrigo said. "This is

my world. In here, I make the rules. I decide who lives and who dies. In here, I'm God."

Rodrigo formed several black orbs of energy and unleashed them. Acheron moved back, creating several orbs of demonflame to counter the black orbs. Black tendrils of power shot out from the wall behind him, wrapping themselves around his body.

"You want to stay in the center of the room," Acheron said, looking down at the tendrils around around him. "These seem to be some type of gelatinous constructs. My demonflame is ineffective against them."

"Stop describing them and break through them," I said, without taking my eyes off Rodrigo. "Do something."

"He can't," Rodrigo said. "I told you. In here, I decide."

The tendrils slowly started pulling Acheron into the wall.

"What are you doing? Let him go."

"I intend to, right into a rending," Rodrigo said. "I was going to make you watch, but I don't have that kind of time."

"Really," I said, circling around him. "You have somewhere to be?"

"I do. You've altered my timetable, but no matter," Rodrigo said. "Everything moves up, right after I take back the weapon."

"You're going to have to kill me first."

"That's the plan," Rodrigo said. "This is the part where you surrender. You can't cast and you're outclassed. Why not die with some dignity?"

"This is still the Vault," Acheron said in my head. *"His power is diminished. Get him to make a mistake. Unleash the Darkin."*

The tendrils pulled Acheron into the darkness of the wall, vanishing him from sight.

"What did you do to him?"

"You've lost everything," Rodrigo said, extending his arms

outward. "Victoria isn't here to save you, your demon is gone, you've even lost your shiny new gun. Give up."

I needed him to make a mistake. He had an ego the size of the city, with a large helping of god complex on the side. I needed to trigger that sense of inferiority he was overcompensating for.

"Is that it?" I mocked. "A few tricks and I'm supposed to quake at your supposed power? I'm not impressed. What did you do? Rig a trap door and some cables? Please, if you're a god in here, then I'm the Ultimate Supreme Being of Power."

"I'm going to kill you slow," Rodrigo said, the anger coming off him in waves. He extended an arm and formed a black energy sword. "Then I'm going to rend your demon to ashes."

I formed the chakram in one hand and extended the claws of the other.

"Is that why Victoria put you in the Vault?" I asked, staying out of the range of his sword. "Your sorcery skills were inadequate? I heard only second and third-rate sorcerers were assigned to the Vault. Those too incompetent to be out in the field."

"You know nothing of the Seven," he snarled. "I slaved away my entire life for a position in the Seven, and what do they do? They promoted that bitch to Director? I should be Director. I *am* the Director now."

"Not from where I'm standing," I said. "You're just a little man no one pays attention to. They locked you away in the Vault and probably laugh at you when your name comes up."

He growled in anger and charged at me. I only wanted to trigger him, not send him over the edge, but pushing buttons isn't an exact science. I dashed to the side and backed up, making sure to stay away from the walls.

You will have to kill him.

The Darkin.

I can't. He has information I need.

Get the information, then kill him. He will not spare you. His intent is clear—your destruction.

I'm getting that.

Let me kill him, I will make it swift.

No, I need to know who he's trading the weapon to. I need the magnifying gem.

No, you don't.

You don't know what you're talking about, you're in my head. I need that gem.

I am Darkin. Searching this place for a magnifying gem is child's play. Even you could do it if you tried. It is in the room opposite this one on this level. That stone is Darkin. It is mine.

"You have it?" I said out loud before I caught myself. "You have the gem?"

"How did you get that information?"

He may as well have confessed.

"How long have you had it?"

"I acquired the gem the day after you attuned to the weapon."

"Ouch, sucks for you," I said, smiling. "Seeing me walk out of here with the weapon must have pissed you off. I mean here you are, lord of the Vault, but powerless to stop me from leaving with *my* weapon."

"*My* weapon, you bitch," he hissed. "You took it from me, you took my power."

"What power?" I asked, still circling. "Little men like you are powerless chihuahuas, all bark and no bite, constantly trying to prove their worth. Real power doesn't advertise."

"I was going to kill you for your weapon; now I have to kill you because you know too much."

"What are you going to do, kill me twice?"

"Once should be enough," Rodrigo seethed. "Before I end

you, where did you get that information? Not even Victoria and her spies knew. She thought I had a buyer."

"It was a lie."

"I was going to kill her at the meet I had set up," Rodrigo admitted, "but killing her with your vehicle seems fitting, plus I can implicate you and your demon."

"Why do you need my weapon?" I asked, looking for an exit. "You're not Otherkin."

"The weapon unleashes the power of the gem," Rodrigo said, pointing. "It fits on the weapon, in the center. You stole it from me before I could get the gem."

I deliberately made an effort to avoid examining the chakram.

"That must have been frustrating," I said, mocking him. "First you had the weapon but no gem, then you get the gem, but no weapon. You really are bad at this aren't you?"

"No, more talking," Rodrigo hissed. "Time to get to the dying."

"Bring it."

TWENTY

Rodrigo wasn't kidding about trying to kill me.

He dashed in ending his forward movement with a blazing fast lunge. His speed at sigil forming translated equally to his sword attacks. I barely managed to parry his blade, as he traced a sigil and blasted me with an orb as he rotated around me.

The orb slammed into my side, knocking me sideways as he slashed at my leg, cutting my combat armor and my thigh. I screamed, more in surprise than pain as my leg burned.

"You are a ruthless, conniving son-of-a bitch."

"I told you," he said, pointing to my leg, "you're outclassed. I'm a sigilsmith for the Seven, conniving ruthlessness is called job security. Give me the weapon. I promise to make it quick, which is more than a dog like you deserves."

"Come take it," I said, taking a step forward and nearly stumbling. "What the—?"

My leg was becoming numb as pins and needles shot all the way up it.

"I don't need to take it," Rodrigo said, absorbing his sword. "My blade was coated with Gorgon venom. Not as effective as shooting you with a Desiccator round, but it will get the job done. In about two minutes, you'll be dust."

Unleash me or we both die here. He deserves to die for this.

It was one of the few times I completely agreed with the Darkin.

He's all yours.

I gave up complete control, and the Darkin unleashed a low growl in my head, followed by a roar, threatening to tear my skull apart from the mental sound. It wasn't until I saw Rodrigo's face that I realized that the sound wasn't only in my head; the sound had come from me.

Scales covered my body, and the scar Gryn had given me exploded in pain and heat as my body transformed. My entire body felt heavier, thicker, and stronger. Everything was just...denser.

A second later, demonflame engulfed my body, forcing Rodrigo to take several steps back, the fear evident on his face.

"You sought to hurt me, little man?" I said, my voice blended with a deeper bass undertone. "You thought you could cut me without reprisal?"

"What the fuck are you?" Rodrigo said, forming his sword again, while taking another step back. "What the hell are you?"

"You thought me the prey as you formed this trap," I said, looking around. "But I am not the prey here."

"You're an abomination, that's what you are," Rodrigo said as he charged forward.

He slashed horizontally with his energy sword. I parried it with the chakram and unleashed a right cross to his jaw, breaking it. He raised a hand to trace a sigil, but I closed the distance, extending my claws and burying them in his shoulder, stopping him.

He screamed in agony as his arm started to burn.

"It's not Gorgon venom," I said, "but it will kill you."

"Fuck you," he spat in my face and kicked my chest sending himself backward. "You think I can't kill some demon freak like you?"

I separated the chakram.

Rodrigo slammed his sword in the floor and began a two-handed sigil. I released both halves of the chakram, throwing them to the side. An enormous orb of black and red energy headed straight at me. It moved too fast for me to dodge. I raised both arms in front of my body in a cross block.

"Die, you bitch!" Rodrigo screamed as the orb closed in on me. "Die!"

"You first," I said, as the orb slammed into my arms.

In my peripheral vision, I saw the halves of the chakram boomerang around the room and circle back through the center of the room—and Rodrigo's neck.

I was only able to catch his final moment of shock and surprise as his head slid off his shoulders. The next moment, the orb blasted into me, breaking both arms and launching me through the Room wall.

Only my scales prevented me from becoming a new Splattered Darkin exhibit in the museum. I landed on the smooth, marble floor with a crash and slid across to a stop at the other end of the atrium.

The scales and demonflames disappeared. Everything ached and the numbness in my leg had started creeping up my side. The Gorgon venom was spreading.

I was dying.

"So this is what it feels like to die," I said as I laid still, looking up at the ceiling. "Not so bad, actually."

Acheron's face came into my field of view.

"Ugh, seems like I'm already in hell," I said, still not moving. "Either that or I'm dead already."

"You're not dead yet," Acheron said, scooping me up from

the floor. "It took some doing, but I managed to break free from that infernal goo."

"Where are you taking me?" I asked, as my vision began tunneling in. "Too...too late. Gorgon venom on his...on his blade. Cut me."

"For once, would you be quiet," Acheron said, his voice filled with concern. "There is a chance, but we must hurry."

He crossed over to the other room. Somewhere in my memory I vaguely remembered that this room was important for some reason.

The gem.

I looked around, and my head lolled to the side, as if I had overdosed on muscle relaxants and my neck could no longer support the weight of my head. I was suddenly desperately thirsty, and I knew it was the venom.

The room was filled with twenty small daises strategically placed around the floor. On each dais rested a small transparent glass cube. Inside each cube, in an ornate display, rested a large gem.

Acheron looked around.

"He's hidden the damn thing in plain sight," Acheron said and looked down at me, his expression one of anger and anxiety. "We don't have enough time to try them all, Nyxia. Which one is it?"

I looked over at the exhibit of gems. Everything in my body wanted to go to sleep. A weight descended on me, and all I wanted to do was close my eyes and take a nap.

"So tired," I slurred. "Can I take a nap?"

"No!" Acheron said, jostling me. "Focus. You can't let them win. They thought you an inferior cast off. They thought you were just trash they could experiment on and discard. Are you going to let them win? You're better than this, focus!"

The intensity of Acheron's words struck me and brought

me back. I managed to fight off the overwhelming sense of lethargy and pointed at the gem that I could sense.

It was a black gem with a blood red center.

"That one," I mumbled. "It's that one."

"Are you certain?" Acheron asked as he placed me gently on the floor. "We don't get a second chance."

I nodded and he shattered the case.

"That's the one, I can feel it. It's Darkin."

"I don't know what that means," Acheron said. "This is a blood gem. "It's either going to help you or blast us both to bits."

"Oh good, that sounds fun," I slurred again. "Blast to bits sounds great."

Another wave of exhaustion washed over me and this time I really just wanted to close my eyes and sleep. I saw Acheron kneel beside me with the gem in his hand. It glowed red as he whispered some words and traced a sigil. He took his glowing hand, placed it on my forehead and yelled some more words I couldn't understand.

Then my world exploded.

TWENTY-ONE

I stood in the middle of the park.

It was mid-afternoon and empty, which was impossible. The park was never empty during the day. I looked around, and saw I was standing on an immense lawn beside the largest tree I had ever seen.

This was not any park I recognized.

"Hello, child," a voice said from behind me.

The Darkin.

"So," I said, turning to face the enormous demon, "I've died and gone to the Darkin afterlife? Kind of boring if you ask me."

The Darkin was even larger than the last time I faced it. Even standing in front of it, I barely reached its shoulder. Its massive head dominated my vision. The scales on its body were a reddish-gold, and made small jingles of metallic sound as it approached me. Flames hovered around its eyes.

"Yes, you have died, but not as you perceive death," the Darkin said.

"What other way is there to perceive death?" I asked, confused. "I have ceased to exist. Haven't I?"

"Yes and no," the Darkin said, and transformed into an almost identical version of me, except for it having flaming eyes. "Right now, your demon friend is implanting a Darkin blood gem into your body, in an effort to save you."

"I think he might be too late," I said. "The Gorgon venom has advanced. I was beginning to sound dopey there at the end. Also, the thirst meant my body was shutting down."

"Yet he continues, why?"

"Because he's an idiot," I said, fighting the tears back. "He doesn't know when to quit and walk away."

"This is your choice," Darkin Me said. "If you accept me, I can promise you many years of pain and hardship. You will be hunted, and persecuted. Many will try to kill you; no one will truly understand you, except for maybe your demon friend."

"What's the alternative?"

"Oblivion."

"Oblivion?"

"Do you not understand this word?" Darkin Me asked. "Your finite minds are so limited. The end—of everything for you."

"I understand it," I said, holding up a hand, "It's just that your sales pitch needs some work."

"Sales pitch?" Darkin Me's eyes flared brighter. "This is not a sales pitch. This is your final choice."

"Are you always this literal?" I asked, shaking my head. "I know what it is. What I don't know is why? Why not just let me go? I'm sure there are other more worthy hosts for your Darkiness, Darkinship?"

"That is why," Darkin Me said. "Your choice?"

"I still have plenty of ass to kick, and my life has always been pain and hardship," I said after giving it some thought. "If I accept you will I become stronger?"

"Exponentially stronger, yes, but it will take some time

before this power is available to you," Darkin me said. "You are still so frail and delicate."

"I'll get harder," I said. "What do I need to do?"

"Accept and let go," it said. "You have never truly accepted who and what you are. Once you do, we can begin."

I nodded and extended my arms wide. The Darkin stepped into my embrace, and laughter surrounded me as my world became flames.

TWENTY-TWO

I opened my eyes and screamed.

Power exploded from my body; the energy wave causing Acheron to fly across the room. The daises and glass cases around me shattered to dust as the stone floor beneath me cracked. Flames erupted around me, covering my entire body.

"Nyxia?" Acheron called from the other side of the room. "Is that you?"

"Fuck, even my hair hurts," I said as I sat up slowly, the flames disappearing. "What the hell?"

"No, hell has nothing to do with it, well at least not directly," Acheron said. "You nearly died."

"Water," I said, my voice raspy. "I need water."

"I would assume so," Acheron said, producing a bottle of water. "Sip, don't gulp. Your body is adjusting."

"What happened?"

"Context?" Acheron asked. "It's been a long night."

"The Gorgon venom was killing me, I was dead, then it gets kind of fuzzy after that. I know we found the gem—"

"*You* found the gem, I just placed it where it belonged."

"Then I spoke to the Darkin, but then it was me, but it was really the Darkin and I had to choose."

"And you chose to be a Darkin," Acheron said gently. "There is no separation now. You, the Darkin, the weapon are all one."

"I'm a—"

"A Darkin, with all that entails," Acheron said. "Good, bad, and worse."

"Including an army of enemies," Victoria said from the doorway. "You need to leave."

"I just got back."

"Doesn't matter," Victoria said. "The OSA, the Cleavers, and the Seven will make you priority number one now."

"Even the Seven?"

"I may be the Director, but you killed a sigilsmith," Victoria said. "You did *kill* the fucker, yes?"

"Yes, in the end, he lost his self-control, and his head."

"Sounds like Rodrigo," Victoria said, and limped over to where I sat. "He had many supporters entrenched in the Seven. It will take time to root them all out. In the meantime—"

"I need to watch my back from the Seven," I said. "You know he planned on killing you."

"The exploding sigil made his intentions clear, yes."

"Not that," I said. "The buyer was a set up. He had the gem a day after I attuned to the weapon. He was going to take you out at the supposed trade."

"But you ruined his timetable by attuning to the weapon," Victoria said. "It means his deception ran deeper than I thought. Where is the gem?"

"Gone," I said, giving her a hard stare. "He tried to use it against me and failed. It was destroyed in the process."

Victoria looked around the destruction and noticed I was the epicenter of it all. She crouched down, and ran a finger along one of the cracks in the floor that still glowed a subtle red with latent energy.

"Considering the damage to the Vault, I could see why Rodrigo tried to kill you in the Room," Victoria said, gazing across the floor to the Darkin-shaped hole in the opposite wall. "Then the battle moved here, where the gem was being stored. The conflict created more damage, resulting in another explosion, destroying the gem and ending the lives of one sigilsmith and a pair of terrorists. It's quite sad actually. He will be honored as a hero."

"Heartbreaking even," I said, getting to my feet with Acheron's help. "Did Eight survive?"

"It was the only vehicle in the garage to do so. It saved my life."

"What? How?"

"At first I tried to contain the blast," Victoria said, as she shuffled out of the room. "I realized soon enough that was going to be an exercise in futility. So I did the next best thing. I inscribed a blood sigil into the floor of your vehicle and rode out the explosion—literally. I drove it out of the garage punching a massive hole in the wall as I went."

"Holy hell," I said. "You are out of your mind."

"A blood sigil?" Acheron asked. "With whose blood?"

"Mine," Victoria said. "There was no other choice."

"That was positively demonic," Acheron said, slightly awed. "I'm impressed."

"I wasn't going to lose the Vault or my life. Not to Rodrigo," Victoria said, with a slight nod and pointed to a wall. "Over here."

We walked over to a plain adjacent wall. She traced a sigil and placed a hand on the wall. A small door opened outward, leading to an empty alley on the side of the building.

"This whole building is an illusion," I said, surprised.

"It was designed that way. That alley will lead to your

vehicle. Take it and disappear for a while, at least until I can deal with the OSA."

I was about to step outside when I stopped.

"I never thanked you for saving my life," I said. "For a long time I hated you for letting me become an Otherkin, but I think I understand why you did it now."

Victoria nodded, as the sound of sirens filled the night.

"I've done many things as Director of the Seven that I regret, things that if I could undo, I would," Victoria said. "Saving you is one of the few things I don't regret."

"But the Seven is still going to hunt me down, right?"

"Officially? With every resource at our disposal."

"Unofficially?"

"Unofficially, you need to get your ass to your tank before this place is crawling with OSA," Victoria said, her voice stern. "I'll see you soon. Now, go."

Acheron gave Victoria a nod. "Director."

"Keep her alive," Victoria said. "Or I *will* be coming for you."

"A scenario I do not wish to experience," Acheron said. "To never seeing each other."

"I should be so fortunate," Victoria said, and closed the door.

Acheron and I made our way down the alley to Eight, who purred when I started the engine.

"She really is a tank," I said, rubbing the dash. "I lost my new gun."

Acheron reached into his vest and pulled out Dark Justice.

"I was keeping it safe for you," he said, as I placed it in its holster. "I knew how attached you were."

I stared at his vest and shook my head.

"Do I even want to know?"

"Not really," he said. "We still have things to attend to,

but we won't need Liv or the portal now. The gem is part of you now."

"We couldn't go to Liv's now even if we wanted to," I said. "The OSA and the Seven will be all over the Grimoire."

"For some time yes, "Acheron said, peering out of the window. "Then things will calm down and I will be able to see Liv again. That will be a good day."

"Thank you," I said. "For everything. I mean it."

"That's what elder kin are for," Acheron replied, looking at me. "I expect weekly visits to Fong's once things quiet down."

"They will never quiet down, you know that."

"Then we'd better get some now as we exit the city, " Acheron said. "I can have Fong pack some Death Noodles for the trip."

"Sounds like a plan," I said, pulling away from the Vault as the sound of sirens grew closer. "We may need to lay low for a bit. But we'll be back."

Acheron nodded as he strapped in.

I stepped on the gas, and Eight roared into the traffic.

THE END

AUTHOR NOTES

Thank you for reading this story and jumping into the darker world of Nyxia & Acheron.

To the NAC: You win lol.

These three stories were going to be all of Nyx & Acheron I was going to write. Honestly, I didn't know if the characters were going to be well received. They are a bit darker than the usual M&S stories and the MC is some kind of demon-human hybrid.

All in all it was a blast to write Nyx and her world.

My thought was to write the three novellas <cough novellas> and call it a day. I thought you would generously and patiently entertain my detour in Nyx's world (because you are great that way) and promptly decide three novellas was enough.

I was mistaken.

The Nyxia & Acheron Coalition (NAC) formed quickly after book one and strongly suggested (demanded with a subtle hint of threats) that I continue Nyx's story after the three novellas. My readers are awesome and if I can write a story you enjoy then I will.

The first full length novel of Nyxia & Acheron will be called DARKIN and should appear some time later this year. The outline is currently being worked on as of this writing. Thank you for reading her story and providing amazing feedback.

Okay to the challenges:

This story was supposed to be 20k words long. The entire collection clocks in around 84k. None of the stories listened to my suggested word counts.

Nyx is stubborn.

Yes, I can hear your laughter from here. I truly do not know why I do this to myself. In my (very weak) defense I can only say that having a set word length gives me some sort of parameter to work with. Said parameter becomes meaningless when the MC decides that 20k (or 30k) is way too short and obliterates it.

This was my dilemma. Keep it short and truncate the story or let it run its course and set it up for the full series? I decided on the latter. Also Nyx's claws are sharp and I don't think I would enjoy being eviscerated. Acheron also gave me a few looks of disapproval when I tried to suggest a shorter story, along with tuts of disappointment.

What I learned (mostly):

First and always, my readers are amazing.

Writing Nyxia & Acheron, while different from writing M&S has become a familiar experience. Nyxia refuses to be managed, censored (she definitely believes cursing is a free expression of who she is), or controlled (*don't tell me what to do* is what I hear from her often). This hasn't changed in any of the books. The only way I was able to end the third book was with the promise of the series. This last 'novella' clocked in at 34k+-.

It was nearly a novel in it's own right.

The key to Nyxia's story and to Nyxia herself, is her fierce loyalty to those she calls friend. Part of it is because she really only has one friend, and he's a demon. For most of this story, Acheron had to act like a check and balance. Her desire for revenge could easily send her over the edge into utter darkness. An unchecked Nyxia would just be a horror story with an immense bodycount, but it's an idea I will explore in her full length novels, which will be darker than this trilogy. Hopefully, Acheron will keep her grounded against her darker nature. If not, all hell will break loose, in more ways than I can imagine.

In these stories, I'm still exploring what is the definition of 'evil' (thank you again Jeanette for pointing this out). In Nyxia's world, Acheron and demons are considered evil by the magical class (sorcerers) to be destroyed. For Nyxia, Acheron is her close friend who always has her back. As she transitions into something else we will go deeper into what it means to be evil and good.

One of the driving questions that came up during edits was: Is Nyxia a Darkin or does she wield the power of a Darkin? I hope I addressed that in the story. The next question that comes up is: What exactly is a Darkin? That will be explored in the full stories of her series.

Yes, Gryn will reappear at some point. Possibly the first book of the longer series...we'll see. He's a great character that deserves more time in the spotlight. Besides, he still has much to teach Nyx (read torture lol).

In this story, I revealed a bit about Acheron's past. I don't know how much more will be revealed at first. I think I will save that, and the time of Nyx's humanity for the series and possibly the first book. I did get a few notes that this story felt like you were thrown into the middle of her world. I like that approach even though it feels overwhelming at first.

Over time more and more of who she is will be brought to light.

There are also other demons to create and introduce as well as other sorcerous types (who want Nyx dead) to bring into play. Overall, I'm enjoying the darker aspects of this world and I hope that comes across as I tell Nyx & Acheron's stories.

I want to express my humblest thanks to each and every one of you (especially the NAC!) for stepping into Nyx's world with me. Each new story and each new world is always a risk. I count myself fortunate and honored to have a MoB Family of readers that will allow me to take a chance on a different type of story and support me as I do so.

I am truly humbled that you have all enjoyed Nyx & Acheron so much. Once I get started on the series, I will definitely let you know.

Thank you again for being so amazing.

You totally rock!

Thank you again for jumping into this story with me.

SPECIAL MENTIONS

Larry & Tammy—The WOUF: because even when you aren't there...you're there.

To the MoB Nyxia & Acheron Coalition: I concede. This is just the prequel trilogy lol. The first book will arrive later this year.

To Dan Fong: Because Fong's is AWESOME!

Orlando A. Sanchez
www.orlandoasanchez.com

Orlando has been writing ever since his teens when he was immersed in creating scenarios for playing Dungeons and Dragons with his friends every weekend.

The worlds of his books are urban settings with a twist of the paranormal lurking just behind the scenes and with generous doses of magic, martial arts, and mayhem.

He currently resides in Queens, NY with his wife and children.

BITTEN PEACHES PUBLISHING

Thanks for Reading

If you enjoyed this book, would you please **leave a review** at the site you purchased it from? It doesn't have to be long... just a line or two would be fantastic and it would really help me out.

Bitten Peaches Publishing offers more books by this author. From science fiction & fantasy to adventure & mystery, we bring the best stories for adults and kids alike.

www.BittenPeachesPublishing.com

More books by Orlando A. Sanchez

The Warriors of the Way
The Karashihan*•The Spiritual Warriors•The Ascendants•The Fallen Warrior•The Warrior Ascendant•The Master Warrior

John Kane

The Deepest Cut*•Blur

Sepia Blue
The Last Dance*•Rise of the Night•Sisters•Nightmare

Chronicles of the Modern Mystics
The Dark Flame•A Dream of Ashes

Montague & Strong Detective Agency Novels
Tombyards & Butterflies•Full Moon Howl•Blood is Thicker•Silver Clouds Dirty Sky•Homecoming•Dragons & Demigods•Bullets & Blades•Hell Hath No Fury•Reaping Wind•The Golem•Dark Glass•Walking the Razor•Requiem•Divine Intervention

Montague & Strong Detective Agency Stories
No God is Safe•The Date•The War Mage•A Proper Hellhound•The Perfect Cup•Saving Mr. K

Brew & Chew Adventures
Hellhound Blues

Night Warden Novels
Wander•ShadowStrut

Division 13
The Operative•The Magekiller

Blackjack Chronicles
The Dread Warlock

The Assassin's Apprentice
The Birth of Death

Gideon Shepherd Thrillers
Sheepdog

DAMNED
Aftermath

RULE OF THE COUNCIL
Blood Ascension•Blood Betrayal•Blood Rule

NYXIA WHITE
They Bite•They Rend•They Kill

*Books denoted with an asterisk are **FREE** via my website
—www.orlandoasanchez.com

ART SHREDDERS

I want to take a moment to extend a special thanks to the ART SHREDDERS.

No book is the work of one person. I am fortunate enough to have an amazing team of advance readers and shredders.

Thank you for giving of your time and keen eyes to provide notes, insights, answers to the questions, and corrections (dealing wonderfully with my extreme dreaded comma allergy). You help make every book and story go from good to great. Each and every one of you helped make this book fantastic, and I couldn't do this without each of you.

THANK YOU

ART SHREDDERS

Adam Goldstein, Amber, Anne Morando, Audra Vroman Meyers, Audrey Cienki

Barbara Hamm, Bethany Showell, Beverly Collie

Carrie Anne O'Leary, Cat, Chris Christman II, Colleen Taylor

Darren Musson, Davina 'The Tao of Comma' Noble, Denise King, Diana Gray, Diane Craig, Diane Kassmann, Dolly Sanchez, Donna Young Hatridge

Emily O'Leary

Hal Bass

Jasmine Breeden, Jasmine Davis, Jeanette Auer, John Fauver, Jen Cooper, Joy Kiili, Joy Mosier-Dubinsky, Joy Ollier, Julie Peckett

Karen Hollyhead

Larry Diaz Tushman, Laura Tallman I

Malcolm Robertson, Marcia Campbell, MaryAnn Sims, Maryelaine Eckerle-Foster, Melissa Miller

Natalie Fallon

Paige Guido, Pat (the silly sister)

RC Battels, Rene Corrie, Rob Farnham

Sara Mason Branson, Shannon Owens Bainbridge, Stacey Stein, Stephanie Claypoole, Sue Watts, Susan Brouillette, Susie Johnson

Tami Cowles, Tanya Anderson, Ted Camer, Terri Adkisson, Thomas Ryan, Tina Johnson

Vikki Brannagan

Wendy Schindler

ACKNOWLEDGEMENTS

With each book, I realize that every time I learn something about this craft, it highlights so many things I still have to learn. Each book, each creative expression, has a large group of people behind it.

This book is no different.

Even though you see one name on the cover, it is with the knowledge that I am standing on the shoulders of the literary giants that informed my youth, and am supported by my generous readers who give of their time to jump into the adventures of my overactive imagination.

I would like to take a moment to express my most sincere thanks:

To Dolly: my wife and greatest support. You make all this possible each and every day. You keep me grounded when I get lost in the forest of ideas. Thank you for asking the right questions when needed, and listening intently when I go off on tangents. Thank you for who you are and the space you create—I love you.

To my Tribe: You are the reason I have stories to tell. You cannot possibly fathom how much and how deeply I love you all.

To Lee: Because you were the first audience I ever had. I love you, sis.

To the Logsdon Family: The words, *thank you* are insufficient to describe the gratitude in my heart for each of you. JL your support always demands I bring my best, my A-game, and produce the best story I can. Both you and Lorelei (my Uber Jeditor) and now, Audrey, are the reason I am where I am today. My thank you for the notes, challenges, corrections, advice, and laughter. Your patience is truly infinite. *Arigato-gozaimasu.*

To The Montague & Strong Case Files Group-AKA The MoB (Mages of Badassery): When I wrote T&B there were fifty-five members in The MoB. As of this release, there are over one thousand four hundred members in the MoB. I am honored to be able to call you my MoB Family. Thank you for being part of this group and M&S.

You make this possible. **THANK YOU.**

To the ever-vigilant PACK: You help make the MoB...the MoB. Keeping it a safe place for us to share and just...be. Thank you for your selfless vigilance. You truly are the Sentries of Sanity.

Chris Christman II: A real life technomancer who makes the **MoBTV LIVEvents +Kaffeeklatsch** on YouTube amazing. Thank you for your tireless work and wisdom. Everything is connected...you totally rock!

To the WTA-The Incorrigibles: JL, Ben Z. Eric QK., S.S., and Noah.

They sound like a bunch of badass misfits, because they are. My exposure to the deranged and deviant brain trust you all represent helped me be the author I am today. I have officially gone to the *dark side* thanks to all of you. I humbly give you my thanks, and...it's all your fault.

To my fellow Indie Authors, specifically the tribe at 20books to 50k: Thank you for creating a space where authors can feel listened to, and encouraged to continue on this path. A rising tide lifts all the ships indeed.

To The English Advisory: Aaron, Penny, Carrie, Davina, and all of the UK MoB. For all things English...thank you.

To DEATH WISH COFFEE: This book (and every book I write) has been fueled by generous amounts of the only coffee on the planet (and in space) strong enough to power my very twisted imagination. Is there any other coffee that can compare? I think not. DEATHWISH-thank you!

To Deranged Doctor Design: Kim, Darja, Tanja, Jovana, and Milo (Designer Extraordinaire).

If you've seen the covers of my books and been amazed, you can thank the very talented and gifted creative team at DDD. They take the rough ideas I give them, and produce incredible covers that continue to surprise and amaze me. Each time, I find myself striving to write a story worthy of the covers they produce. DDD you embody professionalism and creativity. Thank you for the great service and spectacular covers. **YOU GUYS RULE!**

To you, the reader: I was always taught to save the best for last. I write these stories for **you**. Thank you for jumping down the rabbit holes of ***what if?*** with me. You are the reason I write the stories I do.

You keep reading...I'll keep writing.

Thank you for your support and encouragement.

CONTACT ME

I really do appreciate your feedback. You can let me know what you thought of the story by emailing me at:
orlando@orlandoasanchez.com

To get **FREE** stories please visit my page at:
www.orlandoasanchez.com

For more information on the M&S World...come join the MoB Family on Facebook!
You can find us at:
Montague & Strong Case Files

Visit our online M&S World Swag Store located at:
Emandes

If you enjoyed the book, **please leave a review**. Reviews help the book, and also help other readers find good stories to read.
THANK YOU!

Thanks for Reading

If you enjoyed this book, would you **please leave a review** at the site you purchased it from? It doesn't have to be a book report... just a line or two would be fantastic and it would really help us out!

Printed in Great Britain
by Amazon